OPIUM

Salar Abdoh was born in Iran. He now lives in New York City, where he teaches in the Creative Writing Program at the City College of the City University of New York. He is the author of *The Poet Game*.

by the same author

THE POET GAME

SALAR ABDOH

Opium

faber and faber

First published in 2004
by Faber and Faber Limited
3 Queen Square London WC1N 3AU

Typeset by Faber and Faber Ltd
Printed in England by Mackays of Chatham plc, Chatham, Kent

A CIP record for this book
is available from the British Library

Many thanks to my editor at Faber, Walter Donohue,
for all his hard work and patience – S.A.

ISBN 0–571–22117–3

To the memory of Reza;
also to Negar and Ali, and to Sid, of course

I am God

Al–Hallaj, beheaded in Baghdad, 922 AD

Without opium, plans, marriages and journeys appear just as foolish as if someone falling out of a window were to hope to make friends with the occupants of the room before which he passes.

Jean Cocteau

Prologue

It is an absence, opium is. Imagine you are sitting in some subterranean den in a casually brutal land far to the East where, come dusk, otherwise rugged men fall in quietly to take their remedy. They have been doing this since before time. As for you, you are only an interloper, not one of theirs, come from the land of infidels. You do not belong here. But these men take you in because, perhaps, they are hospitable men, perhaps there is honor among thieves, and without quite knowing how it came about, you too have become a thief. It is, in the very least, a more honorable occupation than the obscenity of withdrawal. All your life you thought something was missing. Opium was. You know that now, much as you know the protestations of your own limbs when the remedy is late arriving. And as it arrives, as the long wooden Persian pipe with the enamel bowl and its tiny painted blue dragons bespeaking some miniaturist's fancy is heated and reheated over the charcoal brazier, as the brown substance is made soft over the angry embers, and as the rugged men in tribal clothes and menacing turbans begin to eye the night with glares of approval that follow the vapors' trails into some collective tribal memory, you feel the calm already descending. Or, ascending. It is the calm of expectation. The pipe goes around the circle of men until maybe an old fellow with a scraggly beard and the wide, but misleading, forehead of a saint holds up a piece of reddened charcoal over the pipe for you. Experience has taught you not to be wasteful. So you breathe in deeply. It is the breath of a life of hungover mornings, stiff joints, lethargic evenings and unbroken anxieties. The smoke envelops them like the mother of all things. You do not

1

hear their cries anymore. You do not smoke to be lost but to be found. You are neither weightless nor daydreaming. You are here in this room and you are beginning to feel withdrawal fading. The smoke is a glove with an even, quiet spread. It is democratic and leaves no part of your body untouched. And as it settles, it feels as if you had become that first-ever aerialist who saw the myriad formations of opposing armies in their entirety. Your advantage now lies in the distance, in the perspective. Everything is quiet up here. Stay then, since you have arrived. Home is where opium is.

Wednesday, February 2002

He was standing in Roth's living room staring at a sea of books scattered every which way. The phone rang loudly, sounding false and self-important. A clock chimed. His house had clocks everywhere, for Roth had been a man painfully aware of time. Chase had loved him like a father, but his love for the man was beside the point now. Roth was dead. Getting on for a month, now. And Chase knew he'd been pretty remiss about writing his thoughts down in his notebooks these past few weeks. He'd had to lay things aside for a while. Mourning – real or exaggerated – had taken over. The habit had taken over. The habit always did.

Eleven p.m. He called up the Henrietta Hotel to make sure his replacement was there for the night. The replacement was a Jamaican fellow. A man with any number of dreams, one of which was to save enough money to have his own goat farm upstate one day. The world was full of men like him, Chase thought, guys with routine hits and misses. A goat farm here, a summer house down by the beach in Florida. But he was diverging. Bottom line was that Roth was dead and it had taken Chase a month to get here to his place.

In the kitchen: Roth in a group picture. Year, mid-1980s most probably. He was grizzled in that picture. A band of Afghan guerrilla fighters surrounding him. All the men just slightly undernourished, the way men who have been fighting a while ought to look. They all had guns strapped to their shoulders, except for Roth who only carried heartbreak. 'I won't let you down, Joe,' Chase murmured softly, not knowing what he really meant by those words.

Telephone ringing again. He stood over it and this time noticed that the thing was blinking with a box full of messages. Roth's messages, he thought, were like credit card offers that came in the mail. They kept arriving long after a man was dead. He went back to the kitchen and turned on the gas stove out of habit. Blue flames and hiss. This was what an opium life was – a tinkering with the paraphernalia that made the habit possible – and he was sick of it, all of it. He located the jam jar and the pair of red and yellow McDonald's straws Roth had often smoked through. Afterwards he stood over the phone erasing one message at a time, not allowing the computer voice to get past itself. Then he dialed old Seyyed's number. Soon Seyyed was gliding into the living room smelling of kebab – though that was not really the food he preferred. The old Afghan would sooner eat bread from morning till night; used to it from the old village, Chase figured, a place of quietly flushed lives and missing limbs. Seyyed liked prayer and solitude. He liked bravery to the point of foolishness, even if it profited him little save for small battles won in places where that sort of courage bought time only to buy hunger for another day.

'I called you many times,' Seyyed said slowly. 'Roth was righteous. He left all these books for you.'

'Books didn't help him live. Did they?'

'They may not have killed him either,' Seyyed answered in his own language.

Chase watched the old man watching him. Seyyed's nose turned toward his God, who surely disapproved as much as he of the familiar scent of opium in this apartment.

'What do you want me to do, Seyyed?'

'Collect your friend's books. Give them a good home.

4

That's what he wanted. He said you'd know what to do with them if he didn't make it.'

Not making it was probably a catch-all phrase the old man had adopted from the English language when he meant to say that the world was a ruin beyond all repair. No, Roth hadn't made it. He'd drunk until his liver had turned sour on him. For a man like Roth, opium was only a side-arm he'd keep for moments some old pal from his fighting days might come round. Bourbon was what had done him in. And Seyyed must have loved Roth as much as anyone to bear an infidel's drinking habit for so long.

Chase felt a sense of grandness wash over him, as if he had grown out of his shoes all of a sudden and was now ready to take a few giant steps towards something big. What were Seyyed's plans then? It hadn't been more than a couple of months since the Americans had finally settled an old score in Afghanistan, settled it for all of them – for Seyyed, for Roth, maybe even for Chase himself. And maybe they could have gone back to Kabul and made it right this time. But make what right? Chase, who knew himself to have turned sedentary these past few years, would not be going anywhere. Not alone, anyway. Why did Roth have to die? Why now?

He said to the old man, 'You know, Seyyed, I don't have a home for all these books. As a matter of fact, I'm here because I'd like to rent this place from you.'

Seyyed murmured that Allah knew best, adding that Chase was more than welcome to the apartment. Thankfully, he did not bother asking why Chase didn't want to live in his own furnished room at that hotel up on 43rd Street anymore. In return, Chase didn't ask the old man why he'd left Roth's place untouched for an entire month since his death, why the phone line was still working, why things had been left as if somebody would come and simply slip into the bed Roth had occupied for so many years. It was kismet – Roth's favorite word – that was what it was. Fate.

At least they'd broken the ice between them. They'd both loved Roth for reasons that were theirs and theirs alone – two men who never had much to say to each other without the third man present. Now with Roth gone, Chase could finally call Seyyed 'Uncle Seyyed' as Roth used to, and the old man could mumble that Allah knew best and be on his way.

Once Seyyed was gone, Chase tripped limply on Roth's books lying on the floor. He thought about the lost month of no entries in his own notebooks, and knew that he'd sooner sleep than try to rectify the situation. But then the infernal phone began ringing again. The machine, now emptied of its full box of blinking messages, finally picked up. Twelve midnight and someone calling to hire 'Mr Detective Roth's services' for something. The voice was still talking into the answering machine when Chase closed the door to the apartment behind him.

On East Broadway, two doors down from Seyyed's place, a certain Weinfeld's advertised wholesale Bar Mitzvah sets across from another shop that dealt in Torahs and Tephilim. But aside from these few holdouts from another time, the neighborhood was now almost entirely Chinese. Even at that hour a cluster of lean, overworked illegals, dressed in white uniforms and boat-shaped caps, stood outside of Hung Hoop's Noodles smoking with the urgency of men who were certain they hadn't come to America with Hung Hoop as their terminus. To these men, Seyyed's shop was invisible. No wonder then that the old Afghan's sandwiches were not exactly the rage around here. But Seyyed didn't need the Chinese to make him happy. Only some tenants and a serviceable number of believers in Allah in the near vicinity. This was not too much to ask for. And so Seyyed thrived in America.

A half-hour later, in Billy's Corner Bar on 43rd Street, Chase sat on a stool watching Mette. He'd known Mette for just about five months now. It had come about soon after the terrorist attacks on the Twin Towers last September. For Chase, however, that day – September 11, 2001 – was no watershed at all; it was rather like being jostled back to a past, a Middle East past that he'd much sooner forget. So, like it or not, he'd found himself wanting to loaf in bars again. And there, of course, was Mette. He knew her distantly, from the waist-high sanctuary of a bar counter where conversations could always be severed for long intervals, or for good. Mette's style as a bartender precluded, thankfully, a false sense of solicitude for her customers. Maybe elsewhere in his notebooks he had once described her clumsily as a Venus with an eye at the back of her head. She was no Venus. Though she had fine generous lips. Safely blonde, so that most waterholes around Midtown would gladly offer her a behind-the-bar job, even if she was not quite twenty-something anymore. There was an extra thread of flesh, and it wasn't from drinking on the job. She must know that this could be an asset as long as she didn't force anything. She hung back and actually waited for a refill order instead of seeking it. Billy the bar owner didn't like this, but he said nothing about it to her. He already understood that if things ever got out of hand at the bar, Mette would be the only one of his 'girls' he could rely on totally.

'Where's your little scribble book then?' she was asking Chase. 'I haven't seen you with it in a couple of weeks.' She stood in front of him with a half-hidden face that blocked out most the pinkish light shining off the bald head of a dead boxer on the back wall. The picture made Chase think of words like fleeting, passing, transitory, made him think that a day might come when he wouldn't even remember her name, nor she his.

'It's been a month actually,' he corrected her, 'since I carried the scribble stuff anywhere. I'll take a White Horse, please,' he said. She nodded, with a slight grimace. He felt obliged to explain. 'I discovered it only recently. Among the cheaper whiskies, it's the one that actually has some taste to it.'

She poured him the shot and pushed his money away. 'Tell me, Chase, what do you scribble when you do scribble in your notebook?'

'Oh . . . impressions, I guess. One day I got up and realized everything was changing before I could get a handle on it. I could have bought a camera and some film. A notebook happened to come cheaper.'

'Cheaper like the whisky you drink?'

Chase didn't answer. At the other end of the bar a woman called out loud for a Long Island Ice Tea. Besides the rarity of women here, Long Island Ice Tea was not the sort of drink people asked for at Billy's. Mette – Mette from Norway – made the drink expertly anyway. The drink looked to Chase like a dirty aquarium. So much revolved around prospects and probabilities, he was thinking. Chance that you might come out ugly or beautiful. Mette from Norway, he was thinking. Mette. Scandinavian girl behind the bar with a fair absence of attitude. What was she doing here? And he? He looked several stools down at the woman who had ordered the complicated drink. She had long black hair and was sexy enough, but made too much noise. She rubbed Chase the wrong way. It was taken for granted that the night was hers. He would have liked to brush past her and not look her way at all. Or maybe whisper in her ear something like, 'We're not all on the prowl, you know.' But just saying that invalidated the idea, didn't it? Made it sound like you were being dishonest with yourself. He thought, I should jot this down in my notebook and let it ripen there a while. But he knew he wouldn't. He seldom did lately. He looked back at Mette who was standing in front of him again, talking.

'What of it, Chase? The whole world is changing all the time.'

For a second he was lost. 'Pardon?'

'You said everything is changing. What of it?'

'Nothing of it. It's just that in Times Square, the change is an avalanche. It destroys your sense of time. Maybe that's why they call it *Times* Square.'

'Clever man, where would you like to live then, if not Times Square?'

'I can think of a few places. I'm waiting for my retirement bonus to come through first. That'll be a while.'

'Been living here long?'

'Long enough to record the change I was talking about. Even Billy's has cleaned itself up past couple years. Everything has.'

'But not the dump you live at.' She laughed. 'Yes?'

'One of the last holdouts, that place. I guess they're waiting for me to kick the bucket.'

'The bucket?'

'English expression. Means death. I thought your English was perfect.'

'In Norway, they didn't teach us bucket means death.'

He'd forgotten simple things, like how to tell Mette he wanted to see her outside of Billy's for a change. Desire had long been on vacation. That happened with the habit. It was just as Thomas De Quincey had written two hundred years earlier: opium did overrule all feeling into a compliance with the

9

master key. Which was itself. Afterwards, the only pressing need you ever knew was one of withdrawal. And you learned to fear withdrawal like a second habit. A habit on top of a habit. And at the end of the day you always left trifling matters like a good fuck to other men. You did that and you left Billy's Corner Bar without further intimations of the sort.

Outside the night had gathered a vicious chill that was rare for this mild winter. He quickly crossed the street to the Roswell. It was the same ritual every time. The hotel clerk knew Chase was standing outside but waited for him to ring the buzzer anyway. The clerk didn't like any of the hotel's 'permanent residents'. They didn't tip, for starters. They were in the way of progress. Most of the residents who lived here were octogenarians who had come with the Flood, anyway. They saw thriving Times Square changing all the time and still too many of them were taking their time dying. At the same time, gone were the local whores and sex shops operated by grim-faced South Asians who couldn't smell the funk in the back-end cubicles of their shifty places. Times Square was a family affair now. But the old, old guard still hung on by the skin of their teeth. And until they did, the Roswell remained only a potential money maker. No three-hundred-dollar-a-night rooms for the owner to rent out. So Chase and the others got the cold treatment, while the owner lost money. It seemed like a tolerable enough balance, defiance being a purpose and an end in itself.

He asked the clerk if there was any mail in his slot. It was more out of habit that he did this, since there was hardly ever any mail. But he also did it to get on the man's nerves. Surprisingly, the ageing, one-time low-level Broadway actor fished out an envelope from Chase's box and handed it over without looking up at him. Nor did he bother to explain that it had been hand delivered. Chase noticed there was no stamp on the thing. No address either. All it said was 'For Cyrus Chase, room 303'.

Once inside his own room he tore at the edges of the envelope. A very loud garbage truck halted next door at Billy's where Mette was soon to count her take for the evening. This almost round-the-clock bustle of his street negated the isolation he felt in his room; it contradicted the seared streaks in the brown carpet where he had burnt too many holes while feeding the habit. He took a deep breath. Afterwards, he thought of how he should have guessed what sort of a sentence awaited him. Composed of only one line, a question, the letter read: *Do you think that the door of freedom is as wide as the door of entrance?*

Beautifully put. He could still count on Lotfi's rented eloquence after seven very long years, quoting from a passage of *The Thousand and One Nights* as if every sentence those Egyptian storytellers had recorded there turned out to have a sharp edge some fool was destined to get skewered on. That fool would be Chase himself. And maybe he knew enough to know that nothing remained but stories that caught up with you at last. But it wouldn't do to cry about it. Lotfi was here now. And as soon as the telephone rang in his furnished room Chase knew who was calling. Lotfi the Persian, one of those spur-of-the-moment Third World nationalists who like to call themselves one thing and not another – Persian, not Iranian, and sometimes the other way round when it suited their purpose. As if any of it made a difference to the guy counting his goats in upstate New York.

'Whatever brings you to my side of the planet, Lotfi, old friend?' Chase asked the other man in fluent Persian. He was trying to be casual about it, but the truth was that Lotfi's call the other night, when Chase had been on duty at the Henrietta, had caught him off his guard. He hadn't known what to say, except to make the excuse of being busy at work just then. They had arranged to meet after Chase's shift was over, but he hadn't waited around for the Iranian to show up. He was so thrown by that call that he had the irrational notion if he just disappeared for a couple of days the other man would give up on him and go away.

'You, baby, are what brings me to your side of the planet,' Lotfi answered.

He had said the 'baby' bit in English and laughed nervously. This was not Lotfi's territory at all and his anxiety, coupled with Chase's, jammed the airwaves between them.

'I already got your note,' Chase said coolly. 'I can see you still read *The Thousand and One Nights*. I read it myself. Good book. Maybe you feel bad you didn't write it yourself.'

'We all feel bad we didn't write something good.' Lotfi waited a few seconds before going on. 'I thought we'd already agreed. You were supposed to wait for me at the hotel. Why did you run, baby Chase?'

'I didn't run. I took a walk. Your reappearance into my life hastened a decision I'd been coming to for some time now.'

'Is it so terrible to see me then?'

'Lotfi, my friend – you could say I lost my virginity in your country. I roughed it there for a while and that was good and well when I was younger. But all I want now is a little peace of mind. Okay?'

'You call working in a hotel from night till dawn peace of mind? I'd call it tough luck.' Lotfi laughed again putting some spite into it.

Chase waited for him to finish laughing. 'I could be doing better and I could be doing worse,' he said.

'Can't we have this discussion face to face, Chase?'

'Not tonight, I'm afraid.'

'When then? Where?'

'Bryant Park.' The name of the location had come out of his mouth by itself. He'd known that having to meet with Lotfi was a foregone conclusion. That meeting alone might destroy him. It might land him in jail. Even worse, it might give the Justice Department people a chance to collar him for things he'd never done. He was sure that was what they had wanted to do to him seven years earlier, if only they'd had the goods. But they hadn't, since there was nothing to be had. It had taken Chase all his staying power to persuade them he really was a nobody. After a couple of years when they saw he was nothing but a night-man in a hotel they'd started to lose interest in him. Actually, they'd lost interest in him almost right away. But procedure was procedure and he had to play the game, meeting with them from time to time. He felt like a man on permanent parole. That was all right, though. It beat incarceration. But now if they caught him meeting with an operator from a country that, year after year, the American State Department called a sponsor of terrorism, what would they think? They'd want to screw him. And if he called and told them about it right now, they'd still want to screw him, because that's what they did, especially after they'd laid the 'Trust us' bit on him. No, it made no difference now. He had to wait and see what Lotfi wanted and who exactly he was working for. Was he still in the opium trade, or had he gone over to the Iranian Ministry of Security? Not that it made a difference – in a way, the Iranian Ministry of Security, the SAVAMA, *was* the opium trade.

Chase added, 'Twelve noon tomorrow. At one of the tables by the coffee stand near 42nd and 6th. That's 42nd Street and 6th Avenue. Right close to where I am.'

Lotfi began to protest, asking for some place more private. 'Don't you trust me, Chase?'

'Open spaces cramp me less,' Chase shot back and hung up.

He caught a glimpse of an open notebook of his where a couple of months earlier he'd written something about how he was, or felt like he was, always on the verge of finding God. It wasn't exactly a profound thought and looking at it now he felt a bit embarrassed with himself for having written it. There were other notebooks. They lay scattered about the room. All half-dozen of them. He'd started the practice just about a year ago, writing furiously and wondering if he was not doing something worthwhile for a change. If only he'd started this business of keeping accounts, say, ten, twelve years earlier maybe he'd have a complete story to tell today. Go over old disappointments and make something of them. Lotfi was a part of a not very grand disappointment Chase had thought he would never be seeing again. But now that the fellow had come around, he might as well find out what Lotfi's spiel was. His spiel? Most likely that he wants you, Chase, to enter the game again. He needs you. You think to yourself: The Game? Yes, the game. In the parts of the world where Lotfi and guys like him came from the game was played by men who were janitors and taxi drivers one day, until there was a revolution or a coup or a silly war or a riot of the wretched, and then maybe a pair of fellows who could barely spell their mothers' names became the respective heads of Intelligence and of Counter-Intelligence and learned interrogation techniques from old CIA manuals read to them by little men scared shitless, little men who nevertheless went on to translate for their new bosses, in sorry English, about how to torture a dissident or a non-believer. That was how it was, how it always would be – and the thought turned out to be Chase's insight for the evening to himself, permitting him to think it was a gold standard only a rodent in Lotfi's position could really appreciate.

Again, it was that feeling, like he was due for something, a move of some kind, and his wanting to break the habit and to feel human warmth again, after so long – all that was definitely a part of the equation. It didn't matter that it was Lotfi's call that had prompted his resolve. It was the resolve that mattered. He needed a telephone number. He got it from information and called the bar. Mette herself answered. Chase said an uncertain 'hi' into the speaker.

'Who is this?'

'Chase. The fellow with the scribbling habit.'

'Are you coming back tonight?' She actually sounded glad to be hearing from him so soon again. 'We'll be closing in another hour.'

'I'm calling to make a proposition.'

'It's either too early or too late for me to get married.'

'Maybe we could try shacking together one night before we go that far. What do you say?'

'Why the sudden enthusiasm, Chase?'

'It is not sudden. I've been working toward this moment for some time now.'

'No, you haven't. You've been coming around, waiting, watching, doodling in between your shots of scotch. But that's about it. I'd feel it if it were different.'

'Okay, I haven't,' he admitted since she wanted to hear his admission. 'Truth is there's this fellow after me and tonight I need protection.'

She laughed, telling him that it was probably the lamest line she'd ever heard. Then she reconsidered, adding that she'd actually heard lamer, but on another continent.

Chase stuck to his proposal. 'Will you join me tonight?'

'Why?'

'Because I need to confess my sins, feel a little human touch, both those things at once.'

'Meet me at the bar in an hour and we'll go over to my place.

I only live two blocks away by the Port Authority terminal.'

'I'd like you to actually come to the Roswell and rent a room here. My own's a mess. But don't worry, I'll pay for the room. I prefer not to leave the building tonight.'

Pause.

'I thought your hotel was only for long-term stays,' Mette said doubtfully.

Chase felt that he might lose her there and then. He needed to offer her irony, cynicism, whatever, to make light of it. He said, 'We've had a couple of residents die on us of late, and dead residents mean empty rooms. I told you, this neighborhood is changing all the time.'

He could still feel her hesitation. The trust was gone a bit, but outright fear, thankfully, hadn't replaced it, yet. She declined the offer of coming to the hotel, but before hanging up gave him her address.

Intentions were often such garbled affairs. An hour and a half later when he was getting ready to leave the hotel he still didn't know if he'd go to Mette's or back to Roth's place, *his* place. Billy's bar was already shut. He thought about it: no, it wasn't true; he did know why he wanted to go to her place. The Iranian be damned, it wasn't because of him that he wanted to go to Mette's. It wasn't fear, or loneliness; it was attraction – something that simple, yes, but also the recognition that company had a way of keeping the habit away, and Chase ached for the day when the habit would stay far away.

Across the street he watched a bedraggled homeless man pushing a shopping cart towards Broadway. It was in the same general direction of Mette's place and Chase followed him that way.

She lived over another bar. He knew the place, an unflourishing local blues joint hidden by the bus terminal so that it

16

got terrible musicians and few visitors. The scent of incense was strong in her studio. The floor was on a slant and the wood looked to be rolling back on itself in many places. There was a very small kitchen, a bed and a drawer, nothing else. This is a crime, he thought. She should be doing a lot better than this.

'Are you an out-of-work actress? Are you running from something?' he asked her.

'The second,' she answered without hesitation. Adding, 'More or less,' with some emphasis.

He watched her. Was she being serious? Yes, she was. She kept her story to its outline. In a country like Norway, she said, you were not supposed to fear for your life, right?

It seemed like she'd been waiting just for this, the right ear to broadcast her story to. Or maybe after five months of waiting for him to make his move, she felt like she didn't want to waste time over prefaces. He was tempted to tell her: *Mette, you don't know me that well yet. Slow down a bit, allow me at least to get my bearings in your apartment*. But who really knew anyone, and why should he need his bearings anyway? He had already decided he wanted all of her, because they were here; it didn't matter if it came in bits and pieces or in one unexpected flood of self-revelation. She ended up telling her tale without shame and without crowing about how tough she was for having suffered what she'd suffered. But her story of addiction was of a different class from his own. A nine-year junk habit she realized she could never break out of unless she got out of Scandinavia, out of Europe. He would have told her about the monkey on his own back, but what would have been the use of that? She hadn't come all the way to America to trade hard-luck stories right away. She was on a clean run now, and this dumpy little studio was supposed to be only the first step to a better life for her.

'Who's after you then?' he asked her.

'Not anybody in particular,' she explained carefully. 'It was the habit. I had to get far away from it, from all the familiar places and people.'

'What do you plan to do here?'

'The one thing I didn't do much of during all those years, travel. Junkies never go on the road, you know.'

He looked away. How right she was. Imagine yourself in fresh mountain air while dopesick. What would you do, look at the beautiful scenery? I don't think so. He kept the thought to himself. But looking at her and thinking of all that she'd just said, he felt his instinct hadn't betrayed him: coming here was a step in the right direction for him; he'd been banking on someone like her showing up one day and saying, *You wanna clean yourself up, Chase? Well, let me show you how to do it*. He'd already changed his mind about not wanting to trade hard-luck stories. Soon enough, he thought, he'd broach the topic. He promised himself that.

'And you? Why did you call me tonight?' she asked now.

'Someone really is after me,' he said directly, knowing he'd opened a floodgate with those words. He could still walk out of here and just let the two of them stay as a possibility. Then he saw she was smiling, almost laughing. She didn't take him seriously, and that made him want to prove himself, like a kid.

She said. 'Whoever's after you, do you want me to beat him – *them* – up for you?'

'It's not like that. It goes back a ways. I'll see the guy tomorrow. We'll talk. I'll see what he wants and hopefully that'll be that. I just didn't want to take the chance of him barging into my room tonight.'

'You're being serious, aren't you?'

He nodded. He had her attention now. It was something

he hadn't wanted, but had steered them toward, stupidly. Maybe tonight he needed an ear as much as she did. He said, 'I figured I'd better stick to the hotel, but sleep in a different room. I was on the level when I called you.'

'So you don't really want to sleep with me?'

'Oh, I do. Very much. But I have a problem: I've been kind of preoccupied these past few years, forgot how to sleep with a woman. Honestly. The skill just sort of abandoned me.'

'It's not a skill, it's animal nature.'

'I think that's what abandoned me, my animal nature. I've become too human. Three cheers for my human nature.'

He was making her laugh again. An auspicious beginning. He toyed with the idea of breaking down and telling her right there and then about his own 'situation'. But no, it wouldn't do to escort her back into the confessional mode so quickly. An addict who'd gone straight didn't need a mirror from the past held up to themselves. Tonight, there wouldn't be any *Hey, come and listen to the sad tale I got to offer you*, he reminded himself. Instead, he started to say that his name was Chase, but she cut him off.

'Silly. This is not the first time we've met.'

'No, it's not. What I meant to say is that my name's Chase and sometimes I wonder if there isn't a point to my having this name.' He told her now about the job he'd had over the last few years at the Henrietta Hotel. Living in one hotel in the neighborhood and working in another. But she already knew that too. He was repeating himself. 'They call me the night manager. The work entails one thing and one thing only: staying awake or pretending to be awake at night.'

'And the guy who's after you?'

'Ah that. You sure you want to know?'

'I think maybe *you* want me to know,' she said, giving him a look.

'Okay,' he nodded, already feeling dirty from that budding coyness in his tone of voice that made him seem false to himself. 'Okay, well, talk about wanting to travel! Once upon a time there was maybe a half smart kid back in California who'd finished college early and gotten himself a pointless degree in English literature. One day this same kid was looking around and he realized he didn't know what to do with himself – with the rest of his life, that is. He thought he was ready to hit the road, see much more of the world, but not as a tourist. He needed a real cause, something to give himself over to completely.'

'That would be you.'

'Yes. That would. I felt like I'd already missed all the good causes, that somehow it was too late in the game, you know, to do something heroic.'

She waited for him to continue.

'And then I'm reading the *LA Times* one day and guess what? The cause is staring me right in the face. The cause is called Afghanistan. Some fifteen years later every little snot-nosed kid and his mother will know where that place is, but at the time nobody does. There's a war going on there. Afghans taking on, you know, the good old communist beast and giving it a bloody nose with American money, American guns. People from other places joining up to fight. You want adventure, young man? Go to the border town of Peshawar. Quit wasting your days on Santa Monica Beach waiting for your perfect wave to come in. Go east where life comes cheap but where things happen at least.'

'Did you make it to Peshawar?'

'Sort of. You could say I took a detour. And the detour has caught up with me again. That would be the fellow I get to see in the morning.'

He left it at that and made his move. He really *had* forgotten, he thought. He caressed her face with the back of his hand. She let him.

'It's been a while,' she said.

'Believe me, I know. In *The Thousand and One Nights* a man says to a woman that mountains cannot reach one another but lovers can.'

'Really?'

'Actually I made that up. But it's the kind of thing *The Thousand and One Nights* would say.'

Maybe his confidences to her were only a cheap ticket, making it seem like he'd gone through hell, when in reality he'd only dawdled at its gates and then gone back on his merry American way, content with the knowledge that he wouldn't get his throat slit in some back alley of the Orient as long as he consistently showed he was more naïve than he was – what the rest of the world liked to call an 'ugly American'. So she could listen in now and be curious. He didn't care. He'd noticed her that first time all those months ago in Billy's and gotten hooked right away, stopping at the bar before work, during work, on his nights off, trading weary glances with a member of his own tribe. She was that all right. One knew these things, the same way one knew right away who to stay away from inside a crowded bar room. It was no accident that people who'd known addiction could only pal with their own. For how could you explain to a perfect stranger that just getting up in the morning was worse than grief?

He crawled in next to her and breathed deep, scents of oats and strawberry. She was naked and the upper half of her back was covered with a tattoo he hadn't noticed earlier. A winged rabbit, ferocious-looking, a cross between a hawk and itself, airborne on Mette's back in America.

2

Thursday

Ten a.m. Her rabbit was staring at him still as he left her place. Mette sleeping on her stomach. He'd decided the first thing he was going to do was find a way out of the bar and hotel life – maybe even do it for both of them. He had an idea. But with any idea came questions. If, for example, he could take over his dead friend Roth's one-man detective agency, would he need to get a license? And how did one go about getting a detective license anyway? Was there a test? Did one have to jump through legal loops? Show a clean record? Act like one knew the lingo from inside and out? Was there a book he could read about it?

In another two hours he was due for the meeting with Lotfi. It was about as bad a time as ever for him to be seen with an Iranian. They were a supercilious lot anyways, cursed with just enough history to think they'd done the world a favor by just being around. Lotfi had taken a hell of a chance showing up like this. Chase thought he might be making it easier on both of them by giving it to him straight: *I'm a marked man, Lotfi. Federal law enforcement has a bad-guy file on me here, even if it's only because I misbehaved myself clumsily and pointlessly in that water-starved country of yours. Please go away!* Lotfi would do no such thing, of course; he wouldn't go away. Otherwise he wouldn't have come all this way in the first place. So in the time left to meet with him at the park, Chase decided to get on with two essential tasks whose time had finally arrived. First he stopped by the Henrietta Hotel to drop a note for the manager there telling him he was not coming back to work anymore. Two blocks away, at the Roswell Hotel, he packed up the few belongings he possessed – some clothes and a handful of books, most of them various inept translations of *The Thousand and One Nights*. When the owner of the hotel arrived at his office at a little past eleven, he was surprised to see Chase waiting for him there. He was a burly fellow with the unlikely name of Swan who at one time or another had offered every one of the hotel's permanents a lump sum of money if they'd agree to leave the place. In all, two people had taken up his offer. One had ended up on the street after only a year and the other man had blown all his money at the Off-Track betting parlor on 37th and Broadway before drowning himself.

Chase could see Swan's eyes twinkle when he told him he'd decided to accept his cash offer. Swan didn't hesitate. Of all his permanents, Chase was by far the youngest. Chase could just imagine all the sleepless nights Swan had spent dwelling on resident Chase's furnished room on the third floor of the hotel. Theoretically Chase could stay here another half a century and cost the hotel a fortune, or Swan could give him ten thousand in cash today and be rid of him forever. They didn't bother shaking hands or saying good luck to one another. After Chase had signed on the dotted line and was counting his money, he noticed Swan eyeing the brown duffel bag in which he'd already stuffed his belongings. Swan's merchant heart was calculating, poring over whether he could have gotten a better deal out of all this. Maybe Chase had to go anyway and he could have gotten away with giving him half as much as he had. Maybe he could have given him nothing.

Chase decided to put the other man's mind at rest, saying, 'I wouldn't have left for less than the ten thousand cash you just gave me.'

23

Swan's face relaxed. Misers could easily be assuaged with a lack of options; too many options, on the other hand, often threw them into fits of despair, giving them nightmares about pennies that might have escaped.

Afterwards, there was just enough time to survey the park, gauge the promise of bad faith. As if overnight he'd come to know the spirit of shadow men and stakeouts. The trick, he supposed, was to wear fear like armor. It wasn't paranoia, but rather the full-blooded dread that pervaded everything and afforded you time to witness your own glass jaw breaking. He had not actually seen this in America until after the planes had crashed into the Twin Towers and made them disappear. Less than a month later the call he'd been expecting came. *Chase, how about you come down to the office for a talk next week.* The office was at 26 Federal Plaza in Manhattan, where men he had tried not to give too much thought to since coming back from the East were busy and showed it. It had finally happened. The Twin Towers were no more. And Chase knew even before he'd entered number 26 that the hunt was finally on in a way it hadn't been before, and he could no longer get away by simply being ironic about the subject at hand – terror.

That day at number 26, Chase had had to endure a new kind of hardness from the Bureau. The special agent wanted to go over old territory. *Chase, run this by me again, why exactly did you go to Afghanistan in '87? Or was it '86 . . . '88?* The agent's line of questioning a tactical fraud, but one that sometimes could get results. He knew from the file that Chase had never actually made it to Afghanistan. He'd gotten close, but close was not the same as being there. The agent also knew the precise time frame of Chase's time abroad, but he wanted Chase to correct him and in doing so perhaps reveal an angle that had not been there before. Chase was tired and he knew that the agent would be even more tired before the year was over. *Chase, have any of your old Afghan associates contacted you of late?* He had no Afghan associates, he'd told the agent. Maybe he should pore over the file a second time for confirmation, Chase had suggested next. A hostile look from a special agent his own age, a man in his mid-thirties with good skin and a certain bright lawyerly look that could become a stiff mask in a second. *I can make life real hard for you, Chase. Don't mess with me.* The fellow wasn't the usual agent Chase had had to deal with and, thankfully, he hadn't seen him since. His regular FBI contact, Jay Shanker, must have been on a more important assignment then, but Chase wouldn't push his luck any further by asking the other agent where Shanker was. He left it at that and even managed to mollify his interrogator a bit by saying that if any 'old associates' called, he'd be sure to let the Bureau know about it right away.

But why should he let the Bureau know anything at this point? Lawmen, Chase reminded himself, were always after a confession and he had none to offer right now. When and if the time came, he just might make that call. What he didn't want to do, though, was to go about things arbitrarily anymore – like his going East years earlier to fight what was then called the Soviet menace. He'd ended up, instead, working for middlemen like Lotfi who profited from war's mayhem by shuttling unrefined poppy out of Asia to be processed in Turkish villages before its distribution in the markets of Europe. Vast stretches of the Afghan border were cultivated then. Everybody made out. The Pakistanis. The Afghan warlords. Even some Soviet commanders who had come to a profitable understanding with their foes. The Americans who were the Afghans' major backers tolerated the whole thing because they didn't want to displease the warlords fighting the Russians. All that had been a while back and Chase had gotten into it a bit too late anyway. The Russians had left battered and bruised, the warlords had ended up going for one another's jugulars, and men like Lotfi either continued what they were doing or put on a different mask since the competition only got more stiff with time because of the overproduction of poppy by Afghan and Burmese farmers. As for Chase, he'd come back to the States several years later having had his big adventure, even if it wasn't quite the one he'd gone away for.

Bryant Park. The place appeared safe enough. No sign of Lotfi yet. It was sunny out but too cold to allow him to relax. He waited another fifteen minutes for his man. Lotfi, who had dyed his hair three shades lighter than usual, appeared wearing a loud suit he had to have bought in Eastern Europe on his way to New York City. He'd probably come with a paid-for and legitimate Italian passport and walked right through immigration smiling at the customs people who were mainly on the lookout for brown-skinned men with questionable nationalities. Now, as he was approaching, Chase distinguished something of a transformation in the other man. Lotfi looked like he'd learned to muffle his cynicism, give it a quiet shake that said he knew how to swing but he was keeping himself in check. Chase was picturing him back in Tehran driving around with his pockets stuffed full of local currency, zeroing in on the barely veiled prostitutes who returned his gaze on Jordan Avenue.

'You chose some place to meet me, Chase.'

'This is America. I'm not used to strangers leaving me obscure threats.'

'I'm not a stranger.'

'Time will tell.'

26

Lotfi's pale eyes regarded Chase with the amusement you might feel for a partner who was swimming against the current and hadn't noticed he was swimming by himself.

Lotfi smiled. 'Tell me about yourself. I'm really curious to know what you're doing these days.'

'Not much.'

'I can see that. But why, is the question.'

'Because I don't know too many things. I haven't learned.'

'What's that mean?'

'Mean? It means you come back to where you thought you belonged, and you realize that maybe you don't belong there anymore. Everybody is adding memory chips to their damned computers, learning new software, punching the alphabet on their cellulars, making or losing money in the stock market or at least thinking about doing it. You don't know how to do any of these things. Maybe you can recognize a good translation of *The Thousand and One Nights* when and if you see one, but who needs that kind of a talent nowadays?'

'You've become a philosopher, Chase.' Lotfi trailed Chase's bag with his eyes. 'Going somewhere?'

'I gave notice, quit my job and where I was living.'

'I hope I didn't have anything to do with any of that. Hate to disrupt, you know.'

'I'd been meaning to do this for at least four years now. Just couldn't find that extra push, you know. You're my personal catalyst. I should thank you for making me adventurous again.'

'My pleasure. I've come here to do just that.'

Chase groaned inside. A devotee of the poppy had once described the longing for the habit like the crying of a thousand children waiting for their mothers' breasts. Chase had never been that kind of a casualty. He'd always regimented the habit as best he could. He'd learned to stretch withdrawal into a thinness that was manageable. The discomfort was simply a part of the landscape of his life now. It was hilly country, but as long as you learned to pace yourself you could keep climbing. Dopesick, yet smiling.

They were quiet for a bit, then Lotfi remarked, 'We never quite figured how you got out of the country. How *did* you?'

'The Canadians,' Chase replied easily, noting the surprise on Lotfi's face. 'They're a very helpful lot, those Canadians. I went to them one day and introduced myself. They were shocked, in a Canadian sort of way of course. They had no idea what an American citizen was doing in Tehran. I told them some nonsense about having been across the border before taking a wrong turn one sunny afternoon. Of course they didn't believe a word I said, but they were willing to help. They forged a Canadian passport and sent me on my way. They just happened to send me to New York and this is where I stayed. They might have sent me to Kansas City or Vancouver and I probably would have stayed there too. I was tired, Lotfi, tired and always broke. I had to get out.'

Lotfi's face had turned progressively darker as Chase had been talking. He fidgeted, looking uncomfortably about him, and finally observed, 'New York is where they send a man they're not finished with yet.'

'Who, the Canadians?'

'Don't be ridiculous, Chase.'

'Look, I went through what they had to throw at me a long time ago. It's true, the men you're worried about were there at the airport to greet me when I arrived. I'd have been surprised if they weren't. But what did I have to hide? Nothing. They did their usual fifteen minutes of push and shove and when they saw I was nobody, they left me alone.'

'Not their style, that. Especially not now.'

'All right. So every few months a man from the New York office of the Federal Bureau of Investigation calls up citizen Chase. Usually this happens when someone's been bad on the other side of the world or if they've run out of leads to follow. "Mr Chase, have you heard from any of your old associates lately?"'

Lotfi faded with this piece of news, barely uttering, 'And what would you tell them if they called you today?' Gone was his usual mocking grin. Around him, faces of men and women who didn't belong to his time zone. He could not simply have them cleared, eliminated, erased and deleted with a phone call. He was stuck in America with Chase possibly an informant, though hopefully not. Hope, however, wouldn't earn his bread and butter. Lofti had not come here in order to hope. And sitting now only a few blocks away from the United Nations building he must be wondering whether he was not under surveillance.

To needle him some more, Chase asked if he had flown in under diplomatic cover or not.

'Answer the question,' Lotfi said, looking about him. 'Would you tell the Americans anything if they called on you today?'

'*I'm* an American, Lotfi.'

'Don't play with me. You know who I mean.'

'Maybe I won't have to tell them anything.'

'Why? Are we being watched right now?'

'Are we? I wouldn't know. Starting today I'm just an out-of-work hotel clerk.'

'But they do call on you sometimes. Yes?'

'Yes and no. They're way too busy with the Arabs now. I'm an American, after all. Unless, of course, there's a reason I should call and tell them something. Is there a reason? Is there violence in the air, old friend?'

'Violence is always in the air, *old friend*,' Lotfi said grimly. He got up to leave without another word, satisfied with Chase's apparent confusion over his going so soon.

'Are you going to kill me?' Chase asked with mocking naiveté.

Lotfi turned. 'Why? Have you done something to warrant that?'

Chase shook his head, slipping Lotfi a piece of paper with Roth's Chinatown address and number on it, saving himself the trouble of having to try and spot Lotfi's men following him to East Broadway. 'What is it you want from me, then?' he asked the Iranian. The question was purely cosmetic, an act of defiance even. Lotfi could not make another move until he had spoken to his people back home. The Iranian knew Chase knew this. He also knew that Chase's being in periodic contact with US law enforcement, albeit involuntarily, was a thorn he could do nothing about. Chase could see him weighing up the possibilities: Could Chase be lying to get him off his back? But what if he wasn't? A man like Lotfi didn't need to take undue risks. Besides, their game had a history behind it. Chase had walked away from Tehran on a Canadian passport under their very noses. In Lotfi's world there had to be an appropriate reaction to everything, a strike however trivial, a payback. It was only of academic interest that in the grand scheme of things Chase should mean absolutely nothing to him – Chase had never stolen from him, never slept with his wife or daughter. But what Chase had done was to dare to walk away in a part of the world few did without *somebody's* permission. A Canadian passport – that was what stuck in Lotfi's craw. Something that simple.

Lotfi folded the telephone number Chase had given him into his pocket. 'Don't disappear,' he said.

'I'm not planning to.'

Three p.m. Roth's place. Scouring the newspapers he'd picked up, nothing caught Chase's eye, nothing to warrant Lotfi's presence on these shores. In the headlines there was the usual tit-for-tat between the Palestinians and the Israelis. There was some news of mop–up operations against the Taliban going on in Afghanistan. Several articles about roundups of cells of alleged terrorists in the US and Europe. The Iraqis, too, were starting to get a lot of attention from Washington; in fact, it was looking more and more likely they'd be next to get hit after Afghanistan. But the Iranians? What was their deal? Sure, they were still smarting over the American president calling them a wicked bunch in that 'axis-of-evil' speech he'd given recently. But that meant little. The Iranian Ministry of Security didn't send someone this far because it felt insulted. That was not how those guys did business.

By the kitchen sink was a half–eaten kofta kebab from Seyyed's place downstairs. Chase kept a steady gaze on the flames of the stove, recalling how Roth used to say that the sound of a gas stove was the poppy's best friend. Roth, too, had come to know the habit back in the East. The first time Chase had run into him was in the lobby of the Roswell. Roth had already been living in one of the furnished rooms for some time when Chase had moved there. The older man was polite with the other residents but kept to himself. For the first few months they'd been pretty much invisible to one another. Just two more drifters in Times Square, veterans of everything and nothing. Gradually, though, Roth had gotten Chase's attention because of the sort of people the younger man saw him with. You'd notice them waiting outside of the hotel or coming into the lobby to make a call to Roth's room. Almost always the visitors were his clients, Roth being vaguely something of a detective. *I handle things for these peo-ple. They got no one else to do it for them.* What he really was, was a fixer for a lot of the Muslims in the city who had no one else to go to for their troubles. Roth wouldn't advertise, but business came through word of mouth, and he got enough of it to have a quiet life on his own terms. The two men's friend-ship had not started with the habit, but after a while it revolved around it – so they could avoid discussing too much, especially the details of a waterlogged past on both sides. It was Roth who insisted on it being that way, mostly keeping mum about what exactly it was he had done when he'd worked overseas for the government. Neither could Chase's occasional prodding get him to divulge a whole lot more about it.

'You've been to some of those places, kid. You know how it is,' he'd say. 'Iran was the first official posting I got bug-gered in, Afghanistan the second. If there's a God, or an Allah, there has to be a third one coming, even if it's not offi-cial this time, for the Lord doth it to us in threes.' What did Chase think of that, then? Roth would ask. Chase would per-sist that he wanted to know more about those days. Roth's reply was always the same: knowing more did not necessarily clarify a goddamn thing about the world, did it?

Chase fussed about the gas stove till late into the day. The phone rang several times but he didn't bother answering it and no one left a message. It occurred to him that perhaps he should change the greeting on the answering machine. He listened to Roth's somber voice maybe a half dozen times telling whoever was calling to state their name and the num-ber they could be reached at, then repeating the message in Arabic, Persian and Urdu, his voice sounding a notch more intimate in those languages than in the very language he had been born into. Chase kept the message as it was. In the course of the afternoon he popped downstairs to get a cup of coffee from Seyyed and make it final: he was going to pay the old man for first month's rent and remain there.

It really did hit home that a man was dead when you were confronted with the books he'd left behind. Roth had left too many books. They were everywhere. He had lived sloppily and read ferociously. At some point Chase started to pile the books in precarious columns around the apartment according to the languages they were written in. Occasionally he'd go back to the stove and smoke. He didn't need to, but the ritual itself was comforting, partitioning the day into convenient, elastic segments of withdrawal, satisfaction, and gentle abuse. Opium, after all, was something gentle – the cure to all ills except itself.

Eight p.m. It could be Lotfi ringing. He should have had plenty of time by now to discuss their situation with his people.

'Mr Roth?'

'Mr Roth is dead,' Chase answered without trying to dampen the blow to whoever it was on the other side of the line. He figured that the few people who had known Roth well would not be calling now to ask for him. As for the clients, the sooner they found out the better. They could then choose to deal with Chase or hang up.

'I'm sorry, sir, what did you say?' the voice asked with uncertainty.

'Mr Roth is . . .' The truth was immaterial, he now decided. 'Not in at the moment. If you're calling regarding some business, maybe I can help you.'

'My name is Rauf Khan, sir, Mr Roth.'

Pakistani. Or an Indian Muslim, the song of his voice sounding worried about something that needed Roth's attention, so much so that what Chase had just told him about Roth not being in had not registered at all.

'Sir, I would very much like to hire your services. I'm sure my business will not take more than a day or two of your time. I am told that you are a discreet man, sir.'

'I am indeed.'

Now it seemed like the most natural thing in the world to take over the business as it was. Why not just become Joe Roth, if that was what some people were desperate to hear? It would be doing them a favor. He asked the caller what he wished to see him about. The man replied that he would prefer to discuss his problem in person.

'Tomorrow morning then,' Chase said. 'Say around eleven o'clock?' He gave Roth's address and said goodbye.

He decided to check the other message that had been left on the machine while he'd been out – another fellow who needed to talk to Roth about something. Chase dialed the man's number and got him right off. 'This is Joe Roth. What did you wish to discuss, Mr Najjar?'

Some hours later, he'd given the apartment a slight semblance of orderliness. *You have become an impostor, Chase.* He imagined himself jotting the words down in his notebook. But what did those words really mean? He knew that Roth had most probably been an impostor during his career abroad. So if Chase was pretending to be him then he was impersonating an impersonator. There had to be an annulling factor here, like the multiplication of two negatives. The phone stayed quiet for the rest of the night. Lotfi must have decided to let his subject sweat for a while. Men like Lotfi did that out of a certain sickness once they realized that the ground beneath their own feet had shifted. And the ground beneath Lotfi's feet had.

3

Friday

The first client, Rauf Khan, wanted his wife watched. He was wary from the first moment he stepped into the apartment. Chase was not what he'd expected. The house itself certainly didn't look like anybody's office. Khan claimed he was in the import business. He asked about the going price, to which Chase answered a hundred dollars a day, plus expenses. Probably a ridiculously low price these days, but for Roth's sake he preferred not to err on the side of appearing greedy. This was about all he really knew about the business – a certain per diem plus expenses. The night before, while attempting to tidy up the place, he had come across a set of How-To books with ominous names like *Deadly Doses, Cause of Death, Body Trauma, Armed and Dangerous*. They told him nothing, and probably hadn't done much for Roth either. This uneasy client, Khan, only wanted his wife watched, after all, not to find out who had murdered her.

'Why do you need someone to watch your wife?' Chase asked him.

'I need proof, sir.'

'You think she's sleeping around?'

Khan stayed quiet. His round face was like an earthen bowl pasted with gray fuzz. His eyes showed more shame than sadness. He played with the buttons of his jacket and refused to look up, his existence reduced to feeling disgrace over a wife who might have turned adulterous. If he was back in the old country he might have been able to have had her quietly done away with without anyone giving a second

35

thought to it. It would be the adultery that mattered, not the murder. Here, though, he'd be a laughing stock to his own people if he so much as raised a whisper. He had come to Joe Roth, not for proof but guidance.

'Mr Khan,' Chase said carefully, 'supposing that I were to find out that your wife was . . . you know. Then what?'

'Then I will know what to do, sir.'

'You need pictures?'

Khan started. 'Pictures! Yes, yes . . . pictures would be very good.'

Chase got the necessary information from him, plus a four-hundred-dollar retainer. He felt comfortable. He was in his element now – no more clock-watching behind hotel desks. He'd already located the Canon 35-millimeter camera with zoom lens that Roth had left behind in the bedroom closet. Old man Seyyed had touched so few things. It was almost as if Roth had simply gone on a vacation and was due back any day. But Chase still wondered about all the dirty jobs his dead friend may have done with that camera strapped to his neck, taking incriminating pictures of unfaithful women who'd turned their backs on their veils and their holy scripture. What did Roth think of himself when he did that sort of work? Or did he think about it at all?

Still no call from Lotfi. At a quarter past two in the afternoon Chase caught the N train to Astoria in Queens to meet with the other client he'd talked to on the phone. They sat in a Dunkin Donut shop under the subway overpass and exchanged a few hurried pleasantries. Najjar turned out to be Lebanese. He sized Chase up for a while and then declared awkwardly that he could not possibly be Roth, taking an offended bite of a chocolate-glazed donut. Chase immediately got up to leave. The other man held him back.

'My apologies, but I expected you to be somebody else. Older.'

'Well, I'm not Joe Roth, if that's what you mean.'

'You're not?'

'No. I'm his assistant. Mr Roth charges two hundred and fifty dollars a day, by the way, plus expenses.'

'Money is not the problem at this point.'

'What can I do for you, Mr Najjar?'

The Arab owned a flower shop in Brooklyn's Sheepshead Bay. His shop was one of a handful of non-Russian stores in the neighborhood, just as old Seyyed's was one of the few non-Chinese shops in his. Najjar's story was that he didn't want to pay the local toughs a 'special tax' to stay in business. On principle he refused. If he was going to pay a special tax to anyone, he fumed, it certainly wouldn't be to any godless Russians.

'How much do you know about these Russians, Mr Najjar?'

'Nothing. I only opened my business last month.'

'I see.'

What would Roth have done about this man? Najjar finished his donut and then started on Chase's without realizing what he was doing. He ate ravenously, out of nervousness, his powerful jaws working themselves through a frenzy of chocolate.

Chase asked the obvious. 'Have you thought about going to the police?'

'I am told going to them will make my position more hazardous. Besides, the police don't like our kind very much. I was told that Mr Roth could do something perhaps.'

'Pay the special tax.'

'What?' Najjar asked indignantly.

'Mr Najjar, listen to what I have to say. I could sit here and

37

tell you that there is no problem and that the situation can be handled. I could take your money and maybe even go have a chat with the Russians. Then what? You'll still be left having to live in that neighborhood at the end of the day.'

'But what if they want more?'

'They won't. They'll keep it reasonable, because they want you to be in business. This is the price you pay for being in America instead of Beirut. But at least you can sleep better at nights, and your children don't have to listen to the sound of rockets and mortars on their way to school every day.'

He'd said it like it was – without quite knowing where it came from, that well of advice – but he knew his counsel was right and the Arab would be grateful to him soon enough. It still took him another few minutes to convince the guy. At the end Najjar seemed grateful. He did not offer to pay for Chase's time and Chase didn't ask for it.

As Chase was walking to catch the train back to the city he thought again of Roth and this life he'd created for himself. Roth hadn't been a detective, not really. He'd been more like a counselor, a therapist. Chase saw that better now. He supposed the work had brought enough satisfaction to allow Roth to forget the past – Iran, Afghanistan – unkind places both. He'd invented a different world here and he worked that world like an amused saint.

By 7 p.m. Lotfi still hadn't called. Chase fingered, with some distaste, one of the two vials of methadone he'd bought on his way back from the donut shop in Queens. He'd only bought the vials for the sake of the job, so he could spend extended time on his feet away from the kitchen, the gas stove and the opium. There had been a detour into Harlem to pay for the medicine and to tell the woman he only knew as Fly that he might be back for two more sooner rather than later. Fly

38

offered one of her big-bellied laughs. 'You must have scored something heavy, Chase! What's up?' Nothing was up. Fly should have known better than to ask. Why did anyone go after synthetic trash like methadone unless they had to, unless they had bills to pay, faucets to fix, parole officers to appease and generally act like they were living in the world? Why else, Madame Fly? She was a woman he'd known for a few years, going back to a time when he'd foolishly been try-ing to kick one habit and fallen into the trap of another. Now, with this latest purchase, Fly no doubt saw Chase as being back in the fold, back on that straight path to hell that stretched between the two of them and the hospital nurses in Spanish Harlem where methadone disappeared in the quick-sand of dependence and where nobody ever quit anything except life.

By the time midnight rolled around Chase went down-stairs. Old Seyyed and three other men were sitting in his after-hours shop sipping tea and talking. Spotting Chase walking past, Seyyed came out onto the street to say hello.

'How is it for you, so far?'

'I'm grateful to you, Seyyed. What if I told you I'd taken over Roth's business?'

'What is taken is there for the taking. Or it would not be there,' the old man declared with a cheerless face, as if that said it all. 'It is the same with men,' he then added darkly, 'they are eventually taken. Some earlier than others.' He retreated back into the shop without waiting for Chase's response. Apparently Seyyed had no bones to pick with America, at least not quite in the same way as his friend Joe Roth. Everything, Chase reminded himself, was always a matter of grounding. And Old Seyyed probably wished that Chase too had been grounded in something. *What a poor sub-stitute I must appear to the old Afghan.*

'I moved out of the hotel,' he told Mette.

The bar was uncharacteristically quiet, especially for a Friday night. Mette put a drink in front of him and poured herself a clear soda.

'You didn't call me yesterday.'

Not an accusation, but statement of fact. *You didn't call me, but you're here now.*

'Why did you move out of the hotel?' she asked him. 'Is it because of the guy you said you're afraid of?'

'I don't think I said I was afraid.'

'Did you meet with him then?'

'I did.'

She went over to serve the remnants of a drained airline crew huddled around the middle of the bar. The top of her tattooed rabbit was just visible from underneath her blue blouse. She stood there for a while before coming back, suffering the muddled monologue of an airbrushed fellow who was too sure of himself not to be one of the pilots.

'Why did you leave the hotel then, if you're not afraid of this guy?'

'I've left the hotel life altogether. I quit my job, my room, everything.'

She gave him a funny look. 'And now what?'

'I've become a gumshoe.'

'A what?'

'A private detective.'

She laughed, as he'd expected she would.

'I took over my friend's business,' Chase continued. 'Both his business and his apartment. He's dead, mind you. It's a nice place, downtown. I'd like you to come live with me. I'm serious.'

Laugh again. 'Last night you wanted me to rent a room

with you. Tonight you want me to move in. What's next? A pleasure cruise?'

'I'm serious, Mette.'

'I can tell you are serious. But why?'

'Because – and this is the least of my reasons – I'd like to get off the habit like you did.'

'Habit?' The cloud that passed across her face was too brief and all the more serious because of it. Now their relationship, such as it was, would enter uncharted waters. What would she see in his declaration of guilt? What would she want to see?

'Mette, you've been where I want to go. And I *am* where you've been. This means we understand one another. We can get hitched. Hell, everybody's got to do it sometimes.'

'Hitched?'

'Couple up. Be as one. The great unity of whatever. I don't know, Mette, you deserve more than that place you live in now.'

'I know what I deserve, Chase. And it's not this job and it's not where I'm living now. But I can't live with you, not until you do something about what you just mentioned.'

'That's why I thought you could move in with me.'

'We're all weak creatures, baby. You know what will happen if I move in with you now.'

'I thought . . .'

'You thought wrong. The habit is patient. It knows how to wait for us.'

'And if I do give it up?'

'Then . . . definitely . . . look me up.'

She withdrew back to her airline crew.

Only now did he notice Lotfi sitting alone at the other end of the bar watching them. He'd been so preoccupied with what he'd had to say to Mette that he'd missed Lotfi coming in altogether.

41

Lotfi followed him outside into the cool night air and they caught up together on the other side of Broadway.

'You've had me followed all along,' Chase said to him without much resentment now.

'You'll get better at it with time, Chase. I had to make sure you're not being watched by others, if you know what I mean. Come, we need to talk.'

'About what?'

'You know, about how you're going to help us catch a bad guy.'

4

Saturday

Next morning he started out early. His client's wife came out of the house a little after ten. He'd expected her to be wearing something traditional like a sari. Instead she was dressed in jeans and had on a suede jacket. She was good-looking, early thirties, too young for her husband, anyway. She walked briskly toward the Kew Gardens/Van Wyk Boulevard subway station. The neighborhood seemed mostly made up of immigrants from the sub-continent. Pakistanis. Indians. A lot of Sikhs. Their children biked up and down the street looking blessed. Everybody knew everybody else. Chase thought he stuck out like a sore thumb, going from door to door, sustained and warily efficient on the methadone that kept him on his feet, getting cover by asking home owners if they had a room or a basement to let. A lot of them did and Chase had to be careful to get in and out of their places quickly enough without missing the wife. And what if he did miss her? He had to ask himself that in one particularly ratty crypt he was being shown, a place that smelled of overgrowth and ripe summer evenings. He could just as well give Khan's money back to him and think about his own problems. For starters . . .

But there was no mistaking her when she finally appeared outside of her house, black locks singing down her shoulders like Khan's picture of her. They started walking. The sky was gray, but the weather held and it wasn't all that cold. Chase kept a safe distance until the train and then took a seat behind her. The F traveled the length of Queens until it

43

crossed the 59th Street Bridge into Manhattan. She took out a little mirror and fixed a face that needed no fixing. For a second he thought he even caught his own reflection in that mirror. She rode all the way downtown until Lafayette Street, then strolled east on Houston and waited about a car's length away from a bus stop. Taxis slowed down but she wouldn't flag them. Then the fourth or fifth cab didn't just slow down, it stopped at her feet. From across the street Chase had a clear shot of both her and the driver. The camera recorded them embracing. The driver's coffee-skin face was half hidden beneath a baseball cap. But you could tell he was not much older than she was. He kept one arm wrapped around her shoulders as they drove away. It all seemed so predictable; still, Chase ran across the street and flagged a second cab. And as he did so he noticed a fellow who had ridden the train with them rushing to catch up with him. Probably one of Lotfi's watchers. They could watch all they wanted. The last picture Chase had of the guy was him standing there in middle of the street with his hands in his pockets hopelessly looking on as the two taxis pulled further away.

The woman and her lover ended up somewhere on Atlantic Boulevard in Brooklyn near the Arab district where they parked the cab and walked into a transient hotel. Chase sent off his own yellow cab. Nothing to do but wait. He sat in a coffee house across the street for an hour and played with the camera so as not to raise suspicions once he was ready to take the next batch of photos – feeling ridiculous the whole time he waited. Then, as soon as he saw the couple coming out of the hotel, he shot them holding hands all the way from the entrance of the hotel to the door of the taxi.

For one moment Chase thought of jumping up and following them again. But he let it go. Their car was speeding back towards Brooklyn Bridge and you needed luck to catch another cab around here. He'd already done the job he'd come for; he was finished. Meantime, the methadone was taking its toll. He thought of how far away he was from home and how beat-up he felt. The camera felt heavy. Everything was heavy and redundant and, yes, he was starting to be a bore with his constant grousing at himself. He also thought if Roth was not dead he might even allow himself to feel a little disappointment in his old friend. *So this is what you did for a living, Joe? This is what being a private dick is all about? I'm not impressed with either one of us.*

Time to go home and wait Lotfi out. The Iranian was what mattered most at this point. And last night, after following Chase out of Billy's bar, the fellow had played his hand and come up with a story too unexpected not to be taken seriously:

Lotfi had been saying to him, 'You already know the guy I'm talking about. He worked our *Bicheh* to *Mashad* leg. That dumb Mongol who swore all the girls in Tehran told him he could be a movie star.'

'Tabib.'

'That's what he liked to call himself, Tabib, *doctor*. Maybe the dirty thief thought he was a physician or something. But his birth name is Murad. We used to call him Haji Murad.'

The rest of that exchange had taken place in an empty dispatcher's office on a ghostly block below the Chelsea Piers. The place was like God's parking lot. A lot of Koranic calligraphy scrawled across the walls. A couple of outsize pictures of an apocryphal prophet or two. One of Lotfi's two guys stood guard outside the dispatcher's office, the other inside the main garage itself, surrounded by taxi cabs in various stages of dilapidation. Just God and us, Chase had thought. And for what? Getting briefed on Tabib, of all people. Over a decade ago he'd still been making regular runs with that man, traveling from the Afghan border to Mashad, Iran's holiest city, in one of the northeastern provinces. Precious goods carried on anything that moved – camels, donkeys, or government vehicles that had the blessings of elements from the intelligence service or, ridiculously enough, from the Iranian 'Ministry for the Struggle Against Illicit Drugs'.

'My god, Lotfi! I know that guy.'

'I know you know him. That's why I've come to you.'

'Tabib used to practice his English with me. We're in the desert with enough goods to make a whole caravan of camels see the Prophet twice over, and you know what he wants me to do? He wants me to teach him about English irregular verbs and how to conjugate them. That was Tabib in a nutshell.'

'Funny guy.'

'No. Just damn persistent. After two years he spoke better English than half those fools in your Foreign Ministry. What's he done?'

Lotfi gave Chase a hard look. 'He's killed somebody.'

'So?'

'This is different. We're being pressured to find this guy.'

'Who did he kill?'

'You wouldn't know. Somebody in the *Bekaa*. Lebanon. Except the Arabs there want blood for justice. That's how the Arabs are, hard-headed sons of whores, can't reason with them. I'm supposed to either bring Tabib back or bring *visible* proof that justice has been dealt. But I have to talk to him first.'

Chase thought he'd risk it: 'Tell me, since when did you get to carry a badge for your government?'

A loaded question – which Lotfi was aware of. The man had only been a simple mover of goods at one time. Moving up the ranks inside Iranian security – if that was what it was – meant he had to have kissed a few behinds.

'Things change, Chase,' Lotfi said. 'The good guys, believe it or not, are really the good guys nowadays.'

'The good guys? Which good guys?'

'*The* good guys. I tell you, it's like that everywhere these days. You have to choose sides. It's the same in Tehran, Damascus, Beirut, even Gaza. You play the game or you're out.'

'What game are you talking about, Lotfi?'

'We're trying to clean up the neighborhood on our own terms, aren't we? It's better than having the Americans come in and throw their weight around. We're feeling the squeeze in Tehran. On one side of us we got the Americans in Kabul. Maybe next year they'll be in Baghdad. What after that? Will it be us? We don't want that. We don't want to give anyone an excuse. So we're trying hard to do what's right. But then there are guys like this fellow Tabib. They don't want to give up fighting the good fight. They want the world to end for no reason other than they feel their sisters are getting polluted and their brothers already have both feet in hell.'

'Nice speech, Lotfi. But I'm telling you, this doesn't sound like the Tabib I used to know.'

'Desperate people change desperately. What's this Tabib got going for him? Not a thing. I can't tell you how many men became cold-blooded killers because their mothers didn't breast feed them with tender loving care.'

'I see. And here comes Lotfi. Mr Good Guy, out to save yesterday's freedom fighters from too much enthusiasm.'

'Ah, give the sarcasm a rest, Chase.'

'Give me some names – who do you answer to in Tehran?'

'Who? People with peace on their agenda. Comes a time when peace gets to be more cost-effective.'

'So, you fellows are doing your own policing nowadays?'

47

'We always did. Now we're just vigilant about it. I think there's a business term for that.'

'I wouldn't know about that. I don't know much, Lotfi. But you already know that.'

What that conversation with Lotfi had done for him was to open a door, as if he'd been waiting these past few years for the Iranian to arrive with a bouquet of secrets. All he had to do now was to crack open the fellow's real purpose.

He started by concentrating on their subject, Tabib. What Chase knew of Tabib was that he was a Tajik who'd been drafted into the Russian army during their Afghan war. It wasn't all that uncommon back then for Muslim Soviet soldiers to walk over to the other side and volunteer themselves in the fight against the infidels. Tabib was no hater of infidels, he just hadn't wanted anything to do with that war. He'd somehow worked his way out of the Afghan city of Herat and over to the Iranian border where he'd had a miserable time of it in the refugee camps for a while until somebody figured out that Tabib, knowing Russian, could be an asset in dealing with crooked Russian commanders who gave a nod and a wink to poppy cultivation in their own districts. Chase had done that eastern corridor with him enough times to know that Tabib was not and never would be in the business of killing anyone just because they weren't religious enough. Tabib wasn't that sort. He wasn't a zealot. He loved the West. He was happy knowing Russian but he was hell-bent on learning English. Moreover, the fellow did really believe he should be a movie star and his life's dream was to make it to Hollywood. When Chase decided to beat it out of the Middle East, Tabib was one of the few people he thought he'd actually miss. They'd had a friendship of sorts. Tabib was damned proud to have an American for a friend and given half a chance he would have shouted it out in every mosque and every cubicle in the Grand Bazaar of Tehran. No, Tabib would never kill for faith alone.

Nine p.m. Back at the apartment, he called Mette at the bar.

'It sounds quiet over there.'

'It is,' she said. 'More or less.'

'I'm sorry I disappeared like that last night.'

'The guy who followed you out, is he the one?'

'Yes.'

'What do you plan to do?'

'Ask you to move in with me.'

'You're crazy, Chase. Besides, you already asked and I said no.'

'Did you say no or did you say not yet?'

'Maybe not yet.'

'I'd like to see you.'

'You know where to find me. Customers. Gotta go.'

He hung on to the phone for a bit, waiting, thinking she'd come back. She didn't. What an inhospitable track of time all this waiting was. Waiting now for Tabib. Waiting for Lotfi. Even waiting for Special Agent Shanker of the Federal Bureau of Investigation, who actually used to call on him more often before the Twin Towers had gone down. Chase realized that somewhere along the line he must have disappointed his FBI contact, having turned out to be a subject that had never yielded fruit. Shanker would come round every few months – though not in the pressed dark suits that Chase had imagined G-Men wore; he came often decked out in simple dark checkered shirts that he let hang over his slacks to conceal his automatic. For a while Chase used to think of him as a graduate student in some obscure anthropology department fretting over his thesis. 'I've been wanting to touch base, Chase,' Shanker would say each time. Their meetings were often like blind dates. Settled around two coffees or two beers, there was everything and nothing to talk about. Shanker must have realized this, so now and then he'd play at crossing the line and getting personal. Chase wanted to tell Shanker that he needn't try to ambush him with any form of sincerity. There wasn't anything there to ambush. The fact was, Chase had come to New York on that Canadian passport from Tehran and the rest was history and already a part of his files at the Bureau's headquarters. But for Shanker there was obviously no getting away from the dossier he'd inherited on Chase. Somebody at the Bureau telling him, 'Here's the profile on your boy. Best way to handle him is to be intimate but firm. Threats are not the way to go. He's still searching for brothers, so be his brother if you have to.' But Shanker could not be Chase's brother since Chase could not be his. It was that simple, until the towers had fallen and Chase was summoned to 26 Federal Plaza. A little later Shanker himself would look him up for one of their regular touch-base fantasies. Yet by now the air was thick with a lack of leads or too many leads that were meaningless and Shanker knew that he had to spend time with Chase not to touch but to *cover* all the bases – or his behind at least. Chase had been embarrassed for the FBI agent all of a sudden. Maybe Shanker had been assigned to working on counter-terrorism because he'd taken a course or two in elementary Arabic or Persian, but he was way over his head. And both men knew that what the Bureau really needed now were lost souls like Chase, who hadn't had to learn those languages out of any textbooks, who knew the geography of hell because they had trekked through it. Shanker should have had the courage to take Chase to the Federal Plaza building to tell his bosses he wanted his man on the payroll, so that at last

Chase would have a chance to tell them all, including Shanker, to get lost, that they were way too late on that account. But Shanker hadn't offered to take him there, and Chase was grateful for that at least. At the same time, Chase could breathe more easily because now that the Bureau was having to show that it was hunting for real, he would be seeing far less of Shanker and his ilk, having left the Middle East too long ago to be of value to them.

But there was more to it than that – perhaps much more, the awkwardness of agent and would-be asset going several layers deeper. This had to do with the fact that while knowing little, Chase still knew more about the FBI agent's job vis-à-vis the Middle East than the agent did himself. They both understood at least this much about each other. They were like two men with stuffed noses who had tried following the scent of a trail for too long, only to have to share it with others who had even less of an olfactory sense. Barely five months since that frenzied morning of September 11, there were already whole armies of newcomers who wanted in on the counter-terror bandwagon. Others might think they knew a few things, but the two men knew better; they knew that the whole thing was a charade, that nobody really knew anything for sure. They all were play-acting at best. And it was just as well that the Bureau might finally be about to close the file on Chase for good.

'Let's a share a cab uptown together.' It was Lotfi, coming up from behind him on the street as Chase was heading for the subway to see Mette.

'Don't you ever sleep, Lotfi?'

A cab stopped by them. They'd been speaking Persian; Chase reminded Lotfi that the driver might understand what they were talking about. Lotfi dismissed it. 'They're all Arabs and Indians anyway,' he said in the exaggeratedly nasty tone a lot of Iranians assumed when speaking of their neighbors.

'What if Tabib is around by now?'

'He isn't. I'm keeping an eye on you. I would know.'

'I know what you're doing.'

'What am I doing?'

'Making me nervous. Trying to, at least. Isn't that what you guys do back home, install men outside of some poor fuck's house in plain sight so he'll get nervous and divulge all the things he never did but now believes he's done.'

'Quit making speeches, Chase. What is it you want?'

'Money, of course. You want Tabib. Okay. You're putting me in the middle of all this, so what do I get out of it?'

It was a rudimentary question that he'd been remiss in not asking before – the psychology of betrayal having certain rules which should never be neglected. Asking for money was a sign for Lotfi that Chase was solidly in his camp now, even if the Iranian wondered whether the question itself was not Chase's means of purchasing bona fides for himself. But if Lotfi did ask himself that question, he would have to go a step further and wonder why Chase would want to get tricky anyway. Was it possible, for example, that Chase might feel loyalty for Tabib? But Lotfi could only answer this particular question by looking at things from his own prism, a suspect glass box where men who were stupid enough to believe in loyalty were dead men at best.

Lotfi smiled appreciatively at Chase. 'How much do you want, Chase?'

'I want to be back in the game. I'm bored with my life, Lotfi. I need a change of scenery. Would you like Tabib killed?'

'Not yet. I need to speak with him first. Besides, I never took you for a knife, did I?'

'I'd do it to get taken back.'

'We don't take in Americans.'

'You took me in fourteen years ago.'

'That was a different game. You can't imagine how your country is stressing us these days. They've got their feet on the accelerator and are pushing hard. They want an end to guys in the desert with messianic dreams. We say okay to that. If we help them achieve this lofty goal of theirs, maybe they'll leave us alone for a bit.'

They remained quiet for the next few minutes until Chase was about to get off at the corner of 43rd Street. Lotfi turned and grabbed his wrist. 'You *were* kidding about wanting to join. Yes?'

'Right. But what I wasn't kidding about is the money.'

Lotfi nodded. 'Like the old days. Yes?'

'Better than the old days, I hope. I pissed the old days away and came back to America's graveyard shift. Don't want to do that again.'

'We'll open a trust fund for you, Chase.'

'Just make it a few envelopes, in hundred-dollar bills.'

5

Sunday

He had to make love to her carefully, running a guarded tongue over the silver ball she attached to her pierced navel. Why did people do these things? he asked her. Rings and studs all over themselves, tattoos. What was the point? The rabbit on her back, didn't it carry some kind of immaterial weight? Didn't she feel she might want to be alone sometimes and the rabbit was right there pressing against her skin?

'The rabbit's a reminder,' she said.

'Of what?'

'Screw up, get a small rabbit. Screw up your life, get a big old rabbit.'

The sound of outbound buses for New Jersey rattled the windows to her studio. The natural light was a shade of gray that made them and the room feel dirty. The floor moved. There was a staleness in the air that probably came from the bar below. Her life was a bar life, as his had been a hotel life. Screw up your life, live here, get a big rabbit.

'Is it like a pre-planned kind of thing or something? I mean, is one born with the sign of the rabbit?' he asked her.

'Chase.'

'Yeah?'

'Tell me about your family?'

'Family?' he asked surprised. 'None to speak of. Not any-more. My mother – God bless her – believed in two things: free love and yoga. I kid you not. When I was six years old she took me and a backpack and we headed for Europe and then India via the land route. Except we ran out of money on the way there. We ended up getting stranded in Iran. But it was the early seventies, the country was flush with oil and there were plenty of jobs and cash for Americans who wanted to hang around and smell the East, so to speak. We stayed. We stayed for the next six years and I grew up speaking Persian as my own language. I played soccer in crooked alleyways with local boys and after a while I could imitate the sound of a muezzin like I'd been born to it. It was just the two of us, my mother and I, and we loved every minute of it. She taught yoga and English to rich Iranians, and forgot all about going to India and I was happy that she did. That is, until the Iranians went crazy and had themselves a revolution and suddenly those same kids I'd been playing soccer with started throwing rocks at me because I was an American; the local grocer refused to sell my mother anything. A year later we were back in California. My mother went on teaching yoga, this time to rich Southern Californians. By then I was already thirteen and chasing early-morning waves on Zuma Beach. So . . . what can I tell you? When you ask me about *family* I draw a blank. My guess is families are like that rabbit of yours. A reminder of something. Usually bad. But then when I try reading books about unhappy families, I can't much relate. It's foreign territory to me: Daddy drinks too much, Mommy is neurotic – I don't get any of that stuff. When I was a teenager my mother liked to smoke marijuana with me on weekends and we'd sometimes watch the sunset together by the beach. We were friends. Then I took off, and by the time I got back from the East she was dead. Cancer. She never really knew where I went when I left the States and I never called her to explain.'

'Why didn't you?'

'Because the East had broken her heart. It had rejected

55

her, stabbed her in the back. Don't you see? She'd have never forgiven me for going back there.'

'So you went back to Iran.'

'I did. Like my mother, I got stuck there on my way somewhere else. And like her, I stayed. I stayed because, I guess, it was the easy thing to do. It was like going back home in a way. But I could never call her and tell her that. Or maybe I just wasn't proud of what I was doing over there. Here!' He started to take out the set of six notebooks he'd brought with him the night before. He handed them to Mette one at a time. 'I'd like to keep these with you. Safer. I never showed them to anyone until now. I could use a critical eye, you know. So if you get bored you can glance through them. I'd like that actually. These notebooks are my life. My rabbit. You can find the rest of my story in them.'

She took a long look at the notebooks. 'What are you saying . . . that you don't want to be a blank slate?'

'I'm *trying* my best not to be that. You fill a page and you feel like you're making something happen, instead of letting things happen to you. That's what I tell myself anyway.'

She had to smile. 'If you feel that way, then what am *I* supposed to say? Do you know how many years I was invisible back home? Now I'm here. Clean. Clean but still invisible. Talk about a blank slate!'

'It's different for you. Nobody expects you to piss and mark your territory. You're a woman.'

'Fuck you, Chase.' She turned away.

He turned her back around. 'Look at me.'

'I'm looking,' she said. 'You have the blackest hair I ever saw. I'm guessing you're just on the short side of six feet. I like the turn in your eye. But you look like you could use a little more weight. You talk of *there*, the East – is that where you picked up the habit?'

He nodded. 'I figured the habit would make the days more manageable there.'

'You figured wrong.'

'I was twenty-one years old and knew no better. You'll see what I mean, if you care to read.' He indicated the notebooks again. He already knew why he was so pressing her to read them: all the half-truths he'd told men like Jay Shanker over the years, he wanted to thrust aside by showing this woman how it really had been for him. 'Keep them for me,' he said. 'Okay?'

She laid the notebooks on the bed between them, like they were a margin to be bargained over. 'You *are* afraid,' she said. 'Aren't you?'

'The guy you saw follow me out of the bar, he wants me to kill another man. No, not kill. That's exaggerating it a bit. But he wants me to give the man away, betray him – which pretty much amounts to the same thing.'

'Why are you telling me this?' she said.

'Because I trust you, and because I'm so tired of talking to my notebooks. They don't talk back. It was good for a while, but then it got to be another pointless attachment.'

She waved his words away. Nothing he said settled easily between them. He thought she must be thinking the obvious, that they were strangers who knew too much and at the same time not enough about each other. This allowed her to remain ironic.

'I see. You're not going to kill anybody,' she said acidly. 'That's a start on the right foot, isn't it?'

He didn't know. He wanted to tell her all he really craved now was oblivion. Instead, he admitted that he'd bought enough methadone to start getting off the habit right away. What did she think of that idea? She only scoffed at it.

'That's just substituting one pair of shoes for another.'

57

'Then why won't you let me stay here and go cold. Just sweat it out. You know I can't do it alone, Mette. I need to be able to see the light at the end of the tunnel.'

He felt her skeptical but relenting. 'All right. When do you want to start? Now? Tomorrow?'

'Not now, not tomorrow,' he said lamely, when he should have really been jumping at her offer. 'I'll let you know when I'm ready,' was all he could bring himself to add.

Three hours later, Khan's wife was standing by the door to her home staring beyond Chase with muted consternation. His assurance that he meant no harm was meaningless to her. She seemed resigned to catastrophe, regarding the stranger outside her home as something inevitable, like her marriage. Her look said she knew why he was here. She'd been waiting for this.

'It's best that you let me in, Mrs Khan. Your neighbors already talk about you. Seeing me standing here like this wouldn't be a good thing.'

'Not a good thing for who?' she asked.

'For you. I was hired by your husband to follow you about town. If you want proof, your husband's name is Rauf. Rauf Khan. He owns an import business in the city. I know he's not home because I talked to him today. He's at his office.'

She stood to the side to let him pass through. He didn't venture further than the hallway. As soon as she had shut the door, Chase handed her a large envelope with the pictures he'd taken of her and her lover.

'The negatives are in there too,' he said hopefully.

She looked through them quietly, going back and forth between several of the photographs he'd taken of them at that hotel in Brooklyn, as if she were trying to decide which one to pick for framing.

58

At last she said, 'Why are you doing this?' Her voice slightly shaking. 'Do you want money from me?'

'I already got paid by your husband. He has not seen these. He never will. I am not here to blackmail you.'

'Then why have you come, please?'

'Why?' To do the right thing. Wasn't that obvious? He could sense her drawing back, stunned, angry, but he continued. 'Look, I already lied to your husband. I gave him a full report and told him he had nothing to worry about. But it's you I worry about. I want to make a suggestion: leave him.'

'Leave?'

'Yeah. Free yourself, lady. Go with your lover or go your own way, but do leave. Are you listening to me?'

She said nothing. The envelope fell out of her hands and he had to pick it up and give it back to her. He could see the TV in the living room. Women in a rainbow cloud, dancing. Indian television. They were voiceless – like Mrs Khan, who would not stop gaping at him.

'Throw this envelope in the fire and forget you ever saw me. Good day, Mrs Khan.' He turned to leave.

'Please!'

'Yes?'

'You want no money?'

'Well, if it pleases you, you can pay me for the photographs and the cost of developing them.'

'How much?'

'Not much.'

She disappeared for a minute. When she returned she was holding a wad of twenty-dollar bills. Chase took them from her without a word. He didn't even count the money. It was only later when he was about to get on the train that he realized she'd given him two hundred dollars. It had cost him fifteen to develop the pictures. He put the money away and called Fly, Harlem's methadone queen.

'I may be coming for more of my stuff,' he said.

'Come any time, honey.'

Nine messages on the answering machine, including a potential client who needed Roth to go down to the City Clerk's office to register for a fruit-stand license, and a call from his old boss at the Henrietta Hotel wondering if Chase could work for a couple more weeks until they found someone dependable to replace him.

He didn't recall having left Roth's number at The Henrietta. The only way they would have it was if someone else had left it there for them. Lotfi, of course – Lotfi banking on their man Tabib finding Chase this way. Otherwise, how would Tabib be able to find him at a number that belonged to someone called Joe Roth at the Kismet Detective Agency? I'm learning, Chase thought. It wasn't a bad feeling.

The other seven messages were long silences, as if the caller could not make up their mind whether to hang up or speak. Dialing back on the last number gave him nothing. He waited on that call, letting the day stretch lazily until the phone rang again. The first time he answered, the caller hung up right away. The second time Chase didn't give it a chance:

'It's me,' he spoke quickly in Tabib's native Tajik dialect of Persian. 'It's Chase, T. I know you've been trying to call me.'

'How did you know?'

'Tabib, do you trust me?'

'I don't know.'

'Where are you?'

Silence.

'Tabib, there are people after you. People who'd kill you for a lot less than what you've already done.'

60

'What have I done?'

It hit him: he didn't really know what Tabib had done. There was a certain degree of purity, even artlessness in the way Tabib had asked the question. It was not a challenge, not an invitation to state your purpose; rather, it was like a child's conviction that he was being unjustly punished. He'd caught Chase talking past the purpose of the call, and then easily trapped him with the whine of his innocence. It was an accidental hundred-and-eighty-degree turn to their conversation, which threw Chase completely offguard. He had no answer for the other man. He also recalled how Lotfi had insisted he wanted to talk to Tabib first. If it was a simple eye-for-an-eye job, then what was there to talk about? Something wasn't right about any of this.

'Tabib,' he said delicately, 'I have no idea what you've done.'

'Then what are you saying?'

'It's not what I'm saying, it's what *they're* saying.'

'Who're *they*?'

'Forget it. We can't talk now. Where are you?'

Silence again.

'All right, I'll give you a number to call.' It was a pointless thing to do, but the illusion of security was something doable and he did it. He gave Tabib the number to Seyyed's shop downstairs. 'Call me there in five minutes. Will you do that?'

'Yes.'

Seyyed's place was busier than usual. Seyyed himself was behind the grille calling out the orders to his customers. He gave a nod, as Chase walked over to him, explaining that he had a call coming.

Seyyed smiled. 'Joe would do that sometimes, come here to take a call.'

'Tell me something, Uncle Seyyed: I know Joe had a gun. But I didn't find one upstairs.'

Seyyed looked at him. The phone had already started to ring. Chase walked over to the back of the kitchen to take the call.

'Tabib?'

'I'm in Los Angeles,' Tabib said in rapid Tajik – instead of saying the name of the city, he translated it verbatim into Persian so that it literally became 'City of Angels'.

'What are you doing over . . .'

'Friend!'

'Yes?'

'It is a long story, this. Can we meet?'

'You trust me?'

'I have no choice.'

'You didn't kill anybody, did you?'

'They lie. They lie about me killing. I'm staying near the airport here.'

LAX airport. Seemed only right that Tabib should have turned up in Hollywood. Movie star Tabib. How they'd made fun of this man in those unkind weigh stations of the East. *Who do you think you look like, Tabib? Paul Newman or Marlon Brando?* Him shrugging them off and sticking to his English irregular verbs, knowing his time would come because he was counting on it, almost willing it into existence, seeing himself one day taking that eternal stroll down the avenue of the stars because that was the ridiculous seed that had been planted in him somewhere, somehow. But the stakes now were much more than that simple stroll: Tabib's own bumbling life was on the line. And having made this bet with himself, it mattered little to the Tajik whether he staked his chips here in America or in the ruins of Central Asia where he belonged.

Chase had written a number down on his hand. Now he could feel Seyyed's shadow on him as he hung up the phone.

'Joe had a gun, yes,' Seyyed said quietly. 'I have it. Do you want it?'

'Yes.'

'Are you in trouble, son?'

'It's the nature of Joe's business that calls for a gun, Uncle Seyyed. You understand.'

'I have taken a gun from his room. Will you take it now?'

'I must go away for a couple of days. When I come back I'll get it from you.'

'There is something else. Isn't there?'

'There is. Some men . . .'

'I know. They have been around. They are watching you. I've seen wars. I know when men are watching. You are in trouble?'

'I don't really know,' Chase told him in Persian. 'Sometimes the past catches up with you and you have to play it out, finish what you started. But I don't want to cause you any trouble.'

'It is no trouble. Joe was my good friend. Joe's friend is my friend. I will have the gun for you when you return.'

6

Monday, Venice Beach, California

Tabib had been talking in a monotone about being lost. The idea seemed to turn him resentful. Now he uttered something equally vague about how sunsets were false, promising that the night wouldn't be all that bad. 'But nights are always bad,' he went on sadly. 'They are bad because they are incomplete. Do you know that, Chase, my friend?'

Chase had noticed that Tabib made no attempt to speak English anymore. Making it this far seemed to have finally tempered his enthusiasm for things American. They watched the sun slowly sink into the Pacific. Two women sped past them on rollerblades. The curvatures of their bare legs became a point of contemplation for Tabib, who turned and followed the women with his eyes as if their relevance was something he had to consider.

'Why do they go on those wheels?' he asked, not so much puzzled as annoyed.

For a minute the reflection of the last light made the water look like a sea of chipped glass. Chase's eyes deceived him. The beach's asphalted throughway was like a constantly pulled curtain where you were condemned to witness athletic lives. The two men were strangers to this exuberance. They didn't belong. They heard a bicyclist yell at a pair walking ahead of him to get on their own side of the path. The pedestrians yelled something back and didn't move aside.

'Who will get in the way of their afternoon bicycle ride, that is their biggest worry,' Tabib reflected sadly again.

'You'd ride a bicycle too if you had a beach, old man.'

'I never had a beach,' he said dismissively. 'But you – you lived here. Did you ever do all this?'

'I played in the water, is what I did. After a while I thought a lot about when I could leave this place. I'd walk right on this beach and think about leaving again.'

'And I thought about coming.'

'The circle is now complete, old man. Now, tell me what you've done to get the Iranians after you?'

'The Iranians are not after me.'

'Then who is?'

Tabib hesitated. He really did look like a little Mongol boy who had suddenly put on thirty years, with rosy red cheeks and black hair now thinned to wormy wisps.

'Talk to me. This is Chase. Your friend. How did you get my number, for starters?'

'It was hard work. I found out where you lived before I came. In Tehran they knew where you were. If they had found out right away, they would have come to kill you, but it took three years, so when they finally found out they decided you were not a problem.'

'Well, that's good to know,' Chase said with little faith in his own words.

'Then I arrive here in Los Angeles and call your hotel and they say Chase is gone. You can imagine I'm not very happy about this.'

'No, I wouldn't be either. Good work though.' Chase waited a while before asking, 'So, what's the trouble?'

'I'm a fool, Chase. But I'm not a stupid fool. I take chances because a man like Tabib has to always take chances to make it in this world. I took a chance to get away from the Russians in the war. I took a chance to work with you in Khorasan. After you left like that, I don't know – it wasn't easy. Everything was hard. The Iranians, especially the people

65

in Tehran, thought if I was working with you then I must know where you had gone. They put pressure on me. They wouldn't let me work the border anymore. You really put me in a difficult place, friend.'

'I'm sorry. I felt trapped over there. I thought if I didn't take off then, I might never leave.'

Tabib nodded. 'Exactly. That was how I felt after you had gone. I went back to Tajikistan for a while. But you know how it is there. Fighting all the time and Russians still all over the place. I said to myself, if Chase can get out so will I.' He broke into English: 'Get the hell out, like the Americans say.'

They argued around what should have been the least contentious point for them right now – why it was necessary for them to go back to New York. Tabib didn't want to move from LA. Distances tired him; he wanted nothing to do with them anymore. How much distance did one have to cover during one life until it was finally enough? Wasn't it enough that he had gotten himself this far, past some impossible meridian soldiered and checkpointed by uniformed men who wished to see his kind stay where they belonged? 'Yes,' Chase wanted to tell him, Tabib should be commended for being here, a long-distance traveler, ready to claim what was his out on this California coastline.

Tabib wouldn't divulge much. He avoided revealing just how he had gotten here, under which friendly government's auspices he'd gone past American customs undisturbed. For all Chase knew, Tabib could have easily come here as a Russian, if not a Tajik or an Uzbek or even an Armenian. There was time yet to grill him harder about all that.

'If you want me to help you, you have to come to New York. It's that simple,' Chase persisted.

'But isn't that dangerous?'

It was dangerous, yes. But then again so was everything

else. Chase explained in what he believed was a patient, teacherly fashion that it had to be New York because that was where he felt comfortable operating now. Tabib started to protest and then went quiet. Chase understood what the other man had meant to say: *Hadn't Chase mostly grown up right here? Didn't he belong to this very beach, this very ocean?* But almost immediately Tabib had seen the error in his question and stopped himself – one belonged to wherever logistics were not an overwhelming factor. Chase, for his part, refrained from mentioning that they needed to be vigilant about it all, that the two of them shouldn't even be flying on the same plane to New York. There were passenger lists to consider, as there were special agents whose mouths started to water over such lists, thinking they were finally onto something that would make their careers move up a notch, or two.

'You have a lot of good movies to catch up on here, Tabib,' Chase said, trying to lighten up a bit. He watched the Tajik regard him for a moment as if the American had finally brought him home, reminded him why he had taken the trouble to get to Hollywood in the first place. Then Tabib's plum cheeks expanded and he started to laugh, his laughter carrying them all the way back to the white rent-a-car waiting for them at the parking lot adjacent to the beach.

They drove up the coast past Malibu Park. A loop around the Palisades. Tabib allowing his awe to drift until it went silent on him. So this was America! Chase drove in silence. He wanted to let his companion process it all on his own. No hurry yet. The landscape was big enough for that, generous enough. So much so that you'd forget sometimes just *how* big this country was, how soothing to be out of Manhattan, to be driving for days with no purpose, towards nowhere.

Then at some point past midnight, New York time, he got

out and called Mette at Billy's bar. The first thing she said to him was that he'd disappeared on her again.

'I'm in Los Angeles now, Mette. I'm calling you from a pay phone outside of a deserted gas station in Topanga. I'm in the hills in the dark. The entire city of Los Angeles sits beneath us here, as if we're at the edge of a new wilderness. A new wilderness with lots of Spanish names that make you imagine warm winds in tranquil places – Santa Ana, Santa Susana, Hermosa, Placentia . . .'

'Chase, are you drunk? You're not going to do something stupid, are you?'

'I'm trying to get lost for a bit, if you let me.'

'You don't need my permission to do anything.'

'I would like for a day to arrive when I feel I must get your permission.'

She sighed. 'Oh, Chase! Don't you see that's your first mistake?' There was an abrupt noise. Mette telling somebody in the bar she'd be right with them. Then back to him. 'Asking for permission is a tiresome thing. That's why children and prisoners are always so tired.' Silence. Then: 'Laugh, stupid! It's supposed to be funny.' More silence. 'Okay, there's something serious in what I just told you. I hope you can see it.'

'Mette!'

'Yes?'

'The man who was following me. The one you saw. Has he been around again?'

'He's here at the bar now, watching me talk to you on the phone.'

Four a.m. The place was one of several Persian-language bookshops that dotted Westwood Boulevard by the UCLA campus. A young woman in a black tank-top guided them past the books through a stairway leading down to the basement. He hadn't been here since over a year ago when he'd come for a weekend poppy run through LA's opium underground. The usually labored belly-dance music was, thankfully, subdued. Half asleep, the dancer on the T-shaped platform went through her motions with tired thrusts of her hips. There was one lone waiter with a silver tray fastened to one palm like it had mushroomed out of him. He offered the only thing he had now, second-rate caviar and vodka, with yogurt and sliced cucumber. Maybe a third of the tables were still occupied. Persians and Azeri Turks. Chase picked a table far from everybody else. Tabib glanced over at the dancer and gestured impatiently.

'How do you know of this place? Is it safe?'

'Safe enough. Don't worry.'

The woman who had showed them in returned. Tabib took the rolled cylinder of opium from her and sniffed at it with disdain.

'We're not in Dushanbe,' Chase explained. 'This is what you get.'

He'd brought the Tajik here because experience had taught him that there was a class of men whose tongues grew loose over the poppy. He wanted the other man to talk, even if it meant having to sit and suffer the ordeal of not being part of the act. Chase had already made up his mind to start shedding the habit, seriously, doing it one small skirmish at a time. He only wished Mette could witness what a bloody hero he was being for himself and her.

The men at the other tables clapped lazily off and on in the grimy light, dispassionately inviting the fair-skinned girl over to their table to stuff vodka-soaked dollar bills in her G-string. There was the lingering smell of kebab from earlier in the evening. That and the scent of the poppy.

They sat facing one another, Chase watching patiently while Tabib handled the pipe over the brazier. The dizzying vapors from the charcoal made Tabib's eyes turn. He looked over at Chase almost cross-eyed and finally spoke his piece.

'I have taken a manuscript,' Tabib started. 'That is why they are after me. I know it is worth something. I think it was in the museum in Kabul before the war.'

'Where's the manuscript now?'

Tabib shook his head. In that slight motion rested the absolute limit of the two men's trust in one another. It was no use repeating the question. So Chase remained quiet. They sat staring. Tabib made an offer of the pipe. Chase declined. The belly dancer edged toward them but moved off when they ignored her.

'I have left the manuscript behind,' Tabib volunteered. 'It is not here in America.'

'You left it in Tajikistan?' Chase asked surprised.

'We were not training in Tajikistan. I trained with some god-crazed Uzbeks instead.'

'What?' Chase waited, wishing his ears had deceived him, but of course they hadn't. He should get up and walk away right now. Logic, self-preservation, all that and more told him to. But he stayed. He looked at the other man and asked soberly, 'You said trained – trained for what?'

'It's a long story,' was Tabib's only answer.

Chase glanced at his watch. 'It's five-thirty in the morning,' he whispered. 'I've brought you here, you bastard, and you've had just enough of that stuff to keep you from taking a shit for at least two days. So what we've got plenty of, friend, is time. And I'm all ears.'

'I had to find a way to get to America, didn't I?' Tabib blurted out.

'So you decided to go through the camps?' Chase felt every

muscle in his body tighten. He felt sick inside. He grabbed at Tabib's wrist. 'Tell me, is that what you did? Did you go through the camps? Have you completely lost your mind, T?'

'I made it here, no?'

'And the manuscript? Is it in Lisbon, Milan, Marseilles? I know you guys had to have a leg in Europe, so don't play with me.'

'Istanbul,' Tabib uttered under his breath.

'Come again?'

'I said Istanbul. This is an interrogation?'

Pause.

'And the Uzbeks you were supposed to come here with? Mind telling me what you did with them?'

'Gave them the slip, didn't I? Let them be cursed. I don't want to kill anyone. They do. Let them go do it on their own time and money.'

'While you keep the manuscript.'

'There are losers in the world and there are winners.'

'Which are you?'

'I'm trying to find out about that still.'

They were quiet again. Tabib pulled his chair closer so that their faces almost touched. He looked straight into his friend's eyes. 'Will you help me, Chase?'

Chase exhaled. 'I've gotten too soft for this sort of thing, T. I've been a night manager in a hotel for the past . . . I don't know how long.'

'What is that, night manager?'

'Someone who has to stay awake and watch the clock.'

'Chase, I need your help. We can be rich I think. I'm not sure, but I think.'

'First thing first: what do you plan to do with the manuscript?'

'I plan to sell it to the right person. You'll help me. Yes?'

'How did you get it? Did it just grow wings one day and fly into your lap?'

'Come on! *They* had it. I told you, it was stolen, I think, from Kabul Museum just around the time the Russians left, or a little afterwards, maybe 1990, '91, I don't know. Somehow it ended up north over the border. The story I was told at first was we needed to raise money. The Russians were interested. They sent some people from Moscow and the last minute somebody told them to get lost. Whoever put this thing together figured there was no need for middlemen. Word was the book had to get to America for sure.'

'So you stole the thing and disappeared.'

'That is my story, friend. Please do not be upset with me.'

'And now the Uzbeks are after you for it.'

'Maybe them. Or maybe they sent the Iranians to get it. The Uzbeks, their government's in bed with the Americans anyway. They don't want to be too visible. They still got families back home. And I tell you, over there, it's like this: poof! Make one wrong move and you disappear. You disappear for good, with the blessings of American military advisors.'

'No anti-American lectures from you of all people, please!'

'What do you mean? My knees go weak for America. This is not me, Chase; this is how people talk over there. You *know* that.'

'So what do you suppose the deal is? Why would the Uzbeks have sent Iranians after you?'

'Remember them – the Islamic Movement of Uzbekistan? The Americans mostly wasted the lot when they went in Afghanistan. But those IMU crazies still got a life or two left in them. They're regrouping. Over there everybody is. They probably found out about you and me, how we used to work together in Khorasan. Maybe they offered the Iranians a deal:

get the manuscript and you can keep it, but make sure Tabib is dead.'

'If they want you dead that bad, then they're afraid you'll give them away to the police here. Have you thought of doing that?'

'No, no, no! All Tabib wants now is a quiet life in America, like you. Maybe I too can become a night manager.'

'You wouldn't like it very much.'

'Then . . .' He was stuck for words.

'Talk to me, T. What have these guys come for?'

'I don't know. I honestly don't. Probably bad things. Why else would they come. America puts the squeeze here, you pop up someplace else. They got new expressions for it, "deep thinking", "long-term planning", "mobility".'

'Right!'

'Don't make fun of me. A lot of these guys might be stupid, but not all of them. You think just because you got more airport security now, it's not possible to get in? Some Pakistani fellow will draw you a blueprint how he'll put you on a Greek merchant ship, drop you off in Vancouver and the rest you already know. Easier still, they'll get you as far as Paraguay to this city called Ciudad del Este – you know about it?'

Chase nodded, waiting to see where Tabib was going with all of this. 'I know about the place. It's teeming with sons of bitches we know,' Chase said in English.

'See what I mean? Get you to Ciudad, then up the road to Mexico and before you know it you're sitting by the beach in Los Angeles watching women roller skate past you. It's a difficult ride, but it's there to take and no one can stop you.'

Chase sighed. 'Is that how you got here, T?'

'How I got here is not important now. My point is these men are serious about their foolishness.'

73

'And you just happened to take a ride on their tail because that was what was available.'

Tabib waved his hand, as if warding off a blow from Chase. 'They just got more fierce since you left, my friend. They sit around the fire and talk about stuff. They say if the Yank's got his soldiers screwing their Uzbek women and training their police to kill them, then they'll just have to make sure the next time they hit, the hitters are Uzbek. Do you see the logic of this thing, Chase? It's all up here.' He tapped his forehead with his index finger to make the point.

'T,' Chase interrupted finally, 'stop this political rant. Tell me something specific.'

'Look, I already told you I don't know what they've come for. I couldn't even tell you for sure they've come. They probably got scared after I disappeared in Europe and went under for a while. These guys are not professional.'

'And you are?'

'Chase, I've lived around Uzbeks most all my life. Truth is they couldn't tell you if Mexico is to the north or south of Canada. Two weeks from now these guys will forget about the manuscript. What they want is not to get caught. Another week passes, they'll see Tabib is not telling on them to anyone and they'll leave old Tabib alone, just as the Iranians left you alone after Tehran.'

There was enough material here to grind out another notebook or two at least; it seemed to Chase that they had been speaking for days and days. He felt a bit woozy, and watching Tabib work the drug so greedily didn't help much either. Chase had some methadone on him, but he was trying to be *good*. He'd wait himself out and sweat at least another couple of hours. That's what he was doing now – cold, wet and hungry beads of sweat that made it hard to focus himself.

'Tabib!'

'Yes? You'll help me, Chase?'

'How about I take you to the police and you let them help you? I mean this as your friend.'

Tabib winced, as if Chase had slapped him. 'You hurt me, brother. Why do you say this to me now?'

'Because, one: I think you've dug yourself into a terrible hole. Two, leaving out the bit about the manuscript, I think you could really endear yourself to certain people with your story. People who can give you your American citizenship just like that, with a snap and a phone call. That's what you've always wanted, isn't it?'

'I can buy any citizenship I want when I have that money, Chase. Don't you see I've brought us our inheritance? Yours and mine. It's a beautiful strange book someone would pay a fortune for. I know it. And afterwards, we can relax and be kind to ourselves and to the poor. Yes?'

'Give me one good reason why you won't talk to the police.'

'Why? Because they will chew me and then spit me out. You know that, Chase. You know how they are. And they will do the same to you. Sure, you've been honest lately, but do you think they care? They'll hang us for the sake of their quotas; this is what they'll do. It's not so different here than where I come from. Tell me if I'm wrong, Chase? Look in my eyes and tell me if I'm wrong?'

Upstairs in the bookstore shelf upon shelf of hardbound Persian volumes stared back at them in semi-darkness – solemn tablets from a language that long ago had lost much of its relevance. Chase had been thinking on the way up. He asked Tabib to stop for a minute. The hostess who'd been escorting them gave Chase a quizzical look.

'You didn't tell me what the manuscript is about, did you, T?'

'A book full of ghouls and devils and naked women in hell. It's a nice hell, though. Nobody's unhappy to be there.'

'Miniatures?'

'Yes, of course yes!'

'Devils in hell having a good time?'

'Looked like hell to me.'

'That's unlikely.' It was the hostess who said this. Tabib and Chase had been speaking Persian, as usual, forgetting that the young woman would most probably understand them. They turned to her, unsure if she was angry at them for lingering there or because she had something to say about the manuscript's subject matter. 'I work in this bookstore three days a week,' she said. 'I'm familiar with a lot of miniatures. They have pictures of hell, yes. But nobody is ever having a party in that place.'

Tabib was genuinely offended, swearing on the grave of the woman who gave him birth that he was not lying. Chase asked him the name of the book.

'*Hallaj-Nama.*'

Again the girl butted in: 'I don't know of it.'

'You an art historian?' Chase asked.

'I work here, I said.'

'My aunt Thelma used to sweep floors on Wall Street. Didn't make her a brilliant bonds trader, though.'

She turned to the door, insulted. 'It's very late, gentlemen,' she said coldly. Her long dark hair lapping at her bare shoulders. No doubt she had ambitions that had to do with art, literature and the bookstore part of the place rather than the lower floor.

Chase had been crude, alienating her for no reason. 'Look,' he said, 'all I want is to look through what English books you've got on Persian art or Persian-style miniatures. Maybe there's a mention of this manuscript somewhere in one of them. Even if it's a fake, there might be a mention about it.'

She softened, too quickly he thought – the curiosity of an art-world girl getting the best of her. 'What are we looking for exactly?' she now asked.

'All I can tell you is that this hell manuscript was supposed to be in the museum in Kabul at one time.'

'Kabul, you say?' Head poised and thinking, advertising for their sakes her knowledge of what she thought she knew on that realm. 'Might be the School of Herat, the Timurid dynasty. Though I still doubt it.'

'I'll buy that.'

She switched on a rear ceiling light, then collected a stack from the English-language art section and brought them to the back of the store. The books' covers were full of resplendent pictures of men, women and musicians in odd architectural paradises with animals roaming on flat surfaces. Chase and Tabib looked on while she skimmed through one book after another in silence. The pages depicted the same miniatures you'd see in just about any survey of Islamic art. He'd never been much attracted to them. There was always too much calm turmoil to these miniatures – calligraphy above the still figures portraying the usual suspects: mythic lovers and their predicaments. Kings receiving homage from petrified subjects, princes going hunting, engaging in war and lust in bright colors surrounded by gold leaf in the margins. There was the blood of real people behind the works, and yet the works themselves remained mute.

As the girl went on perusing, Chase picked up a promising-looking and heftily titled volume called *Miniatures from the Time of Baysunqur to Husayn Bayqara*, to do the same thing. Almost immediately he hit on it in the bibliography. Four pages into the back section, he came across the name, the *Hallaj-Nama*, with a reference to page 119 for a visual.

Tabib, who had been standing over him, gave a start as soon as they turned to that page. The color photograph was only quarter-page in size, but more than enough for Tabib.

'That's it! That's the one,' he cried.

All three of them stared now at the image. It was of blackened demons fleshed out in thick woolen cloaks, dancing in a circle of fire that had been rendered in bright gold. To one side of the picture, naked women carried tall gourds and seemed to beckon to the euphoric beasts. The caption said that this was a rare photo of an original manuscript page.

Even the girl showed some surprise. 'I'd never seen this before.'

'Now you have,' Tabib declared triumphantly.

'Could be fake, though. Or it would have been mentioned in the textbooks,' she said. 'The colors are right, but the subject matter is strange. It says the manuscript was *allegedly* located at Kabul Museum. I don't understand.'

Chase answered. 'Oh, you know how it was when the Russians were there. Everything got stolen from the museums. Everything!'

She asked if they wanted to purchase the book. Yes, they would. They would like that very much. Minutes later she was locking up behind them. End of her shift. Her days a revolving door of men who entered the shop for all the wrong things; not miniature reproductions and classical Persian poetry, but second-rate caviar, suspect opium, and worn-out belly dance.

A drive to the hotel afterwards and then to LAX where, despite some misgiving, Chase got them on the same flight back to the East Coast. He saw Tabib produce a real enough California driver's license with a different name but his own picture on it. Tabib was smirking and almost childlike with enthusiasm once they were airborne, ordering drink after drink and telling Chase, 'I told you so. I told you the book was real.'

'All right. But where is it?' Chase asked after a while of listening to Tabib's babble.

Tabib was holding a small key in his palm. 'I want you to hold onto this, my friend.'

Chase took it. 'What is it?'

The Tajik looked at him meaningfully. 'Please! Don't lose this key. I will tell you what it opens later. You'll help me get the book soon. Yes? We sell it together. We two are friends. Partners.'

Chase just sighed. 'All right, T. But then what? Do you think these guys are really going to forget you ripped them off?'

'The whole world ripped off Afghanistan,' the Tajik answered softly, lowering his voice when he uttered the word Afghanistan, even though they weren't speaking English. 'I only ripped off a small part of it,' he went on. 'If I hadn't taken the manuscript who knows where it would have ended up. Probably some pious fools would have burned it to a crisp because they thought the images were blasphemous. I've saved a work of art, is what I've done.'

'Sure.'

'I did it for art, did it for me, did it for you.'

A pause of an hour on the airplane.

'Chase, what are we going to do in New York?'

'See a specialist. See how much your manuscript is worth.'

'How about this guy Lotfi you mentioned?'

'Oh, did I mention him?' Chase said, giving the other man a stare. 'We have to keep you away from him. That's what we have to do.'

'Why not just get rid of the guy then?'

'You don't get rid of men like him; they come off an assembly line.'

'So what do we do?'

'I'm going to leave you in a place called New Jersey. That's just across the water from me. We'll have to be cautious for the time being.'

'Play our cards right, like in the old days, yes?'

'Something like that.'

Looking at Tabib he could not tell if the Tajik was really so reckless or if the gravity of what he'd done had simply made him stupid. Chase thought: And I'm stupid to be with him. It was that time. He went and locked himself in the bathroom of the airplane, tossed a bit of the methadone into its cap and drank it. It would be a while. The bathroom smelled like death, so did the methadone – which took him back to when he was a kid and had to swallow the obligatory pink cough syrup for just about every illness he came down with. His muscles felt packed down, like he'd been given a sound beating. Nobody, he thought, should have to know what withdrawal was. And yet withdrawal was everywhere. It defined everything that people like Tabib, Mette and himself had ever done, accomplished or failed to do. *We're the bastards of the habit*. It was an idea that kept him nauseous and annoyed during the rest of the flight back to the city.

7

Wednesday

It turned out to be another day of many phone calls. Tabib, too, had already called several times from the other side of the river, warning that boredom was going to drive him to do something extreme.

'You've already done something extreme,' Chase reminded him.

'But I want to come to New York. I can see it from here. I've never seen anything like it.'

'It used to look better.'

'What do you mean?'

'Forget it.'

'What will we do about my book?'

'We don't exactly have it in our hands right now, do we?'

Later, a sleepy Mette picked up her phone.

'I've been reading your notebooks,' she said.

'Good. They were written, I'm beginning to think, to be read by no one else but you.'

'No one else? Maybe you have an exaggerated view of yourself, Chase.'

'Maybe an exaggerated view of myself is just what I need to get me through the day.'

'When are you coming to see me?'

'Now if you'd like.'

She asked, 'Who's Joe Roth? You write about him a lot.'

'He's the friend I told you about, the one who died.'

It felt as if he were being graded on the quality of his writing, or maybe the worth of his past experience. She said, 'Chase, you have this particular obsession. You go on and on about it, page after page.'

'You mean my fascination with my own habit?'

'Yes. It must get boring after a while. I know it did for me.'

'Mette, some Frenchman once said that everything one does in life, even love, occurs on an express train racing towards death. Fellow like me, all I want is to be able to get off of this train once in a while.'

'It must be nice to justify yourself with poetry.'

'It's like taking an elegant shit, is what it is. It doesn't mean a thing.'

'*You* said it, Chase. Not me.'

More calls. A man left a message for 'Mr Detective Yusef Roth' in broken English about 'a delicate matter' in Far Rockaway. The Arab fellow Najjar called with many thanks on the good advice Chase had given him about how to deal with the Russians; they'd managed to negotiate something reasonable. 'And may God protect you for protecting us.'

Chase watched the street below from the kitchen window. A man who wasn't Chinese was sitting on a cement block by the bus stop half a block away in front of Ang's Hardware reading a newspaper. No one ever sat on that cement block to read a newspaper, least of all someone not Chinese. Chase thought he recognized one of Lotfi's men from several nights earlier at the taxi garage. He called the old man downstairs.

'Uncle Seyyed, who's in your shop right now?'

'The same man who was here waiting for you yesterday. He's an Iranian.'

'Did you talk to him?'

'I don't need to talk to him. I can tell. Are you in trouble?'

'Often. You have that thing I asked for?'

'I left it under your bed while you were gone. It is a good instrument. I tried it. I left you some other things too.'

Some other things turned out to be two boxes of 9mm ammo. The piece itself was a compact Smith & Wesson easily concealable in pants pockets.

He called back down to the old Afghan. 'Tell the Iranian fellow he can come up if he wants.'

'He's already coming.'

The downstairs door rang immediately and he buzzed Lotfi in without bothering to ask who it was. In another minute Lotfi stood in the middle of the apartment grinning and saying nothing. To make it easier on both of them, Chase began.

'I've made contact with Tabib.'

'And?'

'Currently indisposed. He'd like to take in the sites for a while.'

'What are you playing at, Chase? My men lost track of you. Where did you disappear to?'

'Never mind where I've been. Point is you lied to me, Lotfi. Tabib hasn't killed anyone. That's not the reason you're after him.'

Lotfi laughed. He was eyeing the room and shaking his head. 'Wherever you live, Chase, you live second class.'

'Don't change the subject. Take a seat.'

The Iranian did. They listened to the phone ring. The call was from another Arab who spoke into the machine about needing to go to 1 Police Plaza to apply for a gun license to protect his delicatessen in Brooklyn. He was afraid to go alone and would like 'brother Roth' to go with him.

Lotfi: 'Brother Roth?'

'I'm in the business of helping people these days.'

'Why don't you help us by telling me where Tabib is.'

'He's around. Safe. He doesn't have the book on him.'

'The book?'

'I know about it. No use playing dumb with me, Lotfi.'

'You sure of that?' Lotfi asked more gravely now.

'Sure of what? That I don't want to be played dumb, or that I'm sure Tabib hasn't the book on him right now?'

Lotfi sighed. 'What is it you want, Chase?'

'Look, what do you think you could gain by getting to the guy, anyway? Nothing! The man's a Tajik. He'll spit in your face when you cut off his nose; he'll just laugh it off and die. And then what? Still no manuscript. You're a businessman, Lotfi. Let's handle this logically.'

'This is why I ask, what do you want?'

'I want to bargain with you. For starters, Tabib does not die. There's a simple explanation for this: I have a soft spot for the fellow. Two, you tell me where to find the cell he broke from. If they're in the States I want to know about it.'

Lotfi seemed to consider this. 'What can I expect from you in return?'

'I'll give you the manuscript. But with some further conditions. The thing's worth something. We can talk about that later.'

'Then you do have it?'

'I may.'

Lotfi stood and started to come towards him. 'What if I called my guys in and *made* you tell me where it is.'

'Remember where you are, Lotfi. This is not Tehran, and the law is very jumpy around here nowadays. Very jumpy! I'll call my friend at the Bureau before you can holler into your phone. Or else, what I can do is . . .' Chase pulled out Roth's gun and pointed it at him. 'I can simply shoot you first and deliver you to the proper authorities afterwards. Better yet, maybe I'll go ahead and mail you in little bits and pieces back to the desert you just came from.'

84

Lotfi sat back down, twitching nervously. 'Put that thing away, Chase. You and I don't need that between us.'

Chase stayed firm. 'I will get you the manuscript. And whatever its market price, I'll sell it to you for a fifth of that. That's more than fair. You can relay my offer to Tehran. I'll be waiting for an answer.'

'What about Tabib? He may not like you selling his goods so cheap.'

'He hasn't a choice, has he? He's lucky to be alive. You're doing me a favor by not killing him. Right, Lotfi?' When the other man said nothing, Chase repeated the question, 'You will *not* be killing Tabib, Right?'

'Right. Damn you!'

'Good. Now what about that other thing. I want that cell, the Uzbeks – wherever they are. How about it?'

'How about what? They're not mine to hand over to you,' Lotfi said, raising his voice.

Another phone call was coming in. They were both ears. It was Mette's voice. 'Chase, are you there?'

Lotfi: 'Your girl. You care for her quite a bit, don't you?'

'Don't even go there, Lotfi.'

'So you do care. I'll have to remember this.'

'The cell, Lotfi. Tell me about the cell.'

'The manuscript first. Where is it right now?'

'It's under the seat of Elvis's blue Cadillac at Graceland.'

'What?'

'It's back in Afghanistan where little snot-nosed boys with Kalashnikovs are using its pages to wipe their brown asses with.'

'You're not going to give me the book, are you?'

'I just told you what I am prepared to do. To make it real, I'll give you photographs of several original pages in a few days. I'll include my own hand giving a thumbs-up in the photo to show you it's an honest deal. It's my goodwill gesture to you and your people. So don't follow me around or I may get upset and make that call anyway.'

'The hell with you, Chase!'

'That's fine, the hell with me. But first tell me something about this cell or we have no deal whatsoever.'

'Dearborn,' the Iranian barked.

Chase sat back. He had his answer. The Uzbeks were entirely beside the point; he'd only been needling Lotfi about them to find this out: the fact that the Iranian was willing to give the Uzbeks away so quickly meant that the manuscript was the thing at stake; the Uzbeks were a non-issue. They always had been. And yet, Chase had to act like he gave a damn about them.

He feigned surprise, 'Dearborn, Michigan? That's an Arab enclave. These people we're talking about are supposed to be Uzbeks. What do they have to do with Arabs in Michigan?'

'You're killing me, Chase. Dearborn is the word I have on them, and that's the *only* word I have. That's if they even made it this far after your friend screwed them like he did.' Lotfi rose up huffily and headed for the door. 'Put that gun away! I'll be back in a few days and God help you if you don't have something for me by then.'

'Talk to Tehran. Tell them not to be greedy and they'll get the manuscript.'

'I hope so for your sake.'

Lotfi's exit left a trail of empty threats in its wake. Chase knew that his own threats hadn't much substance either. But at least they held their own. You could bluff your way pretty far before smacking against a dead wall. And even then, maybe you could still keep going.

86

8

Thursday

She told him how she had spent the *best years* of her life contemplating her habit. For some, like Mette, it was a matter of getting on a plane and leaving. For him it was a matter of seeking someone like her out for his own deliverance. She understood this and, thankfully, didn't contest it. Maybe she found his sudden pull towards her amusing, yet she didn't shut him out. This was a step in the right direction. They made love, though it didn't come easy. There had to be a better world for them. A place where out-bound buses to New Jersey didn't rattle your windows every few minutes. A place where you wouldn't have to burn incense in order to obscure the stench of unrequited men from a bar twelve feet below you.

He watched her in the studio's tiny kitchen cracking eggs into a skillet and walked over to kiss her back.

'I'd like you to take a vacation for a while,' he said.

'Why?'

'You said it yourself – all those years you were too deep into your habit to go anywhere. Now's the time. America's a big, beautiful place. I got extra money. I want to send you on a tour.'

'You want me out of the way for a while. Why?'

He kept a steady eye on her. 'Because the guy you saw in the bar, he was at my place last night. He heard you leaving me a message.'

'I thought you said everything was fixed with him.'

'Nothing's fixed until it is.'

'You should have thought of that before you started coming to my place,' she said irritably.

'Mette.'

'Leave, Chase!'

She turned off the stove. Only half-done, the eggs stopped their quivering. At the same time the toaster popped two slices of white bread like a lurid objection to the unwelcome guest in the house. Mette drew distance, perched on the bed now, feigning interest in a free issue of a music magazine that had found its way to her studio. He put on his clothes, but then as he turned to leave she called out to him.

'Chase!'

'Yeah?'

'I've been reading more of your notebooks.'

'Anything interesting?'

'What I mean to say is: quit dwelling on *you* so much.'

'I'd have to dwell on other things then, and other people. That takes time. And some help. You're not helping much.'

It took a few hours at the city's research library before he had pared it down to a meaningful list. From over a dozen names, two stood out, mainly because they had New York addresses. One of them didn't answer. The other was Herman Lund, with a posh gallery address on West 57th Street. Lund turned out to be a specialist in North Indian and Middle Eastern art. Particularly miniatures. Apparently he held a doctoral degree in the subject; before becoming a dealer he had actually taught in Chicago and Ankara. When Chase called him he was cool and impatient. Chase had expected that. He asked some general questions about miniatures and the Herat School and felt Lund slowly warming to the subject. Then, once it seemed Lund might be a man to do business with, he came out with the bombshell, mentioning the

Hallaj-Nama. The title alone pushed their conversation into some kind of hyper-spin. All of a sudden Lund was thrashing for words, asking if they could meet right away. Chase hadn't expected it to be quite like that, the way the mere name of the manuscript could so abruptly open a door. It all seemed a bit too amplified, and he wasn't sure now exactly where his intuition lay on this. But it was he who had made the call, so it was only right that he should agree to the meeting. He gave a false name and stipulated that they couldn't meet at Lund's office. 'You understand, Mr Lund, this is a rather delicate matter.' Yes, yes, the art dealer understood perfectly. Where should they meet then? Chase suggested the fake waterfall spot on 53rd, between 5th and Madison. It was near enough Lund's office, a place where two people might hold a quiet conversation in the open without the worry of being overheard.

Three p.m. Lund looked like someone had put the squeeze to his face. He appeared compressed, like a man whose jaw had more things to do than there was room for. He didn't have to say anything for Chase to be able to tell he disapproved of where he'd been asked to come – a fake waterfall surrounded by skyscrapers, alongside office workers chasing cold tranquility on a February afternoon. He sat down with the offer of an uncertain smile.

'What you mentioned on the phone, Mr Boyd,' the art dealer said, 'I find very interesting.'

'How about telling me a little bit about the *Hallaj-Nama*, if you don't mind.'

'Mind? I certainly don't mind. Though I'd like to know how you came to be interested in this particular work.'

'It disappeared from the Kabul Museum, some time during or after the Afghan/Soviet war. Correct?'

Lund inched closer. 'That seems to be the general consensus. But I wouldn't bet on it. The *Hallaj-Nama* was not the sort of work that could easily be put on display in a strictly Muslim country. In any case, the matter of its exact location in the past doesn't hold my interest now. I'm only interested in the thing itself. A work of rare beauty supposedly. But who can really tell until the thing has been thoroughly examined. It never has. Not to my knowledge. Besides, there are many works of beauty from the era when the *Hallaj-Nama* was supposed to have been put together.'

'So what makes this one so special?'

'Perhaps it's not necessarily the pages of miniatures themselves that are of interest to the connoisseurs, but the subject matter certainly is.'

'The subject matter?'

'Don't get me wrong. From what I know the paintings are supposed to be quite a feat, especially in the way they broke rank from anything that had come before them, or, in fact, came after them.'

'Talk to me, Mr Lund. Tell me about this *Hallaj-Nama*. What is it that makes it so sought after now?'

Lund gave him a cunning look and turned to the fake waterfall. 'You could say that every lover of a certain art form waits out a lifetime for a conversation like this. Tell me, do you possess the *Hallaj-Nama*?'

Chase nodded. Yes. Anything less would get the man thinking, and all Chase really wished for him to think about now was the manuscript itself. Since Lund was here it meant he would not be going to the police. Every art dealer between New York and Tokyo was aware of how much had been looted from Afghanistan. Rare objects continued to flow West, more so now than ever before. Few asked questions. One justification being that it was certainly better to have the treasures here than to leave them in the hands of the *barbarians*.

Look, they said, at what had happened to the great Buddhas of Bamiyan. Besides, you already had American soldiers walking away from Afghan middlemen with two-thousand-year-old coins and pottery, so why shouldn't the professionals get in on it?

Lund spoke. 'How did you manage to come upon this manuscript? Can I see it? Do you have an asking price for it?'

'Easy, Mr Lund. I know the asking price would be substantial. Let's just say that the manuscript is very safe right now. It's not here in the United States yet. But it's not in the wilds of Central Asia either. If asked for, I can arrange for it to be moved to New York very quickly.'

'Then what is it that you wish to know from me?'

'About the manuscript itself. I'll be honest with you. I know little about such things. What I do know is that there are those who would give a lot to get their hands on the work. Would you be one of those people, Mr Lund?'

'I might be. Let me rephrase, I am. I am an interested party.'

'Tell me why.'

'Because the *Hallaj-Nama* is that curious marriage of the sacred and profane in classical art. It's a work of stupendous audacity. It's a series of miniatures done by the craftsmen of a fellow called *Baysunghur* . . .'

'I know that name.'

'Well, actually you don't need to know who Baysunghur was. He was a prince and major patron of the arts in his time. We're talking here of some six hundred or so years ago. The Timurids and some other satellite dynasties. It's all rather confusing. So please don't ask me who the Timurids were.'

'I won't. Go on.'

'I have brought the only known reproduction of the *Hallaj-Nama* to show you. All those years before the Soviet war the manuscript was not allowed to be photographed. The subject matter was taboo. Everything in relation to that book was taboo. They say there was even a time they seriously thought about burning the thing. But there was a great outcry from the West. Soon after that, the country self-destructed and the manuscript disappeared from everyone's radar screen.' Lund gave a meaningful look. 'Until today.'

Then he took a book out of his briefcase and turned to page 119. Of course it was the same shot of the manuscript page from the same book Chase had seen at the Persian bookstore in Los Angeles.

'Imagine,' Lund said, 'there are said to be upwards of three dozen more pages similar to this one, half of them images and the other half calligraphic text, the written words of Hallaj, one of the great, perhaps the greatest, Sufi martyrs of Islam. But the point is this: it isn't that depictions of hell were never done in this form of art. This book I've brought you to look at is something of a survey work and it shows many of the different schools of miniature painting that flourished in that part of the world. Here!' He turned to another page of the book. 'Look at this! This is your typical hell scene. There's the prophet Mohammed resting against a cloud of gold leaves, visiting hell – hell distinguished by its black background. What is happening to these sinners, mur- derers, adulterers? They're having cauldrons of molten metal poured into their gullets by red demons. There's no respite for the sinners. This is the hell we know, Mr Boyd. The hell that's proper to the world of Islam or any other monotheistic religion, for that matter. Now compare this horror scene with the single reproduction from the *Hallaj-Nama*. What is hap- pening here? The same characters at work, excluding the prophet who no longer has any business here, right? You can see the Central Asian, Shamanistic-influenced line drawings of the *Siyah Qalam* school of painting all over the work. But that's only the technical aspect of the thing. What no one could have ever imagined is these sinners and the demons are actually living quite well in hell. Who drew these miniatures? Which workshop, laboring arguably under Prince Baysunghur's orders, was responsible for this radical departure in form and content? We don't know. We won't know until we have the work itself and allow experts to examine it closely.'

'Sounds like a regular feast for art lovers.'

'That's if the thing is real. In academic circles the *Hallaj-Nama* stopped being talked about a generation ago. I suppose rightly so. You can't really talk about something no one can get their hands on. And this one photograph I showed you could easily be a fake. Until we have the original, we won't really know if it's genuine or not.'

'And perhaps when and if its authenticity is established Herman Lund could sell it to the highest bidder in one of the great museums of the West.'

Lund didn't evade the observation. 'Yes. That *could* be the next step. To resell the manuscript. Why not? The Afghan relics are everywhere now. What you are doing is not a crime. I'm almost certain you haven't stolen the book from any legitimate place of safekeeping. Similarly, I won't be committing a crime if and when I choose to sell it. Trust me, I would not have asked to meet with you today if the object in question had come from any other place in the world. I am not a thief, Mr Boyd.'

Originally Chase had half convinced himself he was only coming to Lund for information. But Lund's enthusiasm had had its effect on him and he'd found himself discussing the manuscript's sale without realizing at first what it was he was actually doing. Lotfi and the Iranians would not be amused if they found out. So the only way Chase could justify himself was to quickly relay to those people that he'd found a buyer and that he planned to take his fifth off the top when the deal was made. This was playing with fire; it was far worse than his having skipped Tehran on a Canadian passport seven years earlier. But it was the Iranians who had started this, and Chase meant to finish things better than he'd done last time around.

He spoke intently to Lund. 'I have no problem with all this. I'll deal with you, you deal with whoever you wish. Just keep me out of it. And don't speak a word of this to anyone for the time being. How's that?'

'This is a given.'

He regarded Lund's squashed and expectant face, feeling for an instant altogether out of his depth. What was the next step from here? This was not the Khorasan province of northeastern Iran and what he had to sell was something he'd never even seen or touched before.

'Why the title *Hallaj–Nama*?' he asked. 'What does it mean?'

Lund sighed. 'I'd have to give you a fairly long lecture on that particular subject. It wouldn't do to sit here and begin it now. Most importantly, it wouldn't be doing the great Hallaj justice to approach him so casually. You promise to allow me to lay my eyes on the manuscript and I will tell you about Hallaj until you feel you have known him all your life. Hallaj wasn't just a mystic, he was a prophet, and for that his head was strung on a pole at the gates of Baghdad a thousand years ago. Think about that!'

He *would* think about it. He would think about how Roth had loved reading up on that sort of thing – about fellows like the one Lund had mentioned, and other half-mad

Muslim poets of bygone days who had made a habit of turning their own religion on its head only to end up paying for it.

He was back at the house now, pacing and agitated. He called Mette at Billy's bar. She picked up herself.

'Busy?'

'No, it's too early yet. Where are you?'

'Thinking.'

'Thinking about what?'

'About how we *both* could go on a trip. And I've been thinking even more.'

'I'm waiting.'

'I've been thinking maybe we could leave New York altogether. I got a few dollars.'

'So you said.'

'We could go raise sheep in the country or move to Michigan's Upper Peninsula and give guided tours to adventure seekers.'

'Chase!'

'Aha?'

'Come see me late tonight. After I finish. At home. You sound bad. Do you feel bad?'

'I get worked up when I have to juggle too many things at once.'

'Just stay calm, please!'

The last thing he could do now was stay calm. He said, 'I love your name. Mette! Sounds like a Scandinavian hammer or something.'

'Goodbye, Chase.'

'Please don't hang up just yet.' But she already had.

This was the situation: Lotfi was dead. Earlier, when he'd first discovered him on Roth's blood-spattered bed, single bullet-hole in the back of his neck, he tried to simply dismiss the scene as some trick of the imagination. Lotfi should not be dead. Why should he? Who would kill him? For a long time with the door to that bedroom and that dead man firmly shut, he lingered in the kitchen and sat by his comfort stove, thinking about gorging himself. But he didn't. He didn't because he knew there was not going to be anything lyrical about any of this. No ancient mariners to talk to here. No unwieldy hallucinations to mull over afterwards. In fact, everything, including the Iranian's death, seemed so ordinary, that he was embarrassed at the dullness of it all. He was here with a man's corpse on Roth's bed and no one had ever taught him how to dissolve a body in an acid bath or shown him a pig farm where the owner would turn a blind eye if he fed his animals a cadaver.

The phone rang. It was Tabib. 'I'm bored here, Chase, in this terrible hotel. I want to come where you are.'

'You mean you weren't here today?' Chase almost yelled into the phone.

Tabib's voice broke. 'What are you on about, friend?'

'Are you at your place, Tabib?'

'I am.'

'I will call you in five minutes.'

There was the concerned look on old Seyyed's face when he saw Chase coming round back to use his phone.

'How is the gun?' the old man asked.

'The gun's all right, Uncle Seyyed. But . . .'

'What is it?'

'Nothing. I must use your phone.'

A customer called and Seyyed turned and walked the other way. Chase dialed. When Tabib picked up it was all he could do to keep from screaming at him again.

'You sure you haven't been to the city lately?'

'Chase, my brother, what city? How would I find my way

there? You have me sitting in this room. There are all these people out there on the street. They eat bad food. They are too loud. I don't like it here.'

'*You're* the son of a whore who wanted to come to America. Oh forget it! Tabib, talk to me!'

'What has happened?'

'You don't know?'

'You are killing me, my brother. What? What has happened?'

Chase took a deep breath. 'Tabib, listen to me, I'll come get you later. Very late. Don't go anywhere. Don't open the door to anyone. Don't do anything. Don't even breathe if you can help it.'

The Tajik was silent for a second, and then: 'Okay, I will not breathe. Okay.'

Fifteen minutes passed. There was a lone Chinaman eating a Shawarma sandwich, of all things, in Seyyed's little shop. Chase sat in a corner of the kitchen saying nothing. Seyyed was watching him – in his face a token stoicism that was as old as his native land and just as unforgiving. When the Chinaman left, Chase turned to the old Afghan.

'Uncle Seyyed, close up the shop, please.'

It wasn't quite closing time yet, but Seyyed didn't protest. He locked up and came over to Chase.

'What has happened?'

'I don't wish to say.'

'Then don't. Sometimes it is best that way.'

'Maybe sometimes a man needs a hand, Uncle Seyyed. It is true with the best of men. It was true even with our friend Joe – peace be upon him – who was the best of the best.'

'Indeed he was a man with a fine strong thread to him, a man who backed from no one. I have heard it said that in Afghanistan . . .'

97

Chase didn't let him finish. 'I think this is what I want to know, Uncle Seyyed. About Afghanistan.'

'I was not there with him.'

'But maybe there were those who were. Men who would have done anything for Joe Roth. Men whom he could turn to in times of trouble. I need one of those men now. Joe mentioned a man like that once. He said if I was ever really in . . . trouble, and if Joe himself wasn't around . . . he said I should seek this man. But I've forgotten, Uncle Seyyed. I've forgotten. I can't remember. It was some time ago when he told me that.'

A moment of edgy silence. Then: 'Perhaps the man you want, his name – I have heard him called "The Black".'

'Where can I find him?'

'I do not know.'

'The Black? Joe didn't say that name. Where was he from? Was he an Arab?'

'No, he is American.'

'Are you sure of this?'

The old man gave a don't-insult-my-intelligence look. 'I have seen him. A big man. He was in Afghanistan when Joe was there. I know this much.'

'Uncle Seyyed, I need to know if he would do anything, absolutely anything for Joe.'

'For Joe, yes. But you are not Joe.'

They were quiet for a while. The old man put a sponge to the grill and began cleaning up. Chase was lost for words, imposing himself as he had. Who was he, after all, to this old Afghan? The old man hadn't come all the way to America to be burdened with infidels and their follies. Chase couldn't tell him there was a dead body here in Seyyed's building. He couldn't tell him anything except to apologize in his own lumbering way.

'I will go away, Uncle Seyyed, if my presence troubles you.'

'You pay me rent, son. But you are also a guest, as Joe was. Seyyed does not turn away guests. Your trouble is my trouble. What is it you wish from me?'

'To find this Black fellow.'

'The Saaliheen mosque in Queens is where you must seek him. Many Afghans go there for prayer. Someone would know what has happened to The Black, I think.'

'I can't go up there, Uncle Seyyed.'

'You have problem with Afghans?'

'I have problems, Uncle Seyyed. Yes. There are one billion Muslims in the world and the world is still a small place. I did not fight like a man over there like Joe did, like The Black did. I'm not proud of what I did.'

'Maybe there are men at the Saaliheen mosque who would recognize you?'

'Everything is possible.'

'Then give me until tomorrow morning. Somebody in Flushing will know about your Black. Men like him disappear, but they do not die easily. I've heard said that he, like Joe, was the best of the best at what he did.'

'What did he do?'

'He fought for Islam, of course. He fought for the faith.'

9

Friday

A corpse puts things into motion, forcing a situation beyond itself. He imagined flocks of paunchy, bearded men dressed in rumpled white shirts, having just woken up from their two-hour siestas, scurrying about obscure offices of a Middle Eastern capital wringing their hands, wondering how they'd explain a disappearance and an operation gone awry.

In the meantime, Chase thought cold.

He put Tabib and himself to work. After fetching the Tajik from across the river, the two of them scoured the bedroom and then went on a grim trip, buying enough ice cubes to keep the dead man cold inside the bathtub. Lotfi wasn't easy to move. Once under the ice, he looked remote. Chase watched the rigid face of the man whom he'd known in the desert and felt no stirring from within. Lotfi had meant nothing to him. His death only an inconvenience.

'Maybe I know this man?' Tabib asked in a ghostly voice.

'Maybe? He came here to kill you for that manuscript.'

'You think I killed him?'

'No, Tabib. I don't think you did. I know you – it's not typical of your work to put such a clean hole in a man's neck like that. Besides, you're rather stupid when you lie about dead people and you're not lying now.'

'What do we do about him?'

'That's my worry. What do we do about your book? I've talked to someone.'

'A buyer?'

'We need to get the thing from Istanbul. Don't tell me no.'

'And what about this guy?'

Chase shook his head. Neither of them minded Lotfi dead. It was appropriate for him to be where he actually was, under that ice. 'Somebody killed him,' Chase said, stating the obvious.

'Chase, my friend, I know he was killed. But why?'

'What do you think, for sport? He was killed because someone didn't want him to find you and wanted me to know that.'

'Do you mean I have friends in the world?'

'*I'm* your only friend. You don't have any friends, T. Somebody else is after the manuscript and for that reason and that reason alone they want you alive for it. Alive for now.' He watched Tabib's round face sink. 'You'll have to stay here,' he told him.

'I don't feel safe here, my friend.'

'Can you think of a better place? People are after you, T, yes. But you're not a kid. You're new to this country. You'll learn your way. There's a fellow downstairs, his name is Seyyed. He's trustworthy. If there's trouble he'll call up and let you know about it. I'll talk to him on my way out.'

'Where are you going?'

Chase indicated the frozen corpse. 'Keep feeding our man fresh ice from the fridge. I'm going to try and find a way to get rid of him.'

'Don't leave me here alone,' the Tajik pleaded. 'They're watching us. I'm sure of it.'

Chase took Tabib's hand like a child's and guided him into the kitchen and the gas stove. He sat him down, let him smoke and saw him calm down after a while. Then he handed him Roth's gun and watched him tinkering with it as if it were a magic lamp waiting to be rubbed just the right way so that all his troubles would vanish.

'Protect yourself.'

'What about the police?'

'If the police show up – which they won't – then you'll have to come clean. You have no choice. You're not an assassin, just a dumb thief. These guys appreciate the difference – if they feel like it, that is.'

'What do you mean if they feel like it?'

'Forget about it.'

'I don't understand you anymore, Chase my friend.'

'I'm talking American to you now. It'll take some getting used to.'

'Will I ever learn?' Tabib asked tiredly.

'You learned English, didn't you? From here on, it will be easy. Stay here and be a quiet guest now. Don't get bored. Don't watch TV. Do everything in silence so you can hear things. Do you understand silence?'

'It's a horrible thing, silence. I ran here to get away from it and now it is the same. I guess we can't choose the mother we came out of, can we?'

'Even if we could choose, we'd still be complaining.'

'Uh-huh,' Tabib laughed nervously. So did Chase. He locked the door behind him and made sure Tabib latched it from the other side.

A couple of words in Uncle Seyyed's ear downstairs. The old man looked up and nodded and then wrote something down on a piece of paper.

'I went to the Friday prayer at the Saaliheen mosque for you,' he said, 'and asked around for The Black.'

'Yes?'

'People are not trustful, you know. They say soon the police will send their people into the mosques too. Nobody wants to say anything. They're scared. You say good morning to them and they look the other way. I would do the same.'

'So you found nothing?'

'Yes, I found something.' The old man passed on to Chase the note with the address he'd written on it. 'The Black does not come to the mosque anymore. But some men still remember him. He has a place. This is the address.'

Chase folded the piece of paper away giving the address a quick glimpse – Fulton and Nostrand, a half-hour ride on the blue line into Brooklyn.

'You're a good man, Uncle Seyyed.'

'I am what I am,' the old man said dismissively.

'Have you thought you might go back to Afghanistan? Things are getting better there now, you know.'

Seyyed looked at him. 'Better for who? I will stay here.'

Chase nodded. 'Will you keep an eye on my friend upstairs?'

'Something is wrong again?'

'Yes. Joe shouldn't have died so soon.'

Four p.m. Lingering smoke and the scent of incense, street vendors, dreadlocked men with vacant eyes, Arab store owners watchful of the cheap wares they sold to locals they despised. Once in a while you'd see a Hassidic Jew hurrying across towards nearby Crown Heights. Chinese fishmongers, Bengali sandwich makers, Hispanic deli owners, white cops. Africans selling dubious watches and other knick-knacks. More white cops.

The address brought him to a side street off Nostrand where a sign on a closed shop announced Dakari's Used Furniture. The name didn't ring a bell; he couldn't remember if that was the name Roth had mentioned. The shutter on the place was drawn. Nothing to see through to the inside. He'd hit a blank wall, literally. He stood a while just staring at that sign. Who was Dakari and what did he have to do with

The Black and how could he find him? After a while the neighborhood went curious on him. A kid riding an under-sized red bike cruised by.

'He don't work Fridays.'

'Hey!'

The kid stopped and turned to look without a word.

'You know him?' Chase asked.

'What you want from him? He don't much talk to people.'

'Is that what he said?'

'I know him.' After some thought: 'Not for real.'

'You know where he lives?'

The kid looked up over at the building where the furniture store was. There were another two floors above the place.

'Which one?'

'Number two, I think.' He shrugged. 'He ain't talking to you.'

Chase watched the boy ride away and yelled 'thanks' to him, to which the kid shrugged again. *White fool asking for trouble.*

But he, The Black, did answer his bell and he did talk.

'You are?'

'Name's Chase. I'm a good friend of Joe's. Joe Roth.'

'Joe's dead.'

'I know that. That's why I'm here. I don't know your name, mister. They call you . . . The Black over at the Saaliheen mosque. But maybe you don't like that name. Dakari maybe?'

The man nodded, saying nothing. They were still standing by the outside door and it felt like the entire block was watching them by now. The Black, Dakari, wasn't big, he was enormous, in a historic kind of way, a bulging presence. Chase felt daunted by him, though the other man seemed quite accustomed to being related to this way.

'Shall I call you Dakari, then?'

'Kari is fine,' he said in a deep voice. 'What do you need?'

'It goes like this: I got a dead man in my bathtub and I was hoping you'd know what to do with it. I sure as hell don't.'

Kari sighed. 'Joe's friend, yeah?'

'Best friend.'

'No, his second-best friend. Maybe you'd like to come upstairs and explain a little?'

'I'd like that.'

The austerity of Kari's place was that of a mosque stripped of its only ornament, God. There were a lot of books, though, perhaps as many as there were at Roth's place, but not much of anything else. There was a threadbare oriental rug that covered most of the living room; no tables and chairs, not even a pillow to lean against. It was odd that the man ran a used furniture store and there was none in his own home.

Kari turned to him, reading what was most immediately on Chase's mind: 'I gave it up a while back. You won't find any "Allah akbar" signs here, if that's what you're looking for.'

'What happened to Allah then, Kari? Did you lose him on the way or something?'

He motioned for Chase to sit. 'Yeah, that's what happened. I lost him on the way.'

'No longer convenient?'

The big man shook his head. 'I was barking up the wrong tree. And I was barking hard there for a while.'

'Why are you telling me this? You don't have to.'

'I figured you might show up. I know a little about you. Joe mentioned you more than once. He was about the only man I saw regular the last few years. When that old Afghan fella, his landlord, had him buried, I was sitting in my car watching from a ways off. I didn't see you there. Why?'

'I couldn't make it. I had my own problems. I have my own problems now.'

'Like?'

'I'm living at Joe's place.' Kari raised an eyebrow. 'And I got a dead Iranian in there.'

Chase watched Kari turn away. Already he was starting to fall in love with this guy. It was the big man's presence, a serenity Chase had looked for over a lifetime in, say, opium, and of course never found. He wanted to shout across the room to Kari: What's your secret? How did you get to want so little when I want and need so much?

'Was he an operator,' Kari asked, 'the dead Iranian?'

'He didn't used to be. He ran a short end of the opium road from Herat and Balkh, through Tehran to Istanbul, when the Russians were in Afghanistan.'

Kari shook his head. 'You're not that naïve, boy. Anybody on that road back then was some kind of operator.'

'I wasn't.'

'You don't count. You're an American. What were you doing there anyway? Roughing it for a while?'

'I was doing what I had to do.'

Kari's smile was full of bitterness. 'I'm talking about the natives. Over there a man switches loyalties without having switched a thing. Just changing hats. You think there's a difference between an Iranian dealer and an Iranian operator? None. What I know about you from our mutual friend is that you were on the other side of the border back then. You never made it to Afghanistan, did you?'

'Not quite. Not in the sense you and Joe did.'

'Don't feel left out. It was the same shit in Peshawar. You didn't miss much not having a crack at being a hero.'

'That doesn't help the fact that I got a dead fellow in Joe's bathtub right now.'

'No, it doesn't. What did the man want from you?'

Chase told him most of it – about Tabib, Lotfi, the manuscript, and the Uzbeks supposedly hiding out in Dearborn, Michigan. After a while he started to sound shifty to himself. No man in their right mind would be telling all this to someone they'd met for the first time. If Chase had his Jay Shanker, why shouldn't it be possible that Kari had his own Fed to report to? But it was already too late to think along these lines. So he continued talking. Kari listened, saying nothing, until the very end when Chase asked him what he'd come here to ask him: 'Will you help me?'

The man wouldn't, at least, *not* help him. The calm in his face and his roughly charitable look said as much. Now Kari said, 'Whoever killed Lotfi is also after the manuscript. I assume you know that.'

'Yeah. That is a given.'

'Getting rid of the dead body won't solve your problems.'

'It's a start.'

Kari thought for a while. 'All right. But now you're probably going to ask why I'm willing to do this for you.'

'I was getting to that.'

'Ask me some other time. Ice melts. Even on a dead body.'

Saturday

Morning. Mette should have been home, but it was her answering machine that picked up the call. 'Mette, think about what I said – a trip for two, anywhere you like. America on wheels, nothing beats it. Grand Canyon, Yellowstone National Park, the Badlands. You name it. Mette, give me a call when you get this message. No, forget it. I'll call you myself. Mette, I love your name.'

Tabib was sitting by himself in the kitchen next to the stove, smoking again. The fellow was starting to put a serious dent into Chase's resolve. But Chase held off. It was as if those vials of methadone were a kind of piggybank, and every time he withstood the assault of withdrawal he was putting another penny into a coffer for himself. He still felt sick though, and it didn't help a bit that all night long he'd been drinking from Roth's last remaining bottle of bourbon.

Drinking and waiting. A string of client phone calls for The Kismet Detective Agency. The last one from a Yemeni restaurant owner named Al-Awlaki. His name had apparently been confused with another Awlaki on a Bureau watchlist, and . . . 'Detective Roth, these men are driving me very much out of my head. Please help me!'

Tabib buzzed Kari inside and held the door open for him. The big man's eyes immediately zoomed in on the now almost empty bottle of alcohol next to Chase. He snatched it, glanced at the label, and threw the bottle into the trash without looking at either Chase or Tabib.

Chase felt completely used up from the drink. 'Hey,' he

called feebly, 'that was a memento from Joe. What did you throw it away for?'

'You don't need that garbage. Same way Joe didn't need it.'

'You don't like booze, Kari? But I thought you'd given up Islam,' he said for the sake of having something to say.

Kari looked back and forth between Tabib and Chase. Disgusted. Concerned. 'You asked for my help, I said yes. I've taken care of the business. It wasn't easy work, but it's done, and done right. You don't need to know where your friend Lotfi ended up. What you *do* need to do is act straight. That means don't get yourself wasted right now. And you!' He turned to Tabib. 'Get that shit off the oven and out this house.'

Nonplussed, Tabib looked at Chase. 'Who does this man think he's talking to?'

Chase answered in English. 'Do what he says. You don't look a gift horse in the mouth.'

'What?'

'Nothing. The man just saved our skin. Don't make him upset.'

Opium, bourbon – they were invented limbs, appendages. Kari was their man, the one who got things done, always out-living his mistakes to fight another day. And feeling as indebted as he did, Chase wasn't sure what he should say to Kari now. He remained still. Time passed. A dullness came over them all. Kari went and stayed in Roth's bedroom for a long time with the door closed. Tabib lingered in the kitchen pouting.

The next time the phone rang Kari came out of the bedroom and pulled the cord out.

'You don't need to be answering any phone calls,' he said.

They examined each other for a time. Chase asked, 'Were

you resting over there?' He turned to look into Roth's bed-room.

'Checking out the books by his bed. I never came here much. Joe came my way,'

'You're welcome to his books if you want. I don't read much anymore. I just read one book these days.'

'Yeah, *The Thousand and One Nights*. Joe told me about it. You're an oddball, Chase.'

'And you're not?'

'Meaning what?'

'Meaning why would you risk your quiet retirement to help a man you've never met before? I only came to you on a hunch.'

Kari seemed to be digging deep for something really meaningful to say, but finally came up with nothing more than 'I owed it to Joe.'

'That answer's too vague for me, Kari. You risked a lot.'

'I risked it when I went to Peshawar. It makes no difference. A fellow does what he has to.'

'You didn't have to do this.'

'I did.'

'How does that work? You give up on Allah, and so you think you have to go around being good to men who got dead bodies in their bathtubs?'

'It wasn't just anyone's bathtub. It was Joe's. Him and me went back too far for me not to do this. I'm not one to get nos-talgic for the old days. Screw the old days. They were rough and we got the short end of the stick. Especially Joe. I saw him go down. Take the fall. I saw it coming, but there was nothing I could do about it. This here, today, it was some-thing I could do. It was my little part. Too little, too late, but still . . . As for your other problems – kid, take my advice, watch your back. Get out of town and stay out. And if you want to send Joe's books my way, I'll be glad to take them off you.'

Then taking a pile of Roth's books, Kari made for the exit. Chase got up anxiously.

'You can't leave me like this, man.'

'Why? You got more bodies in the bathtub?'

'It's not that.'

'What is it, then?'

'I need to know what happened to you guys in Afghanistan. To Roth. What made him slowly kill himself like that? Come on. I too got a need-to-know. I'm living in the man's house, for God's sake, I'm taking over his business. What was it did him in? I know it wasn't the whisky. That came afterwards.'

With the door ajar Kari stood there looking at Chase. 'What about your friend?' he asked, indicating Tabib.

'Him? Tabib's life can be summed up in a stolen manuscript and a silly off-and-on habit that maybe I can help him get rid of.'

Kari put the books back on the table between them. 'What do you want to know, boy?'

'Afghanistan.'

'It wasn't just Afghanistan. Joe and me went back way before that. I was in Iran when he was stationed there.'

'You were with the Agency in Iran?'

'No. I was never no Agency man. That's nuts. I was in the service. An embassy guard. You already know the story of what happened: when shit hit the fan with the revolution against the Shah, they got most of us out. But not all of us. I found out about it much later. Joe was on everybody's shit list from early on. He kept sending reports back to Langley. Reports no one ever bothered with. He'd say things like, there were no operatives in-country who could speak the damned language. He complained of rampant incompetence. That's how he put it: rampant incompetence.'

'And the suits didn't want to hear it.'

'No. When Iran fell they spread the blame. The beautiful people back in Washington called it a failure of intelligence. Okay. Whose failure? Whose intelligence? Joe turned out to be a fall guy because he was one of the few who'd been sending danger signals all along. Nobody could stomach that. Men don't like prophets, unless the prophet's got blood on his hands. They bottled him up in some desk job until Afghanistan got the new DCI's attention. After that they needed him again.'

'And you?'

'I got out of the service.'

Kari was staring at the younger man, his look saying he knew exactly what question was coming next.

Chase asked it: 'Why Islam, Kari?'

'Why anything? I got tired of blabbing on the race thing a long time ago. But the race thing is there, a dead stinking elephant in the middle of Fairytale Avenue. You're a black man and you're too damn tall and you can't step into a grocery store to buy a piece of gum without some Korean grandma thinking about reaching for her shotgun. How did I get here? Let's ask instead why's my so-called real name Marcus Johnson? How come my old man got stabbed and died in prison? I know, kid . . . it's all bullshit. It's all been said before. But only because it needed saying and it still does. I saw those crowds in Tehran, marching right in front of my nose and saying they wanted their freedom. I came back to the States and converted a little later. I thought that maybe there was something to this freedom thing.'

'Was there?'

'Yes and no. But those crowds didn't want freedom; all

they wanted was to get even with someone, *anyone*. That's the only thing revolutions are good for. It wasn't about Islam. But I fell for it. At least for a while.'

'Kari-the-convert. Has a certain ring to it. Kari the convert went to Afghanistan to kill a few Russians.'

'Didn't you try to do the exact same thing?' Kari asked scornfully.

'Hey, I'm not judging you, man.'

'Fuck your judging me or not judging me,' he said furiously.

'I'm sorry.'

They stayed silent. Then Chase plucked enough courage to ask him about Afghanistan again.

'Afghanistan . . . Jesus! That's where Joe and me, our paths crossed again. I saw him in Pakistan, in Peshawar. Of course, I could guess what he was up to, and he already, it seemed, knew everything about me. Hell, we got close. And it wasn't like he was running me or anything. It was a meeting of equals, exchange of information if you like – or whatever else you want to call it. He wanted to know what the Arabs there were up to and how many other Americans like me were involved. He suffered. From day one he was off on the wrong track again in Afghanistan. The Agency was giving the bulk of the guns and money to the biggest scumbags you ever saw. The Pakistanis were skimming their share, milking the war for all it was worth. Like always, Joe had to open his big mouth. He sent off more dispatches. Fell between the crosshairs of his own people at the station there. Accused the sons of bitches of all sorts of things. Just about got on a goddamn pulpit and started preaching. Said things like, "While you thieving bastards are robbing the Afghans blind, I got men going against Russian tanks and helicopters with sticks and stones."'

'He wasn't lying.'

'Sure. But Joe always forgot he wasn't a journalist, he was an operator, or was supposed to be at least. He was in the wrong trade.'

'"Iran was my first piece of bad luck," he'd tell me, "Afghanistan the second."'

'Joe's bad luck was neither Iran nor Afghanistan. It was his occupation. That's all. Langley had him bagged. It was they who accused him of incompetence this time, even negligence. They put him on the polygraph and watched his heart go thump. 'You're not telling us the whole truth, Joe.' He told them to go fuck themselves and got out. I didn't see him again till I came back to New York. He was a changed man by then. So was I.'

'Islam disappoint you?'

'I always had a feeling it might. It worked out fine for a lot of other guys like me who had gone down to Afghanistan to fight. It didn't for me. Not quite. I wanted peace in my soul, not decrees and verdicts. But I had to give it a try at least. Besides, Afghanistan was a good cause. Say, where did you grow up, boy?'

'Southern Cal.'

'Go back there. Forget all you ever knew. Pretend the only thing there for you is sunshine. Tell yourself the color of truth is white and it wears a bikini. Get out of the business, unless you want to end up like Joe.'

He didn't wait for Chase's answer. After collecting the books he'd laid on the table, he marched out angrily, slamming the door shut behind him.

Right away Tabib stepped out of the kitchen. 'What's wrong with the black guy?'

'He's tired of all the little people in the world. He counts you and me among them, I suppose.'

'What do you think he did with the body?'

'Did the right thing. Men like him don't make mistakes.'

'Nor do we,' Tabib said forcefully.

'Maybe. But that's only because men like us – you and me – we don't even know that much, how to make mistakes.'

11

Monday

He lost a day, waiting. But the phone, now plugged back, stayed relentless – Mette first, then several more clients – including a fellow who wanted to know if detective Roth would be willing to travel to Morocco to mediate over a transatlantic child-custody battle. Tabib almost never moved from the stove now. Lotfi's murder had really shaken up the Tajik, tossing him into a torpor that smoking could redress for only a little while. Chase would periodically come to check up on him. Then they'd take turns keeping a watch from the kitchen window to see if Lotfi's men, missing their boss, might be out there staking them. Chase took the gun he'd given Tabib and kept it by his side. You could call this digging in – and Istanbul sounded about as far away now as its name. The manuscript sounded even further.

Noon. Both of them jumped at the buzzer.

'It's a woman,' Seyyed called from downstairs.

In a minute his client's wife, Mrs Khan, was standing in front of them with a bruised face. She looked over at Tabib, reluctant to talk. She was an apparition to Chase. He pictured himself clicking away with Roth's camera while lady Khan and her lover stepped out of their hotel in Brooklyn, heard himself calling on Khan to tell the fellow his wife was clean, telling the wife to take back the photos he'd taken of her, telling her to leave her husband.

'He beat me,' she barely uttered

'Who, Khan? Your lover?' She wouldn't answer, so that Chase ended up having to needlessly apologize, then silently

116

berated himself for apologizing. He started over: 'Your husband beat you, Mrs Khan?' She gave him a silent yes. 'How did you find my place?' No answer. 'What would you like me to do for you?'

'I'm afraid.'

'Maybe your . . . friend – the taxi driver – maybe he can help you. Yes?'

She said nothing, her silence carrying centuries of baggage. Even Chase could see that. She was something tarnished. In her world, being found out was a bigger sin than the sin itself. Slowly he pulled the story out of her. The lover had apparently contacted Khan and told him everything before he'd disappeared. Why had he done that? Could it be this was his regular routine and he got periodic hush money from cuckolds like Khan?

Mrs Khan wept. Tabib forced a cup of tea on her. The absurdity of it all made Chase and Tabib disinclined to so much as catch each other's eyes. They could not simply wish this woman away. Nor was she a dead body they could keep iced until they knew what to do with it.

The sound of the phone ringing again was a welcome relief from the impasse. He started to pick up to see who it was, but decided to wait it out. There was a slight pause on the machine, and then Khan's voice stormed into their space. His venom was spectacular. *Roth* was a liar and a cheat, he said, for taking his money and not telling the truth about his whore of a wife. He should be blindfolded, his tongue chopped off, his mouth sewn and filled with lead; he should be thrown off of the Empire State Building.

'Why the Empire State Building?' Chase asked when he finally picked up the receiver.

'Huh?' Khan sounded disoriented and still wasn't sure he was no longer talking into the machine.

'You silly man, you beat up your wife. I can have you arrested for what you did.'

'My wife is not your business, sir!'

'Oh yes, she is. She's here right now and we're going to the police.'

'My wife is there?' Khan asked incredulously.

Chase explained that his clients happened to be many, that Khan's wife had sought his services the same way he had. 'You should have believed me when I told you your wife was clean.'

'But my wife is not clean.'

'That's what a stupid taxi driver told you. Am I wrong? How do you know he didn't have this whole thing planned to get some money out of you? How do you know he hasn't done it to ten other fools like you in the past year?'

Khan gasped. Chase glanced over at Tabib and Mrs Khan standing behind him in the sepia landscape of the living room and imagined them as some Hansel and Gretel duo who had forgotten to piss their way back to paradise. They were both his charges, unable to negotiate their way through the New World.

Khan said, 'You are lying to me, sir.'

'Suit yourself.'

'Wait!' he blubbered desperately in the telephone. 'I would like to hire you, again.'

'What for?'

'To find out if the driver was . . . you know, with my wife or not.'

'Get lost, Khan!'

Hanging up, he turned to get a read on Mrs Khan, but she was no longer there. The door of the apartment was open and Tabib was looking down the stairway.

'She ran out,' Tabib said offhandedly.

'Why didn't you grab her?'

'Grab her for what? We have our own problems.'

In a minute Chase was watching her through the kitchen window. Running across the street. Her long black hair brushing against the side mirror of a parked car as one of her heels gave way and she stumbled. In her right hand a little red suitcase he hadn't noticed earlier. The little red suitcase and Mrs Khan running together. He would have run after her. But Tabib's words had more force than the woman's desperation – they *did* have their own problems. He followed her as long as the angle of the window permitted it. When he finally turned around he saw that Tabib was sitting by the stove again, smoking. He'd have liked to hit the Tajik, bent his arms back till they broke. Mrs Khan was nothing to Chase. He didn't know where she was hurrying to. He didn't want to know. But Tabib – this maladroit bandit was like a brother he wanted to slap on the back of the head. Tabib was all there was now – a problem, maybe a deliverance, depending.

Chase turned the gas off just as Tabib was reaching for a broken-off metal clothes hanger left on the fire. Tabib took the cooler part of the red-hot rod anyway, put the lit end over his pipe and smoked before the rod went totally cold. Then he looked up at Chase and smiled.

'What is it with you and these strange people, my friend? I have a book we can sell and be happy.'

'Tell me about this book, then. Why leave it in Istanbul? I know you're lying to me, Tabib. You're sitting here, lying to me all the time.'

He watched another grin forming at the edges of the Tajik's faint lips as he blew some of the remaining smoke into Chase's face. He waited for an instant, then grabbed Tabib by the shirt collar and threw him against the wall. The Tajik's instincts were those of the disloyal conscript he'd once been. He gave a short jab in Chase's face so that his head snapped back and he let go. Now it was Tabib who was doing the grabbing and soon they were rolling on the kitchen floor. First Chase was on top, then Tabib. Chase had lost it. He was cursing in all the languages he knew. Tabib was taking the curses as they came. They didn't hurt him a bit. He was laughing, and the laughter seemed to throw him out of himself and make him forget he was a hunted man.

'What are we fighting about, friend?' he asked Chase good-naturedly, as if the two of them were a couple of kids only messing around in the dirt.

'The book!'

'I promise you, it *is* in Istanbul. Remember that key I gave you before? Now, where do you leave a book you don't want anyone else to find? You leave it in a locked box.'

'Okay, a box. A box in Istanbul. That's a start.'

They were still locked on the floor – two lovers who had found nothing in this life but linoleum and tiles and each other. The phone started to ring.

'Leave it,' Tabib said. 'That thing is evil. It never quits. You are not this man Joe Roth. Who is this Joe Roth on your machine?'

'A guy better than you and me.' Chased pushed off of him. From the living room came the FBI agent Jay Shanker's voice.

'Chase, what are you up to these days?'

'I'm still here,' Chase sputtered into the cordless as soon as he'd reached it.

'Where's there? You all right?'

Chase got his breath back, explaining quickly that he'd left a message at the New York office with his new Chinatown address and phone number. But of course Shanker already knew that or he wouldn't be calling. It was always as if they were throwing this ball back and forth between them, and Chase couldn't help wondering what would happen if he were to spill everything to Shanker all of a sudden.

Shanker was silent for a bit and then said that he'd called earlier but hadn't left a message. 'The announcement goes on forever. I mean, how come your machine says it's Joe Roth? And what's the Kismet Detective Agency all about? What a name! Kismet.'

'Come on, Jay, you know what it means. It means destiny, fate. It works like this: Mr So-and-So was destined to have his wife screw behind his back, so now he has to hire someone to follow her around and take incriminating pictures. Kismet.'

'Hell of an occupation.'

'Actually all I'm doing is cleaning up a bit, tying up some loose ends of the business for an old friend, Joe Roth, who died.'

When Shanker asked a second time who Joe Roth was, Chase countered by asking why the special agent bothered being so disingenuous. He left it there – implicit in the question that he already knew everything there was to know about Chase's life, including his friendship with Joe Roth, who Joe was and what line of work he had done. There was silence on the line and he couldn't be sure if Shanker was still there or not. He was. He heard the special agent rumble something under his breath. It came to him that Shanker, who was neither a stupid nor an uneducated man, nevertheless was not quite sure of that word, *disingenuous*. Maybe he was trying to figure out if Chase had just insulted him or if he'd called him a genius – with that dollop of the sarcasm people usually hold for cops. Chase felt obligated to explain.

'I mean, why do you ask questions the answers to which you already know?'

'That's a part of my job,' Shanker said simply. 'You have anything for me, Chase?'

'No, it was you who told me when we first met to always keep you posted of my whereabouts, and I'm doing just that. I'm keeping you posted, Jay.'

'Okay,' Shanker said a bit roughly, sounding impatient and dimly annoyed about something. 'I got you down in my book.'

'And I got you in mine.'

'What?'

Chase said the word 'nothing' into the mouthpiece and heard the sound of air getting sucked out of a water pipe from the kitchen. Tabib was sitting at the stove again, unmindful that a few simple words from Chase on the phone could make his days in the old Soviet army in Afghanistan look positively agreeable. Shanker now chatted back and forth for a while longer. But then Chase asked him how he was doing with his Arabic language lessons and Shanker quickly clammed up. Perhaps he took it for a sign that Chase was fishing for some kind of news from him.

Then there was a subject change. 'So you in Chinatown now?' Shanker asked.

'Yeah. I like watching the old people do T'ai Chi in the mornings. It's like every one of them is a little Confucius or something. And they got a statue of him, too, by East Broadway to make it all real.'

'Try to stick around there for a while.'

'I have no more plans to move. I'm turning a new chapter.'

'I wish success for you, then,' Shanker said without sounding cynical.

'Same to you, man,' Chase returned, as he heard Tabib break a glass in the kitchen – probably that homemade pipe he'd been smoking through.

Six-thirty p.m. Mette was put off by his thin desire in bed. Of course, she couldn't know his body was in minor hell ever since he'd decided to go straight. He had continued to be stingy with the methadone, administering it to himself in carefully counted droplets, gauging the arc of his illness from hour to hour. It would take time. Everything would take time. And he saw no reason to tell her what he was up to just in case his will eventually failed him, as it had many times before. He didn't want to disappoint her; rather, he wanted to surprise her with a clean bill of health. And that was worth all the little insufficiencies of the moment.

She watched him with some concern. 'You don't look well, Chase. What do you want? I mean, what do you want me to do for you?'

'I just want your companionship, Mette. You're what I've been looking for. I already told you that.'

'But you don't know me. Maybe you're just in a hard place these days and you need me like you need a rest-stop. What then?'

'Then nothing. What am I supposed to do? Just because no one knows no one in this world, I should quit trying? Besides, what does it take to know someone? Can you tell me that?'

In the room there was nothing to sit on except her bed. Chase was trying and half succeeding at blocking things out for a bit – Tabib back at Roth's apartment, Kari living over his used-furniture store in Brooklyn, the art dealer Lund waiting for his call, Lotfi dead.

She said, 'You're asking me what does it take to know someone? Well, time helps. Time even brings love sometimes. You can start with that.'

'Mette, I'm not sure if I know what love is. What I've always been looking for – without knowing that it's what I've been looking for – is safety. Does it matter if you know another person for two months or two years? It only matters if you're keeping score. In this country everyone's always keeping score. The whole place is a goddamn baseball game. Everyone's got their pencils and pads at the ready. Scratch my back, and I'll scratch yours. I'm not too good at these things.'

She let her hair down. Her skin looked softer than it did in the bar. In the bar too much was performance. Men walking through the narrow aisle, ordering drinks from her and waiting to see if she'd smile at them. They'd often linger if she did. Slowly the softness in that face drained with each successive Budweiser she plopped down for the customers. Most of them bland, good-natured domestic-business travelers staying across the street at one of the hotels.

Looking forlorn all of a sudden, she said, 'You know, I was always afraid to make a move, do anything to change things for myself, until I came here. And now . . .'

He cut in. 'It's me who's afraid.'

She rubbed herself against him, seductively, but his urge stayed dead. She began apologizing now for speaking like a self-help zealot, a schoolgirl, but then she went on to talk about how only in the past few months had she begun to feel she had a personality at all, a being removed and separate from what she'd been in Norway. She wanted to explore this new territory. It was like discovering herself for the first time. Not rediscovering. But *discovering*. She was born again. 'Mette's renaissance'. Maybe, she said, there was some breadth to her that Chase could see, something that she hadn't yet discovered about herself, being so new to the game of knowing who she was. She laughed then and swore she was becoming religious.

'Will you tell me about myself, Chase?'

'I feel safe with you. I can tell you that much.'

'Safe? Then why do you keep going to the window to look outside?' she asked.

'Come here.' He called her to the window. 'Look over there where that old homeless woman is standing. There's a man near the corner, almost on 9th Avenue. That's my problem. That man.'

'He's following you?'

'He and another guy who's probably sitting in the Indian deli around the corner. They take turns. They're not too good at this. They're just doing it because they don't know what else they should do. Their boss is gone missing and they're an ocean and a continent away from home. A street cop could come and ask for their identification and it would be the end of them.'

'What's the story?' she asked, pulling him away from the window.

He shook his head.

'What do you want me to do then?' she asked.

Her voice was calm. As if in a flash she'd come face to face with the object of her desire: to make up for lost time, to do things, become adventurous, in the same way Chase had tried to be, over a decade earlier, only to end up pleading his case at the Canadian embassy in a country that had given him adventure, yes, but also grief. If only he could stop her dead in this particular track! It wasn't adventure she needed, but peace. There were no adventures left in the world anyway, only the overblown talk of pint-sized reporters looking for gore and media awards.

'Mette, here's the noblest short speech I've ever given. And that's 'cause I'm feeling like a bloody saint right now. I really want you to go away. Disappear. And when this is all done and dusted, I'll come get you and we can start a life together. I think we can do it.'

'What about the guys following you around?' She pointed to the window.

'They're not your problem. I mean, they can be handled.'

She gave him a queer look while he asked her for the telephone. 'Here, take these too, then.' She handed him an extra set of keys to her place. 'You're part of the family now, you bastard. You, me, my keys, your noble speech and the stinking bar downstairs. I'm going to work. I won't be back till late.'

He nodded at her without saying anything. Just as she was opening the door he called out, 'Those fellows outside, they won't do anything to you. Don't worry.'

'Anything else I *shouldn't* be worried about?' Silence. 'See you later, Chase.'

After she'd gone, he tried willing the sickness out of his system. He stood in front of the mirror and breathed as evenly as he could. He took out the beeper number Kari had left for him and dialed. Kari returned the call after a few minutes.

'What's on your mind?' he asked.

Chase tried confirming with him that their line was clean. Kari dismissed the caution. 'We're not in the movies, boy. What's up?'

'I got a couple of strays hanging about outside.'

'Lotfi's?'

'Yeah. Don't know what to do with them.'

'Do nothing. They're zero. I spotted them before. They can't stay here, and they might not be able to go back. You've made orphans out of those poor fellas.'

'Kari, I'm not in a mood to have to look after anybody. What'll I do with them?'

'If you like, go have a very brief talk. I'm not kidding. Tell them to find the quickest way back home. It's to their advantage.'

'There's something else.'

'I'm listening.'

'I didn't tell you, but I got a Bob.'

'A what?'

'From the Bureau, I mean. Someone I have to chat with once in a while.' Kari said nothing, so he felt obliged to justify himself. 'You know how it is when a man gets back with credentials those guys crave.'

'So you got a fucking chaperone?'

'Not everyone's as tough as you are, Kari,' he said, pleading again. He told him about how Jay Shanker and he had talked today. 'Just routine stuff. "Hello, how are you" type of conversation. We do it once in a while and we do it a lot less ever since last fall. The guy's got real work to do now. But I *am* supposed to stay in touch, so I do. There's no more to it than that. I swear.'

'Why do you even bother telling me this, then?'

'Because I thought you should know. That's all.'

Kari stayed quiet on the phone for a while. Chase wanted to take his silence to mean that maybe Kari, too, had had to answer some questions when he'd come back from Afghanistan. A guy with some type of a badge tells you they won't press charges after all, because you're more innocent than you're not, and maybe you end up running with that as far as you can. And so what if you have to act grateful and pretend they've thrown you a bone. What mattered was to stay free. It paid to remember that, and Kari, descendant of sinister plantations, probably hadn't forgotten. He told Chase finally not to worry about it.

'I got some stuff to do now, kid. Call later. But best you don't beep me from Roth's place. And like I said, don't worry about the two shadows; they'll only push if they get too desperate. And they're not important enough to get that desperate.'

'They just get on my nerves.'

'People getting on your nerves is the least you got to worry about now. Call me later.'

'Kari, wait!'

'What?'

'Why are you so good to me?'

'Because you're so damned pathetic. That's why.'

Lotfi's two guys were standing together when he came out of Mette's building. They looked out of sync, cold, and generally miserable in their old clothes. But they showed relief when Chase went up to them and asked in their own language if they could break a dollar.

'How do you break a dollar?' one of them said, too innocently, as if now that Lotfi was not around he expected Chase to teach him the ropes about how to survive in America, take him to the Immigration Service, fill in an application for him for asylum, vouch for his character, make sure he landed on his feet and on the right side of the fence here.

'Let me see your change.' Chase took three quarters off the Iranian and passed him a dollar. 'Your lucky day today.'

'Yes?'

'A quarter here is worth two hundred *tuman* where you come from. You can catch a cab or bribe an idiot with it back home.'

'Where's our boss?' the bigger fellow asked. He had a chip off one front tooth and periodically he sucked on a cigarette like it was painful for him to inhale. But he wasn't hostile or intimidating, just a tad grimmer than the other man who had just made himself twenty-five cents.

'Lotfi is dead.'

'Dead?'

'I'll explain in a minute.'

While they considered what he'd said, Chase threw change into a payphone on the other side of the street and dialed Herman Lund on his cellular. The art dealer played at being furious. Why hadn't Chase called him earlier? Did he have the book in his possession or not? Should he consider taking this story to the proper authorities?

'Who are the proper authorities, Lund?'

'The police.'

'To tell them what? About a mystery book from Kabul that might or might not exist? Think they'd care? Do you know how many homicides they have to deal with in New York City every month? Nice knowing you, Mr Lund. Goodbye.'

'Please!'

He watched Lotfi's guys across the street, cold-footed and superfluous. Like their dead boss, they too came off an assembly line. You saw their kind all over the Middle East, ruling their little roost, driving in their tinted patrol cars, clobbering college students for stepping over their shadows, stopping teenage girls in the streets and hassling them about their lipstick, their polished nails. Yet in America they were just two more aliens who had to mumble before they could even order a Pepsi for themselves. They were throwaways, expendable. No one had ever told them that they were here to be shoeshine boys, that they were part of a caste system, that there were hierarchies, gradations of abuse and ignorance even – no, especially – to clandestine careers, and those who didn't matter couldn't know they were never part of the team to begin with. Chase thought about this and about what he needed to say to them. But he still had Lund on the phone. He wasn't sure about letting the art dealer have the address to Roth's place, but he gave it to him anyway. Lund told him he was driving in from Long Island. He'd see Chase at that address as soon as he could, but that would probably take him another hour or two.

He went back over to the Iranians. The big guy spoke. 'How do you know Lotfi is dead?'

'Because I saw him that way.'

'What are you talking about?'

'He's dead, for God's sake.'

'Who killed him? You?'

'As if I'd be telling you about it. Look, brothers, just go home. Tell your people that Lotfi probably got greedy and the Uzbeks found out about it.'

'What Uzbeks?'

'Shut up and listen! The Uzbeks are not your concern or you'd know about them already. But you don't, since your salary-grade is not high enough for that back in Tehran. And count yourself lucky because of that. Tell your people if they want to pursue this matter, I'll be glad to oblige. But I'd suggest they leave it alone. Tell them in Tehran to stick to their own miserable piece of real estate and quit meddling in other people's affairs. Tell them whatever you want to tell them, but . . . if I were you I'd get out as fast as I could.'

'Who says?'

'My aunt Thelma.' Chase started to walk away.

'Who?'

He continued to walk away shaking his head. It had started to rain all of a sudden, as if the sky had suddenly become appalled with this cockamamie show of theirs. Lotfi should have stuck to the opium trade. There would be no memorial anywhere for the dead man. As Chase was turning the corner – a long east–west block nearer 8th Avenue – he heard one of the Iranians call out his name. He didn't bother to stop or look around. The wind drew him anywhere but home. Lund wasn't due for a while anyway. There was time yet for home.

He muttered to himself about how tired he was of babysitting Tabib behind the kitchen stove. He'd walk in the rain for a while. He heard another faint echo of the Iranians and then he dropped away out of sight.

Eight-thirty p.m. Usually Mette handled the entire counter until later into the night. Chase spotted Billy, the owner, at the end of the bar playing his usual solitaire game on the video machine. He was a tall ex-boxer, a white guy with eyes in a permanent squint. He'd been a heavyweight and his place was full of pictures of himself with a procession of black men who had made fortunes in the ring and lost bigger fortunes outside it. Mette noticed Chase as soon as he popped in. There were no empty stools. She was running from one end of the line to the other taking orders. Too many people too soon tonight. He realized why, save for Mette's relatively recent arrival, he'd never really liked this place: it was thin on the authenticity it labored so hard to achieve. Thin – like the pictures of white Billy and the numerous champs on the bar's walls. Wallflower winners, yellowing with the light and the cheap booze Billy had taught his girls, including Mette, to underpour.

'I didn't expect you here,' she said surprised.

'I went for a long walk, ended up here.'

'So what's up?'

'Quit tonight, please! Let's move to the West Coast.'

'Sex on the beach?'

'A scotch will do for the time being.'

'I meant – from what I could tell this afternoon – you couldn't if you tried. Know what I mean?'

'Ah, Mette!'

She laughed and went to pour his drink. A man from the other end of the bar yelled for her. When she didn't answer, he yelled again, throwing 'bitch' into it this time. Chase pretended he hadn't heard. Mette poured a double and went over to see what the noise wanted. Chase downed the drink quickly and kept from looking up. All he could hear was an overflow of voices pushing against his endless withdrawal. His knees seemed to wilt and as soon as the last-shift construction worker next to him got up from his seat, Chase took his place and plopped himself down. Mette returned.

'What did he want?'

'Attention, what else?'

'Want me to deal with him?'

She disregarded what he'd said. 'You look pale. You all right?'

'I don't know. What do my notebooks tell you?'

Another call from the other end of the bar. Same guy.

She kept her eyes on Chase. 'That you wish you'd done a few things differently in your life.'

'I'm sorry, what?'

'Your notebooks, that's what they say, that you wish you were better at being you.'

The next time the man yelled, Chase pulled back on his chair to see who it was. He only saw Billy at the far end playing his solitaire game.

'You want me to call Billy for you?'

She shook her head. 'The guy's a spender. We have to put up with him. Double?'

'Yeah.'

She poured and left him alone. This time the voice got even louder. He could hear Mette's voice, too, rising. Another 'bitch'. He finished the second double and started walking that way. Billy had gotten up too and they were both moving towards the source. Billy saw Chase and gestured for him to pull back. Chase didn't. He was angry. It was an artificial anger, born from too much of everything and the absence of opium. But now it had located an excuse and refused to let go. The two quick double-shots of whisky had had the effect of slapping him around. He took another uncertain step. Billy tried to push him back, but somehow Chase ducked from under the big man and got to the other side. The fellow who'd been giving Mette a hard time turned out to be a South American who owned a knick-knack tourist trap around the corner on Broadway. He had a moustache, no neck, incongruent green eyes, and white hair on beefy cheeks.

'What do you want?' Chase asked him.

Billy grabbed him from behind. 'Chase, get out of here. Now!'

'I want to know what this guy wants.'

'I want you to get out of my face, is what I want,' the fellow barked.

Chase took a false step back. Billy let go, and as soon as he did Chase threw both thumbs in the man's eyes. After that, mayhem. The bar went into a spin around him. Maybe the whole thing took less than a few seconds, but when they were done he was lying in a corner of the bar with blood pouring from his mouth. Mette was standing over him with a wet rag and a glass of water. There was screaming from the other side. Billy looked like some overgrown Jesus holding his arms out so that no one could get to them.

Mette smiling: 'What did you do?'

'I proved my love. I think. Will you come to the desert with me?'

'Okay then, the desert.'

'Thanks. Give me a shot and let me out of here.'

'No way. Billy wants to put a bullet into your head right now. Can you walk?'

'I think so.'

She pointed to the back way. 'You got keys. Go to my place. I'll see you tonight.'

'Not tonight, baby. I got . . .' He looked at his watch and realized how late it was. 'I have to go.'

'Where to?'

'Business.'

She helped him up and they retreated to the back and out.

'I'll see you tonight, Chase?'

'Tomorrow.'

As he hit the pavement on 43rd Street, he felt a small chip from a tooth on his tongue. He let it fall out of his mouth and onto the ground. He picked it up like a penny. Good luck charm. He stuffed it in his pocket and felt, too, the warm flow of blood in his mouth. His knees were giving again. A fire truck sped up 6th Avenue. A Japanese businessman walked ahead of him into a karaoke bar. The knees sagged twice in ten steps. He stopped, waited for a cab, and when none came he waited some more until one did. Then he told the driver: 'East Broadway, on the double.'

'Double?' the Indian driver asked uncertainly.

'Means fast. Go fast.'

'Aha!'

'Go real fast.'

Nine-ten p.m. Bad things had happened. After dithering for a minute in the kitchen, he took the old homemade pipe he'd thought Tabib had already broken and smashed it against the wall anyway. The bottom flew out, hit the window and landed near where Tabib's lifeless body was sprawled on the floor. Tabib was dead. A blunted old cleaver in one hand as if he'd meant to allocate his fate more democratically. Knowing him, he must have put up some sort of a fight. Not that it had helped him much. A hole in the ribs, another in the neck

134

which had probably killed him instantly. Blood on the floor which would have to be cleaned up right away. The house was a colossal mess; the books, which Chase had taken such trouble to pile up neatly, tossed every which way, suspended in unlikely places like they'd suddenly grown wings and just as suddenly lost steam and settled where they could in mid-flight. Those who had done this were looking hard for something. Chase pulled out the gun he'd taken back from Tabib and laid it on the counter. He should have let the Tajik keep it. Tabib dead. Lotfi dead. In another part of the apartment, a bathtub filled to the rim, with Lund also doubled over and suffocated in the still warm water. They could not have left here more than half an hour ago. *They* . . . who? He called downstairs to Seyyed. Seyyed told him he was busy. 'Too many customers tonight.' The old man sounded happy about that. Obviously, he knew nothing about what had happened. Back in the kitchen Chase managed to find both slugs from the 22. Not always loud enough to catch people's attention, but effective if drilled into the right part of the body. God damn you, Tabib! God damn you! He stood over the dead man like a disoriented priest. If only, what? If only he hadn't gotten into that ridiculous fist-fight at Billy's? *This is how I've taken care of your place, Joe. I've ruined everything.*

The telephone rang. It was Seyyed, wanting to know why Chase had called. 'It's nothing,' he told the old Afghan. 'Just wanted to see how you were doing.' The old man's answer was to utter *shokr-khoda*, thank God, a couple of times. And Chase thought: Yes, of course, thank God. You do that, Uncle Seyyed. You just go right ahead and thank that guy. He left the phone on top of the television set to go outside for the call he needed to make now. Before he got to the door the thing was ringing again. He hesitated, then walked back to pick it up.

It was his Bureau contact, Jay Shanker.

'You shouldn't have moved so far downtown, Chase. Now we got an excuse to see each other more often.'

Chase's first response was to bolt. But he controlled himself. Shanker's voice sounded thoughtful, even subdued, and it was just possible he meant what he said, since from the Federal Plaza to this end of Chinatown was but a fifteen-minute walk.

'You there, Chase?'

'Yeah. Such a surprise, Special Agent Jay, calling little old me twice in one day.'

'I wanted to tell you earlier, but I had to think it over a little more.'

'Tell me what?'

'I'm almost done here. I can be at your place in a half-hour. We'll have a chat, have a drink. I want to see your new digs anyway.'

'Ah man. I'm still cleaning up after my friend. I got two thousand books on my floor and can't decide if I want to find shelves for them or throw the damned things away. But tell you what, I'll meet you in the neighborhood.'

'That's all right. Where?'

'There's a place called Triple Pleasure. Little bar on Center Street just below Canal. It's halfway between you and me. You know it?'

'I'll find it. Say ten?'

'Ten.'

Hide the bodies. Clean up. Make yourself less suspicious. You got twenty minutes to do it in. Instead he stood there in the middle of the living room unmoving, engulfed in all that bad luck. Then when there was just five minutes left, he forced one foot in front of the other and ran out of the apartment, heading for the Triple Pleasure.

*

The Triple Pleasure was in the heart of Chinatown, run by a tight-knit group of young Japanese. Most of its clientele, though, were white kids who came because they got a kick out of the name. Being Monday night, it was pretty deserted. Plus the place now seemed to bear the feel of some late-night bar that soldiered on as the world fell to pieces around it. Even the air felt like it still had soot to it. While Roth's place was tucked away and hugged the very eastern edge of Chinatown, where mostly the Fujian people did business, from here there was only a short beeline to the monumental debris that had been the Twin Towers. After five months, desolation clung fast to the neighborhood and would not let go. Traffic remained light and few hung about at night. Chase recalled the feeling in the air in those first days when the police had blocked off cars below 14th Street and kept most pedestrians from going past Canal. It was something the cops had to do, but their caution was especially cruel to Chinatown and a lot of folks had had to close up shop. Chase had not wanted to venture out during those days anyway. If he did, it was only to visit Roth.

Roth was ill, but there was no hint at all that he would die in another three months. He'd been dying for years. Nothing new in that. Together they'd sit by the TV and take in the war that America was about to unleash over Afghanistan, Roth's face glued to that screen watching the parade of old Afghan players, some he'd known and apparently liked, others he'd despised. Chase could feel what Roth was thinking: Afghanistan, like Iran, was *his* turf. He was the one who should be there now. Nobody was more qualified. Nobody had more contacts. Sidelined, all Roth could do was to draw harder on the booze. It was painful to watch. Leaving him at his place, Chase would meander downtown and absorb the odd enchantment that had befallen this part of the city. Deserted roads, people ambling in the middle of once busy streets. The day after the end of the world might look something like this. But then you'd turn a corner and an improvised memorial would have been set up for the victims. There would be guitar and conga players sitting at sidewalk spreads where candles and incense burned late into the night and people got gooey and hugged each other. At first Chase had been drawn to the tender magic of it all – especially since he felt somehow culpable for having been in his furnished room in an opium stupor on that September morning. So he'd walked the streets for a while, but then he couldn't bear it anymore. He started to take refuge in bar rooms, sitting in them at angles where the television would be least in his face. During those days he'd also try to avoid walking by firehouses as much as he could. Most of them had lost some of their crew in the Towers. There was one ladder company only a block away from his hotel on 43rd Street. They had the picture of one of their missing guys on the outside. Every time Chase passed the place he had to look away. He felt those eyes closing on him, accusing him through his past – as if somehow Chase was responsible for the man's death, as if the verdict was still out on Chase's loyalties.

Later on, when the tourists had started trickling back to the city, there would always be folks taking pictures and chatting with the firemen. Those same tourists would corner him at nights behind the hotel desk to ask him how best they could get to the disaster site. It was his job to tell them. So he did, with a grimace. Then one night he decided he couldn't tell them anymore. He'd had it. Fact was that he'd escaped the Middle East to get away from the madness of that place, and now that same madness had come and perched right at his doorstep. Soon, before he knew it, Roth would be dead. A little later Lotfi would come knocking. Lotfi would die too. And now? He might as well drink up and wait for his fate. Thankfully, the Triple Pleasure had no TVs to have to turn away from.

He'd ordered a beer and two separate shots of whisky for himself and was waiting at a remote table. Some college kids had shown up, lingering by the counter. The juke-box was at the right decibel and it alternated between Chinese pop songs and traditional country and western music. The selling point to the place was its self-conscious irony, and it worked. Shanker was already late. He ended up not showing up until after ten-thirty, and when he did he looked sapped and unhappy.

Chase let him sit and went to the bar to order him a Heineken. That was what Shanker always drank. When he got back to the table, Shanker tried to shove a twenty at him and asked if he'd get him a shot of whatever whisky he was drinking too. Chase took the money and put it back in front of Shanker. He went and got the whisky, placed it on top of Shanker's twenty and then sat down himself.

They were sitting at a ninety-degree angle to each other instead of face to face. This made for more intimacy and allowed them to talk at a reasonably low volume. Chase's initial panic had gone. Maybe the liquor had helped him. Whatever it was, it took him off that edge and he thought he might even be able to hear his own voice without being terrified by it. The two of them looked only slightly incongruous here among the college kids and the pair of Japanese bartenders with spiked, painted hair. Shanker didn't have on one of his checkered shirts tonight; he wore a suit and a beat-up tie, knotted loose and twisted to the left of the collar. Chase eyeballed him while the other man took a long sip of his beer.

'What gives, Jay?' He'd never addressed him like this. It hinted at a familiarity neither man had been able to cultivate in the past.

Shanker turned to him. 'It's a jungle out there.'

'It's a jungle in here.'

Shanker gave a half apology about being late. He mumbled something about the office and let his sentence get lost in the next shot he took from his drink.

Chase took a chance. 'Are they stressing you guys to produce results?'

Shanker looked at him. 'So you read the papers.'

'I don't have to read the papers, Jay. It's the way it always works.'

'Guys in Washington couldn't put their finger on a map till yesterday and say here's Iraq, here's Yemen, here's goddamn Afghanistan. Now all of a sudden they've all become real go-getting cowboys. They're already leaking to the papers about how they want action, and blaming us in the field for not getting our priorities straight. I tell you, it's only gonna get worse.'

'Let me guess – New York, for instance, is out of touch with the new reality. You guys are supposed to still be more interested in the Italian mob than terrorism, because that's what you're supposed to know best. That's what they say. Right?'

Shanker took another sip, closing his eyes. 'We got one new Harriet downtown now, pushing for my transfer out of New York.'

'All right, Jay, what do you want with *me*? I'm a source that ran dry long time ago. You know that already.'

'Actually, I don't agree with you on that at all.'

'Are you suggesting something?' Chase felt a tinge of panic, but he checked it and it passed. He reminded himself that Shanker had no need to suggest. If he knew something, it wouldn't be here that they'd be sitting. Shanker wasn't answering the last question, so Chase changed his tack a bit: 'Anyway, you sure it's kosher for you to be talking to me like this. I mean, all this inside politics.'

'Give me a fucking break, Chase. I'm talking straight with you for once after all these years. Let me have a little bit of the same. Everybody knows what's going on with the Bureau these days.'

'You didn't call me tonight to tell me you want to quit.'

'Maybe I should have been a New York City detective. Better yet, one of NYPD's horse-riding jokers in Times Square, the ones tourists love.'

'Well,' Chase said, 'it's nice to know you're not an asshole after all.'

Shanker did a double. 'You really thought I was?'

'All this time you treated me like I was mentally challenged, you know. Like if you just put your hook out I'd come biting. Hell, you might be doing that now, but more cleverly. Guess that means I'm biting.'

'You're not biting on anything, Chase. And no, I never did take you for a sucker.'

'In that case, I repeat: what gives, special agent?'

'I need eyes and ears out there.'

'Come off it, man! You know full well what I've been doing past few years. Nothing. You want a career boost, you have to see guys in the business, not me.'

'I want you to get involved in the community. Hang out at mosques. Show your face. A lot of these people know you. They trust you. You can talk their talk.'

'Is there a bonus in it for me? Is it the Bureau asking or just you?'

'No bonus. Strictly me asking.'

'What makes you think I got the time for that sort of thing?'

'Since you and I talked today, I've been thinking. You're right of course, I know all about your old buddy Joe Roth. I know what he did and who he did it for in this city. Private-eye to the Muslims of New York. You said you were cleaning up the loose ends of his business. Well, I'd like you to do more than that. Carry on the work, won't you? You're in the position to do that. If you want, I'll even help you make it legit. The work will give you room, open some doors. People are going to be calling you to do all kinds of jobs. You'll have some access.'

'Did you ever approach Roth for this?'

'Your friend Roth was one angry guy. Besides, I got word long time ago he was off-limits. Guess he had a bad run at the Agency or something. My condolences anyways.'

Chase was playing with his two empty glasses. He surprised himself. Even the cold sweats were gone all of a sudden and withdrawal waited outside the door for the time being. It was temporary, but God! how he appreciated the breathing space. And for once Shanker and he were truly on the same wavelength, especially in regard to Roth's business. He said, 'You sure this doesn't come from higher up? Just you?'

'What higher up? They want to transfer me.'

They listened to a Chinese version of what sounded like the Beatles' 'Across the Universe'. It was an infectious song, even in Chinese. And less than halfway through it, both men started murmuring along to what they recalled from the English version, their voices getting louder and coming together just at that refrain where John Lennon would have crooned 'kangaroo days, la-la-la'. Instinctively they looked up and caught each other and Shanker broke into a grin and continued more boldly to the end of the song. Chase waited. Then after what he figured was an acceptable break, he gave the okay he knew the other man expected.

'Jay, I'll do it.'

'You don't have to,' Shanker put in for form's sake. 'I'm not making you. Is that clear? It's a favor.'

'Yeah, yeah. Can't you guys do or say anything anymore without worrying about the consequences?'

'No, Chase. We're living in a world where the consequences determine everything we do beforehand. And because we worry so much about the consequences we end up doing nothing at all. This is my job, basically. My job and almost everybody's I know.'

'You're an unhappy man then.'

'No, I got a wife and two beautiful daughters. I never told you.'

'Thanks for sharing it, even if you're lying to buy my sympathy. If you are, let me tell you that you don't need to. I'm doing this because I wish genuine success for you. Better you in New York City than transferred to Boise, Idaho or some place like that. Besides, I had planned to do just that, take over Joe's business. So you and me, we understand each other.'

Shanker laughed. Without wanting to, Chase visualized what awaited him back at Roth's apartment a few blocks away from here. It was a vicious reality check. He told Shanker he was going to stay for a while and drink some more. He needed to see Shanker leave well before he did.

Shanker said, 'What happened to your face? Why is it swollen?'

'It's one of the hazards of this new occupation you wish me to pursue. I'm still learning the ropes.'

'You got any good cases yet?'

'I advised an Arab fellow out in Sheepshead Bay that it was in his best interest to pay off the Russians than not pay them. I also followed a Pakistani merchant's wife.'

'Whoring around, is she?'

'Well, I wouldn't call it *that*.'

'So she was.'

'She was looking for love in all the wrong places.'

'And you told the husband.'

'No. I lied and told him she was faithful. I told him she just liked to walk around the city a lot.'

'Ah, Chase, you're a romantic.'

'So are you, Agent Jay. Or you wouldn't be here tonight.'

They went silent on each other after that. The last thing Shanker said was that he was going to depend on Chase to call him regularly. 'I need a more personal read on these people, you understand.' *These people,* Muslims, the very folks who were going to be calling the Kismet Detective Agency to trust him with their troubles. It wasn't a favor that Shanker was asking, but a demand applied with some moderate leverage over a shot or two in the Triple Pleasure bar. For Chase, whose history to a man like Shanker was written in dirt, saying no was like an invitation to have himself and his new life ravaged. *So Chase, you want to be a private dick for the believers of New York? Well then, this is what it's going to cost you . . .*

When Shanker finally pushed his chair back and stood to go, Chase didn't even look up at him. It wasn't that he wanted to show he was brooding over the issue, but he did want Shanker to think that he took this *favor* he was asking for seriously enough. He wanted the FBI agent to think he was a witness also to Chase's categorical loneliness – wanted him to feel that by having this meeting tonight Shanker had scored a point of sorts. For if life was strange – which it wasn't – it was only because there were too many connections. And the only thing that separated Chase from Shanker was a heartbeat somewhere in the past and a road not taken by one or the other man. Chase could not imagine himself with a wife and two daughters. He wondered if Shanker could. He almost called out a farewell as Shanker left the bar. A few minutes later Chase, alone, got himself another two shots of scotch and put enough coins in the juke-box for seven straight Hank Williams songs. The first song happened to be called 'Long Gone Lonesome Blues'. One of the Japanese bartenders called out to Chase that he'd get a free drink for choosing that song, since the staff had decided that was going to be this Monday night's theme song. Chase nodded, smiled briefly and remembered Tabib. Long Gone Lonesome Blues.

12

Tuesday, 2 a.m.

'Keep letting people get killed in your place and your own number is likely to come up soon.'

'I didn't plan it this way, Kari.'

'You don't plan, period. That's your problem.' Kari looked around the apartment. 'Why's the place like this? They came for the book?'

Chase shrugged. 'It's not like they'd come up here to look for a six-pack of beer. I just don't get it.'

'What don't you get, son?'

'Why would they kill Tabib?'

'He probably gave them no choice. I saw that cleaver in his hand. Don't brood. Now's not the time for it. Who's the ass-up white dude in the bathtub?'

'Lund. Art dealer. The one who was supposed to take the book off our hands.'

Kari looked at Chase in disbelief. 'You told him to meet you here? You told him to come here while Tabib was here? Who opened the door to him? Tabib? And where were you when all this was happening?'

Chase remained quiet. Kari strolled about the living room, kicking books and pieces of broken furniture out of the way. 'You gotta clean this place up.'

'What's the difference now?'

'Wasn't it you who told me a few hours back you got to kiss some policeman's ass now and then?'

Chase didn't balk. He'd thought this one through and come to the conclusion that telling Kari about his meeting with Jay Shanker earlier in the night would only complicate their rapport. Kari might even walk out on him. To Chase that was not acceptable. Shanker and his request were his own problems. They had nothing to do with what was at hand – at least that was what Chase wanted to believe. Besides, being asked a favor by the policeman meant that a certain level of trust was being bestowed on him, and if he was being trusted he was not being watched. It was a plausible and convenient way of looking at things and Chase was not about to contradict himself on that. So to Kari he only said, 'You hurt me, guy. I already told you what my deal with the cops is all about.'

Kari embraced the air with his large hands and let them drop to his hips. 'Supposing your man called and said he was coming by in a half-hour. What would you do then?'

'I would shoot myself. But the point is he won't. I'm nobody. These guys are way too busy listening to overseas traffic nowadays.' Chase watched the other man shaking his head. 'What? I say something wrong?'

'You don't get it, do you? If Tehran sends that man Lotfi to see you and he turns up missing, you don't think someone's gonna pick up a telephone over there and call one of their own here about you? What'll you do if your name comes up on some NSA surveillance between Tehran and New York? You think the cops will still be too busy to drop in on you?'

'They wouldn't think twice about it, would they? They'd accuse me of every act of treason in the book.'

'There you go. Man ought to always know what he's getting into before he gets into it.'

'That what you did when you went to Afghanistan to fight for God, Kari?'

'I won't even stoop to answer that.'

'You don't have to.' Chase looked around, sullen. 'I don't even know what I'm into anymore.'

'That's 'cause you've been acting like a damned amateur.'

'So I'm an amateur. Now what?'

'Tell me about the manuscript. I mean, really tell me about it.'

Chase pointed to where the bodies lay. But Kari didn't seem to be interested in them right now.

'The book first.'

Rain outside. The sound of it lending the disarray here a fleeting order. Chase was thinking how so very little touched him anymore. Tabib's death was already like distant news. The dead man belonged to a different landscape, to Central Asia and its always imminent disasters. Better to imagine he was never here. It was a mistake, his appearing and that hole in his neck keeping him so still, so dead, in the kitchen.

'The manuscript,' Kari persisted.

Chase repeated the stuff about devils and monsters, about the Kabul museum and how the *Hallaj-Nama* had supposedly disappeared from there around the time the Russians had left. 'All this over a manuscript,' Chase said. 'I don't understand why I'm still alive.'

Kari had his eyes closed by now. His hands resting behind his neck and his feet on the table, listening. There was a silver Magnum in his lap. 'Where were you when all this mess happened here? Why weren't you around?'

'I was in a bar on 43rd Street getting drunk. I got into a fight.' Chase brushed his hand over his swollen face to make the point. 'Strange world, Kari. Kismet. Roth had the right word for his detective agency.'

They stayed silent. One of the half-dozen clocks in the apartment that had been hanging precariously from the top of a smashed glass cabinet finally fell to the floor and a pair of batteries rolled out of the back of it. The telephone started to ring.

'Turn that thing off.'

Chase went over and pulled the cord out. 'What do I do, Kari?'

The big man opened his eyes. 'Sit down. Look me in the face and tell me something. Tell me who you think killed these two guys. These two guys and that other fellow, Lotfi. Who'd go to all this trouble?'

'The Uzbeks? The Uzbeks Tabib was supposed to have come here with?' Chase asked uncertainly.

Kari looked away and let out a tired sigh. 'What type of job did Tabib say the Uzbeks were coming here for?'

'Didn't really say. He was too vague. Anyway, if they came, they probably came as Russians. I'm sure that's how Tabib came. I found nothing on him though. No passport. Probably it was taken.'

'Look, I fought alongside and against Uzbeks in Afghanistan, kid. They're not the brightest people I ever met. But try to put two and two together – do you think even those guys would be so dumb as to hang around New York, kill three people who more than likely had nothing to do with their original plan and just wait to get caught? Think about that for a minute and answer me honestly.'

'I don't have to think about it. Even an idiot wouldn't do this.'

'So who do you think did it?'

'Somebody who wants a certain book real bad?'

'Right. And they *have* been watching you. You made the mistake of getting this guy Lund to come over to your place. Can you read the rest of my story?'

'They came thinking the manuscript was here by now. Something went wrong.'

'Something did. Your friend Tabib tried to be a hero. They shot him. They didn't mean to, but they did. Unless, of course, they had already got him to tell them where the manuscript is. But,' Kari surveyed the apartment again, 'by the looks of how they went about ransacking the place, I don't think they ever got that far. They killed Tabib by mistake and then realized what they'd done. They turned the place over. No manuscript. Lund was here or got here. A stupid bystander. They had to finish him too. That leaves you, kid. Do you know where the manuscript is?'

'Yeah. You want to know where?'

'None of my business.'

'What's your business then, Kari? Why don't you just get up and go back to your furniture store and leave me to my misery?'

'You really want me to do that?'

'Of course not. I just don't understand why you'd do anything for me. Who am I to you?'

'Roth's friend.'

'That doesn't seem enough. Does it?'

'Does to me. Besides, I may have a bone or two to pick with God ever since Afghanistan, but that doesn't mean I've forgotten him.'

'I don't know what you're talking about.'

'I'm talking about the devil, kid.'

'Oh, that guy. I'd almost forgotten about him.'

'Come on.' Kari slapped him on the back. 'Cheer up. Us and the stiffs, we're going to take a trip together right about now.' He stared at the dead clock by the broken cabinet. 'Yeah, now's a good time for it. On our way, maybe I'll tell you a story.'

It would be three in the morning soon. Observing him, Chase could swear that Kari was thrilled to be doing all this.

The big man started by fishing out the unlucky Lund from the bathtub while Chase stood to the side watching.

'Kari.'

'What?'

'I was careful. I never called Lund from my place.'

Kari let go of Lund. 'But you did call him. Here!' He took Lund's phone out of the dead man's pocket. 'Smash this thing to pieces. Don't leave it hanging about.' Chase took the phone from him. Kari went through Lund's other pockets, found a piece of paper and handed it to Chase. It was the address to the apartment. There was also a ticket for a parking lot down the street. 'We'll have to transport the gentleman and his companion in his own car. You understand?'

Chase nodded in agreement.

'Let's hope for your sake, and mine, that it's a twenty-four-hour garage.'

'It is. I know the place. It's around the corner.'

'I guess it's just another lucky three a.m. for you then. Give me a hand with this antique lover, will you?'

'I don't touch dead bodies, Kari.'

Kari let go of Lund again and gaped at Chase.

'Just kidding!'

They lifted Lund, took him to the living room and started to wrap him up – like you would an antique.

Eight a.m. Kari drove. The inside of his brown Cherokee was decked out in a burst of colored fabrics one might see on the walls of a West African restaurant. His selection of music, mostly old Motown. The vehicle, a contradiction-on-wheels to the austerity of his pad. The last few hours had been a numbing crash-course. Kari had gone into operational mode while Chase tried to hunker down with withdrawal. Bad timing. The big man did most the work. He got Lund's car out of the garage without much fuss. They checked to make sure there was no surveillance camera on the lot. The late-shift Chinese attendant was too sleepy to care who was coming for the van or who had left it there earlier in the day. They drove the thing around to the front of old Seyyed's building and did the transfer from the basement steps where to inquisitive eyes it would look like garbage was being put out from Seyyed's kebab joint. Lund's van – no doubt purchased for hauling art – was an easy fit for the two bodies. No one could have seen them dumping anything into the vehicle – Chase hoped.

Later, parked in front of Dakari's Used Furniture in Brooklyn, another transfer. For the next forty minutes Chase found himself sitting cross-legged between Lund and Tabib's lifeless bodies in Kari's own car. Curiosity was a luxury that vanished when things started to go from one wrong to another. He didn't ask Kari about the purpose of switching cars. The big man had simply taken Lund's van and driven away with it. Chase was not interested in the fate of that van. And when Kari returned, he didn't bother asking him how he'd gotten back without it.

'I don't know who my enemy is,' Chase heard himself complaining to Kari.

Kari smiled for a change. 'Don't take yourself too seriously, kid. You're not important enough to have enemies.'

'What am I then?'

'You're somebody's obstacle, but also their last hope of finding what they want. But let's not get into all that now. We still have work to do. Why don't you come sit up front with me and leave the dead to themselves.'

The most nerve-racking part of the drive had been when they'd had to cross the bridge from Manhattan to Brooklyn. The tight security on the bridges had lightened up a bit since that first couple of months after September, but there was still a chance they'd get stopped by the National Guard. There had been a shared moment of anxiety then as they'd come onto the Williamsburg Bridge. It was a risk to be taken; they'd stayed silent and ridden it out to the other side. No one had stopped them. A sigh of relief. Now, a quick drive took them across the Ridgewood section of Queens. They passed a succession of blocks of rowhouses until the railway tracks. Then they were nowhere, as if New York City had abruptly fallen off the edge of the world. There were very few lights here. Some industrial buildings, that was all. Kari stopped in front of one of them.

'Where are we?'

'A mosque.'

Chase's skepticism brought out an explanation from Kari. 'Some budding Albanian gangster they used to call Hasan Handsome bought the place a few years back, decided he was going to make a mosque out of it as his way of redeeming himself to the world. Then things went bad over in his old village in the Balkans and he decided he was going to go back home and kill as many Serbs as he could get his hands on. I heard he barely made it to the old village before the Serbs made a soccer ball out of his head. As for this mosque . . .' Kari glanced at it in the darkness, 'it just sort of stayed what it always was. They used to dismantle cars here and sell the parts. Sometimes they'd dismantle body parts – human parts. I guess Hasan Handsome was just getting himself ready all this time to meet his fate.'

'Kari, you sure we're not going to get ourselves caught with two dead guys tonight?'

'We might. We might not. It's the risk a man takes when he helps a brother.'

'Am I your brother then?'

'You're a shithead way out of your depth. But I have this bad habit of helping your kind. What do you think the Afghans were? A whole bunch of shitheads who wasted my time and Joe's. Let's go in.'

Kari opened the main gate with a ready key and backed the car in with the lights off. The flashlight settled on a place that reeked of old manufacturing grease and rusting equipment parts. It was certainly big enough for a mosque, though Chase could have never imagined it being turned into one. He thought of the Albanian fellow's headless torso lying rotting somewhere in Eastern Europe and the only thing blessed about this would-be mosque of his was that Kari had a key to it.

'What do you plan to do?' he asked Kari.

'I don't plan to bury Mr. Lund just yet. I gotta do a more thorough job on him.'

'We're just setting him here like this?'

'I'll take care of him later. That's my worry, not yours. Besides, there are dogs around.'

'Oh, Kari!'

'It's a joke. I know, poor man didn't even get to see the *Hallaj-Nama*. Never had the satisfaction. Roll him out of his sheet and set him on the ground. He'll be all right here. I'll be back for him soon enough.'

An old beat-up green Plymouth sat in a corner of the shop. Kari tinkered with it until he got it started. They left Lund's body there in the shop, then took Tabib's out of the car and lowered him into the back of the Plymouth. A short drive up Fresh Pond Road, then under the Long Island Expressway and they came upon a sprawling cemetery.

'Welcome to Mount Zion.'

'Why here?'

'Lesson one: never leave two corpses in the same place.

154

That's when some nosey son of a bitch might put two and two together.'

'What – are we going to give Tabib a proper burial then?' Chase asked.

'The only proper burial's the one old Zoroastrians used to give. Left their dead up in their Towers of Silence and let the vultures come pick them clean. That's a proper burial for you. It's called the art of the recycle. Those Zoros, I think, must have been the original environmentalists.'

Mount Zion split into two parts right under the expressway. Kari waited, checking his watch off and on.

'What are we waiting for?'

'Making sure the nightman is not on this side of the cemetery.'

Kari jumped out of the car and quickly opened the gate with another set of keys while Chase drove the car through.

'You have a lot of keys,' Chase commented.

'I only have the ones that matter. A lot of them do. So I have a lot of keys.'

With the lights turned off and Kari giving directions, Chase followed a number of switchbacks to higher ground and a corner of the cemetery that sloped too close to the expressway. There was a mix of regular tombstones and bigger crypts that must have been here for a very long time. The cars on the expressway passing so near appeared like hurried ghosts on solitary joyrides. For a minute Chase was transfixed by the view: the skyline of Manhattan a hulking chimera with its blinking glow.

Kari called out to him and when he turned round he saw that the big fellow had propped Tabib's body next to one of the crypts behind them. Then as he walked towards Kari he noticed that there was a stone vault already ajar. He looked into Kari's eyes.

155

'That's right,' the other man said before Chase opened his mouth to speak. 'All the keys that count.'

'Do we just leave him?'

'That's the general idea.'

Chase felt strange asking, 'And the smell?'

'It's a heavy vault, son. And it won't matter by the time they discover him, *if* they discover him. It's not like your friend had a social security number or anything. Trust me. Anything else?'

'Yeah. Are there any other unlucky guys in there?'

'You mean besides the original unlucky guy? Not in this tomb that I recall. But maybe in one up a quarter-mile. Belongs to another Italian, Giovanni something.'

Chase smiled despite himself. 'Tabib always did like Italians. Thought they dressed well, or had class or something.'

'Man's in good company for eternity then, ain't he?'

After picking up Kari's car, they spent the next couple of hours on an aimless drive watching the sun come up in the east. Smokey Robinson and the Miracles played on the CD player – 'Tears of a Clown' was the one song Chase could recognize. He thought of how Tabib had been a clown at his best moments, irritating at his worst. They drove on – over the Verrazano Bridge, heading back to Brooklyn after a long aimless loop through Staten Island. Kari asked him where he wanted to be dropped off.

'Istanbul would be nice. Will you come help me fetch the manuscript?'

'Not that fast. First you have to deal with some unpleasantness right here.'

'Let's hear about this unpleasantness, then. I know you've got something on your mind, Kari. You've had it all morning.'

Kari turned and looked at him for a moment, but then said nothing for the next few minutes until they were off the bridge. Finally, when he did say something, it was something that threw Chase off completely.

'You must quit the shit you take, son.'

'Huh?'

'Don't huh me. I know all about it.'

'I'm trying, Kari. It's going okay, I think.'

'The stuff, it ain't evil, it just slows you down. Changes your priorities.'

'What it does is change the nature of your priorities.'

'Don't go poetic on me now. Hear me out: you got work ahead of you.'

'Me? Alone?'

'Hey, the bad guys are watching *you*, not me.' Kari let out a long sigh. 'You know, back in the days . . .' He didn't continue.

'Yeah?' Chase prompted him. 'Back in the days what?'

Kari parked the car close to the water and they got out. It was a neighborhood somewhere on the edge of Sunset Park and Bay Ridge. Morning joggers chased after their dogs on the bicycle path that rounded the waterline and disappeared in the distance under the bridge. A couple of fishermen stood idly chatting. A ferry passed close to their end of the shore.

Chase turned to Kari, thinking nautical: 'Why do they have to have all these different names for ships and things? What's a dinghy or a trawler? Where exactly are the bow and the stern and the starboard? What do they mean when they talk about a jib or a mizzen? I don't know any of this shit.'

'Ignorance is bliss, son.'

They could hear ice-cream-truck jingles from somewhere behind them. It was a strange backdrop for their talk. Chase watched Kari and wondered what exactly happened to a man when he lost the belief he'd worked so hard to embrace. Kari was looking in the distance. After a while he began again on the same note: 'Back in the days – in the war, I mean – you had all kinds of nutjobs and crazies coming to lend a so-called hand. That's what war does, brings out all the bad actors. People who like to think of themselves as soldiers of fortune, stringers looking for a story, bullshit spies. You name it, they were there in those days in Peshawar. Dealers and thieves and real pious fellows alongside evil sons of bitches who'd cut your throat on a dime.'

'What's this have to do with the *Hallaj-Nama* manuscript?' Chase asked.

Kari looked at him for a second and looked away. 'When you think about it, not much really. What I mean is, you had everybody who had a beef with the Russians, or thought they did – Brits, Poles, Turks, Americans, Paks, even Japs. Some were for real, some were fake, and a few here and there were after nothing but loot. Forget about this museum in Kabul. That's one old country over there. Everywhere you dig you're bound to come up with something. We heard people were digging, sniffing, taking and selling. It was war. What did you expect? We heard about manuscripts here and there and we said: "Okay, whatever! Let's go kiss" – I mean "kill some Russians and forget about the rest of it." Myself, and a lot of damn fools like me, we'd gone there to fight for the faith. Faith with a capital F. I didn't need to be thinking about gold and jewels and antique manuscripts. You with me?'

Chase looked out at the water and pointed to a vessel. 'I think they call that thing a tugboat.'

Kari said nothing. He was elsewhere. Afghanistan maybe, thinking of lost years, lost causes, a lost friend, or a lost faith with a capital F. The silence dragged on for some minutes. An old guy walked by with a small white dog that wouldn't quit barking. Dogs, thought Chase, are a problem of identification very much like ships. I know what a German shepherd is, but that's about all I know of dogs.

'Kari!'

'Aha?'

'But this manuscript isn't just any old antique. Supposedly it celebrates the devil. My question is, do some folks want it because they want their own devil's bible or something?'

'That's just child's talk, son. Devil's bible! What in the hell is that? Your book is worth something. That's why people are hunting for it. And I tell you, with all these dead guys on our hands so far, I can guarantee we're not dealing with just one set of hunters.'

'Think they're watching us then – all of them?'

'I'm thinking they can't be watching us right this minute at least. They've forced themselves into a bad situation with all the killing. They have to be rattled a bit. Lying low. Waiting to see what you'll do next. They probably figure, with your background you got a phone number you need to call. They're going to see if you'll go running to the Bureau or not.'

Chase swallowed hard. 'Should I?'

'Should you what?'

'Go to the cops.'

'No way. Unless you're tired of living outside of jail. What are you going to do? Take their hands and show them three dead bodies?'

'I'm waiting for your brilliant idea then.'

'It's not brilliant, but it's the only one I got. You have to play like you're still trying to figure out who's behind the killings.' Kari snapped his fingers and turned to face Chase. 'Where did you say that first dead fellow, Lotfi, told you the Uzbeks were supposed to be heading?'

'Dearborn, Michigan.'

'That there's a lie. The Uzbeks would be fish out of water in Dearborn. The law nowadays watches them Arabs like a hawk in places like that. To be honest with you, son, I don't think the Uzbeks are around anymore. And even if they were, they'd be wetting their pants from fear right about now. But you still have to go to Dearborn.'

Chase thought he understood where they were going with this. 'To pretend, you mean?'

'Exactly. If the word's out about Dearborn, then they'll be expecting you to go there. They'll get suspicious if you don't. You're going to show our boys you got it into your head to go avenge your pal Tabib's death.'

'And then what? Wait for them to come catch me?'

'That's the general idea. They won't touch you in Dearborn. That place is too small and the Arabs there already feel the heat. But someone *will* be waiting for you when you get back here.'

'And where will you be?'

'Watching your back, but only after you get back.'

Again the air seemed thick with many unanswered questions, especially one: Chase asked, 'Why would you do this for me, Kari?'

'Are we back to that? Listen: maybe I lost my faith in Afghanistan. But I didn't lose faith in faith. You understand the difference? It was people like them, bad men, who stole it from me. They plain lifted the burden off old Kari and stuffed it down the toilet. Now, maybe you think this makes Kari look like a weak fellow. Then maybe Kari *is* weak. Who isn't weak about *something*? But I still got a bone to pick with the wicked of this world. My best buddy, Joe Roth, went and killed himself because of people like that. Maybe I was just waiting these past few years for you to come and ask me to take your hand. I need the burden, son. It makes me feel whole again. I haven't felt this way in a long time!'

'The wicked,' Chase muttered to himself.

'That's just my name for all nasty seed. They spit on what's righteous. And I've been waiting to spit right back at them all this time. And don't be acting smart now asking me if that means I consider myself righteous. 'Cause I damn well do!'

Laughing, Chase asked him if this was the point in the conversation where they would kiss and hug.

'No,' Kari said. 'We do that only after we get the manuscript and sell it. You and me.'

'Kari!' Chase was laughing harder now. 'You're finally beginning to make sense. You do like money after all.'

'Money yes. Sense, yes. But you can't sell the devil's manuscript until you get rid of the devil first – the devil will be after you otherwise.'

'All right then, I'll go to Dearborn.'

'And quit smoking that shit.'

'I told you I'm on it, man. It's not easy, though. I'm like some guy who's had his legs chopped off but still feels them itching all the time.'

'You're like an itch looking for a pair of legs to feel. Get out of here. Best take the train back by yourself. You'll be all right now.'

He felt his feeble knees giving way again after only a few steps. A swift crew of very intent bicycle riders zoomed by, wearing rainbow helmets, knee-pads, and spandex riding gear. It was true, opium did forever change one's speed. It almost seemed like a mistake, an error of nature, that these riders and Chase should both be moving about on the same piece of real-estate, breathing the same air in the world. It was an unhealthy superimposition, this. He'd have liked to share the thought with Kari, but wondered if the big man would quite appreciate the idea.

He turned and called out at him. Kari was still looking out at the water, the fishermen were still fishing. 'Kari, this itch . . .' Chase started to say.

'Just throw it in the sea,' Kari shot back without looking at him. 'Put the itch in a bottle and drop it in the water.'

Chase turned and walked on, having no idea what exactly he'd meant to tell the other man.

Nine a.m. Dearborn straddled the west side of Detroit and was known for two things: the origin of the Ford Motor Company, and the biggest population of Arab immigrants in North America. Kari had been right about the place. A band of Uzbeks would stand out ridiculously here. Chase could actually picture them being just about anywhere else on the continent but in this town. And even if they'd come here for the sake of meeting with a contact, what would make anyone think they'd show their faces in any of the dozen immigrant restaurants and coffee shops that lined Warren Avenue? The whole town was something of a sprawling Arab mini-mart. An amalgam of concrete and neon with store names like Lashish and Shatila. He found a cheap motel on Warren itself where he could register without having to show an identity card. He kept on a ski hat and a pair of semi-tinted glasses the whole time, then spent most of Wednesday going from one eating house to another ordering tea and single skewers of kebab. You could feel the tension in the air. Arab men loafed in circles in the coffee houses watching out for the nuances of betrayal. Their eyes said they didn't believe anybody would be here just to take in the sights – and who could blame them? When he tried to initiate conversations, they turned away excusing themselves. They had a hardened, somewhat ruined and yet deeply masculine pride. It made the air bristle with resentment. And after a while Chase felt foolish being there at all.

Finally, in one of the kebab houses he managed a curious

conversation with an Iraqi exile after risking it all and coming right out to tell him he was looking for friends from Uzbekistan. The Iraqi bobbed his bony face to one side and asked, 'Uz-who?'

'Bekistan. That's in Central Asia.'

'Are you from the FBI?' the Arab asked matter-of-factly, no hint of panic or aversion in his voice. It made Chase think that the man must either be a local snitch or the neighborhood clown – which would pretty much amount to the same thing.

'Why the FBI?' Chase asked, already feeling edgy about being in a town that was probably under every federal law agency's observation. It didn't help either that just then a local cop car parked across the street and the other men in the place immediately started giving the Iraqi tortured looks. The Iraqi caught Chase noting the police and smiled before starting to answer.

'Why FBI, you ask. Ah, because, these are the questions they ask us now: "Do you have a friend from this place, that place?"' He laughed nervously all of a sudden, probably recalling that he'd have a few things to answer for once Chase left. He drank his tea and grinned, revealing a set of teeth weeping for a dentist.

'But these Uzbeks are my friends,' Chase now said. 'I've come to look for them.'

'Oh, bullshit, *habibi*! You are police, take your hat off. It's okay. We have nothing to hide,' he said loudly, looking at the men at the other table for their approval. 'Police come to us too much now. God help you catch the bad guys. You need his help. You are not very excellent at catching them yourself.'

After that episode he imagined that every other Arab on Warren Avenue was trailing him with curious looks. Chase was still not convinced he'd ever needed to come here, but he persisted with the act because it came from Kari.

He spent the rest of Wednesday driving around, checking out the Ford headquarters from a distance, eating a lot of Arab sweets, more tea, another odd conversation – though not about Uzbeks this time, but about ice hockey and why Canada, which happened to be only a couple of miles from Dearborn, was not a part of the United States.

He went to bed late. He'd bought more methadone before coming here. Now with his medicine dropper ready, he counted out the dose and then doubled it out of boredom. He called Mette in New York and when he didn't get her, he replayed their last conversation from the day before:

'How much money do you have in your bank account?' he'd asked her.

'Why do you ask, Chase? Do you think I'd just pack up and let myself get sent off because you tell me to? By the way, Billy doesn't want you in his bar anymore.'

She stood naked in front of him, her hair disheveled. He thought about the coldness of Norway. She spoke English with a deep-throated masculine voice. That was the only trace of an accent in her.

'I'll pack you and you'll pack me,' he said. 'Then we'll get on a train and go to another state. Where would you like to go?'

'Texas?' she said with an unaccustomed chuckle while throwing her light blue blanket over her head.

'Why Texas?'

'Everyone in Europe wants to see Texas. It's like being authentic or something. Cowboys and Indians. The Alamo. Guns sold in the supermarkets.'

'Okay, we'll go to Texas.'

'No, we'll go wherever you say.'

'Is that a yes? You'll come with me?'

'I already said yes.'

Before leaving, he had written her a check for five thousand dollars from his account – exactly half of what he'd gotten from Swan, his former landlord at the hotel. He explained that she should deposit the money as soon as possible.

'Five thousand dollars is not that much money for travel,' she said. 'I already have that much in my bank.'

'Good. Now you'll have ten thousand.'

From that moment on he had made the uneasy discovery that his habits, such as they were, were starting to multiply. They all had a consistency that allowed them to become a part of a troubled whole, a sort of mother-habit that contained everything in its bosom – starting with the opium habit he was trying so hard to break, to a sick preoccupation with his notebooks, and now . . . a newly forged fixation over money.

He thought of money all night long in his Dearborn motel room where cable TV had a 24-hour news show in Arabic. Ministers of barren, faltering states faded in and out of the silent tube while Chase waited for sunlight. Then on Thursday morning he squared the hotel bill with cash and went to Yasmine's bakery next door to get an Egyptian honey cake with coffee to go. In that freezing Michigan morning three Arab men lounged in improbable white summer lawn chairs on the sidewalk and looked on as he pulled out of the parking lot. To them he was just another watcher that came and went. He'd never be back here and they wouldn't want him to.

New York. Midnight. He'd been back at the apartment since early afternoon, spending the rest of the day tidying up, getting rid of smashed bits and pieces of wood and glass and putting the books in order again. He hadn't been able to find Mette. And whenever he'd call the bar, the owner picked up and Chase had to hang up. No messages on Roth's machine. No client calls at all, which was a little odd. He called Kari from downstairs several times. Kari never got back to him either. But, at last, the phone did ring, and as soon as it did he had an instinct that the moment had come. A mechanical and, at first, alien-like voice on the other end said that he wanted to hire Roth for a job. When Chase asked about the job, the voice hesitated just long enough, as if the hesitation itself was an assignment to be gotten through. Then he admitted that because of the urgency of the situation he happened to have been waiting by Roth's place and would like to come up.

'Now? This time of night?' Chase asked, letting his incredulity slip.

There was silence at first. 'Yes,' the voice finally said. 'Right now.'

'By all means.'

The first thing he did was to slip Roth's gun under his shirt. Then he tried dialing Seyyed right away, but whoever had called from the other end hadn't hung up yet. Seyyed would have most probably closed up shop by now and gone home anyway. *Kari, wherever you are, big man – I hope you've got me covered.*

There was a knock on the door. Not even a ring from the buzzer downstairs.

The man who walked through the door was of medium height, built like a wrestler, with bulky shoulders and chest. His hair was short and flecked with a neat trim of gray. The eyebrows were very thin, almost not there at all, which from a certain angle made him look as if he were rippling through himself. There was a small scar up the right side of his neck.

His eyes were narrow gashes, and his skull looked like it had come out of a ball press. It was his black leather jacket, though, that was disconcerting. Chase had been expecting something less informal.

When he asked the man to come in, the other said that he was already in.

'Take a seat then.'

'Do you know why I'm here, Mr Chase?'

Chase turned to him, feigning a worn-out surprise at the man's knowing his real name and not thinking he was Roth. The voice sounded different from what he'd heard on the phone. He spoke good English. The accent was Russian, while the timbre itself belonged to a man who might have drunk a lot of vodka in his time and smoked plenty cigarettes. It was gruff yet strangely intimate. Chase said to him, 'You called me less than a minute ago. But then you didn't even ring my bell. You came right up to the door. Were you already in the building when you called?'

'Now you'll ask why I even bothered to call at all,' the stranger said. 'I could have just knocked. Yes?'

Pause.

'I can't place you, Mr . . .? Where are you from?'

'Why should that be important to you?'

'Well, you *have* asked that I do a job for you.'

The man laughed. 'Pretty broken up here,' he commented.

'How do you know my real name?' Chase asked him.

'People I know left something of a mess behind in this apartment. The least I should know about you, I think, is your name. I must say, you did an efficient job of cleaning it up. These men I work with . . . let's just say they're not as good as one wants them to be. They make mistakes. I had to make sure things were done right this time, so I came myself.'

The fellow stopped talking and stared intently. A number

of things occurred to Chase in uneasy succession now. He could act like he was enraged at what the other man had been saying and make a show of jumping him. This would seem like the natural thing to do under the circumstances. It would, for one thing, establish his sincerity at being angry about Tabib's death. Or he could do away with putting on an act and try to shoot the fellow for real. But there was always the chance that he'd get accidentally shot himself. Accidents did happen, as they had with Tabib.

His unhealthy cerebration brought objects into sharp focus. Roth's books appeared as if they were swimming around them in diabolic fashion. The fellow sat down and regarded him with an easy smile, and just as Chase was thinking of how to break out of this impasse he heard the other telling him to call him Max.

It was as if the name was Chase's signal. He lunged with both arms outstretched. Max dodged, allowed Chase to smack into the sofa, then chopped him on the side of the face. The sofa and Chase turned over and he crashed his knees on the hard floor surface before doubling in on himself. The pain wasn't too bad, and he waited to get used to it. It took him a while longer to get it together. When he dared open his eyes again, he saw that the sofa had been put back up while he remained on the floor. 'I don't feel too good,' he moaned. As if by saying this, he was somehow taking refuge in the other man's control of himself.

Max offered him a tired laugh and then his hand. 'Come! Get yourself off that floor and we can talk.'

'I should have just shot you,' Chase muttered.

'I'd still be faster. Let's go!' Max pulled him up. 'Let's just be nice and civilized to each other. Okay? I don't wish to hit you again.'

The phone rang and stopped. Max patted him down and

took his gun. Max's own piece was bulging from his side. He waited for the phone to ring again and then picked it up and whispered something that Chase couldn't hear.

Half an hour later Max had confirmed he was indeed a Russian. When Chase asked him why his English was so good, the other told him that that was none of his business.

'Max your real name?'

'That's none of your business either,' the Russian said. But then added, 'Maybe I spent a few years in some jail where they spoke only English. How's that?'

'That's okay with me.'

'Maybe in that jail I had a sugar daddy who liked to call me Baby Max. Do you buy that?'

'No, but it's good enough.'

Max picked up one of Roth's detective books off a pile from the floor, leafed through it casually, then threw it back down and let his gaze rest on Chase again. 'Look, there's been too much mess already. Three people killed . . .'

Chase broke in. 'Yeah. Three people. Right here in this place. Your guys are not very neat about this kind of work, are they?'

'Just who do you think *my guys* are?'

Chase shrugged. 'How would I know!' He thought a little more, then recalled something Tabib had said. 'My dead Tajik friend said something about Russians wanting to buy the book off his people on the cheap. Am I getting close?'

Max didn't back away from the question – he didn't have to. 'I spent two years in that fucking war in Afghanistan. The only thing I came away with was a leg wound and an old Enfield rifle I took off a dirty Afghan before I shot him in the head.'

'Making up for a lost cause then, are you? Who're you

working for now? The Uzbeks? No, that couldn't be. They hate Russians. Must be the Iranians then?'

'Iranians, they're overeager pests. But they know who to look for to get a job done. It's what you call a marriage of convenience.'

Chase shook his head. 'Max, I know all about you Russians in Tehran; I know what kinds of jobs you do for them. Tell me, how many destitute old Soviet nuclear physicists did you lure off the streets of Moscow and sell to the Iranian Atomic Agency?' He waited for Max's answer, but the other man only laughed. 'Not enough, I guess. Or you would have retired by now. So you're just trying your hand at a different commodity this time.'

'Hey, I've been after this manuscript for a while.' Max stared hard at Chase. 'I'm going to have it.'

'And you think the Iranians will let you just walk away with it?'

'The Iranians and me, we understand each other – up to a point! The only reason I came here myself tonight was I didn't want another screw-up. All this killing and nothing to show for it.'

'So what am I supposed to do now, just hand over the manuscript to you?'

'I could try to beat it out of you right here. But I don't think that would quite work? What do you think?'

'I haven't seen three men dead in my place to give you what you want so easily. I'd be a dead man myself if I did.'

'You're smart.' Max tapped his own forehead. 'You're thinking. That's good. So what if I told you that you and me, we could make a deal, cut the Iranians out and split the money ourselves.'

'I'd say you were lying through your teeth. I know these people. They might be messy, but usually they won't stop until they finish a job. And something tells me they want this book pretty bad.'

Chase was sitting on the couch. Max, who'd been standing near the kitchen for the past five minutes, came over to him and lightly held Chase's chin to the light. It wasn't a hostile gesture, and for a second Chase thought how just a touch of anger could help him now. He almost didn't know what real anger was anymore. Ten years of opium had seen to that. The closest thing to knowing fury was back at Billy's bar where he had tried to stand up for Mette. Other than that, everything seemed drearily tolerable in his life. One minute he could be sitting having a drink with Jay Shanker, a cop; next minute he was on a burial trip with a black Muslim who had lost his faith and was hugely bitter about it, and now . . . this. The fact that the Russian, too, had an Afghanistan history behind him made Chase feel that much more insubstantial. It was like he kept getting struck with souvenirs of his own shortfall.

'What are you thinking?' he said to the Russian.

'Thinking that I can work with you.'

'But?'

They heard steps coming up the stairway and then there was a knock on the door. Chase had been praying for Kari, but he could already tell it wasn't the big man's footsteps. He got up off the couch as Max withdrew to the kitchen.

'One of your guys?' Chase asked quietly.

'No, but answer it.'

'What if I run?'

'You won't get far. And you have nowhere to run to.'

It was Seyyed. He had a plate of olives and bread for him. Chase was surprised. He came out into the hallway so the old man wouldn't see the broken furniture in the living room.

'Thank you.' Chase took the plate from him. 'It's very late, Uncle Seyyed. I thought you'd be home.'

'I was having tea with friends. I saw your light. How are you? You have had a difficult time.' Seyyed pointed to a light bruise on Chase's face.

'It comes with the job.'

'A man can know pain and live, and a man can know it and not live,' Seyyed said meaningfully in the Dari dialect. 'It all depends on whom he chooses to damage him.'

Chase gazed into the old man's eyes, thinking that he finally understood what this Afghan desired most in the world: it was to dispense wisdom. Simply that. And yet, here, in America, he remained a prophet to an impossibly hurried people.

'Thank you, Uncle Seyyed. Peace.'

Back in the apartment Max had not made any attempt to get closer to the door. Now he took the plate away from Chase and started munching on the olives. Chase would have liked nothing better than to rattle his confidence. At the same time he wanted to prove to the other man he could be on the level. 'I have a contact,' he admitted, as if his confession was the other thing he had up for sale besides the manuscript. 'A cop. Calls me up once in a while for information. There's usually not much information. But then again . . .'

Max waved his hand, dismissive. 'By the way, did you find any Uzbeks in Michigan?' he asked, totally disregarding what Chase had just said. 'How was it there, anyway? Arabs hospitable? They usually are. Hospitable little rats. I hate them all – Arabs, Iranians, Afghans, Uzbeks. They're all vermin to me.'

Chase looked away, allowing Max his satisfaction in having read through his little bluff. Now he felt obligated to ask, 'So are these Uzbeks planning something here?'

'I wouldn't worry about any Uzbeks and what they might or might not do. You already know they're not your problem.

So your trip to Michigan was a waste.' Max paused, and after reflecting he added, 'Listen, Chase, your acting as if the human condition is something you really worry over is an insult to me. Do you take me to be stupid?'

The Russian's observation left him feeling embarrassed. The truth was more or less what the man said: he was feeling less and less over Tabib's death, Uzbeks were foreign soil to him, and the human condition was a tide he couldn't afford to surf.

They'd been standing in the kitchen for this exchange, and now Chase was nose to nose with the other man. He said to the Russian, 'You're right, I don't care about the Uzbeks and what they're here for. Not my business.'

Max gave him a look. 'Chase, are you trying to impress me now all of a sudden?'

'Maybe.'

'Ah! Why?'

'Because you seem to know what you're doing. What made you risk coming to my place alone?'

'The Iranians showed poor judgment shooting your friend, and I wasn't here to stop them. Now they're feeling jinxed. I couldn't take the chance they wouldn't do it again. Besides, you are not a very difficult subject. I have little to fear from you.'

How much time had already passed! Chase was starting to feel like Max's pet, was aware of having been neutralized, simplified to his most basic component, that of a man for whom the solace of his own body took ultimate precedence.

'You say you want the *Hallaj-Nama*, but what makes you think Tabib told me where it was?'

'He did tell you,' Max said smiling. 'And you'll tell me.'

'At a price.'

'You wish to sell me the manuscript then?'

'Yes.'

'For how much?' Max asked softly.

'Well, that man Lund, before your partners had him dispatched, he was talking about a sum in the millions.'

'Do you believe this is a sum I'd give you?'

'Not you, because you don't have that kind of money. But the Iranians, that's another story.'

'The story is that you are dreaming if you are asking for millions.'

'I know, so I won't bother asking for that. But with half a million dollars, I'm sure I won't have to go back to being a night manager at a hotel anymore.'

Chase could see the other man actually considering the proposition, thinking how he might be able to persuade the Iranians. It would be a sort of bridge loan for the Russian anyway, because afterwards he'd try to kill Chase himself or have his employers send someone to do it.

'This much I've already learned,' Max was saying, 'the manuscript is somewhere in Istanbul. The Iranians got that out of your friend Tabib before he decided to play with knives and get himself shot. The fact that we have this bit of information diminishes your asking price by a half.'

'I think I can live with a quarter of a million dollars,' Chase said faintly just to keep the flow of their conversation going.

'Good. Turn around now. Close your eyes if you wish.'

'Are we taking a trip?'

'Did you think we wouldn't?'

Chloroform. Its sweetish vapor administered on the classic white handkerchief of gangster movies. The vapor permitted him an instant of time when he imagined Max and himself as two inseparable sinners falling into an abyss where God, Uncle Seyyed and Kari were not permitted to pass through. And then, he was out.

14

He could not tell what day it was. The length of the room seemed to shift in and out of focus when first he opened his eyes. He was aware he was drugged. There was a lot of noise outside. Sounded like mothers shouting at their kids in distant corridors. Children running up and downstairs shouting back. The empty room itself a sick shade of blue that made him feel horribly boxed in. He was lying on the floor.

He tried getting to his feet, but it wasn't easy to do. There was a small window and through the half-open shade he saw that it looked onto some shaft where there was nothing but pigeons cooing. He didn't manage to stand. His legs felt like they belonged to a foal just come to life. His head was spinning. He called out Max's name weakly, thinking no one would have heard him, but then Max himself entered the room. To Chase he appeared taller, though it could have been the trick of looking up at him from the floor.

'What have you done to me?'

'Animal tranquilizer,' Max said.

'What am I supposed to do with it?'

'It will pass.'

Chase thought he could see another man standing in the room. His vision was still blurry. Maybe it was from the drug they'd given him. No, he was sure about it; there was someone there, maybe even two people.

'Who's he – I mean they?' But Chase felt too heavy to continue. He looked again and saw that the man or men weren't there anymore. Maybe he'd imagined them. He watched

Max leaving. An air of disappointment hung to the room. Chase called to him, but the Russian didn't turn around. The door shut behind him and Chase heard the lock click.

He lay there, very still, wanting to sleep but not being able to. After some time he tried to crawl but didn't get far. Later – he didn't know how much later – he was back in his corner, sweating. The come-down from the tranquilizer was wreaking havoc on his nerves. It almost cancelled out all his efforts of the past few days to clean himself up. The thought of this actually made him more depressed than his being held captive. He made some noise but no one appeared. He managed to get up and walk to the door. Locked, of course. The pigeons were still on the windowsill outside. They must be about five flights up. There was nothing out there but blackened brick and another window across the way, with its curtains drawn. Chase hobbled around the room, clutching at thin air, waiting, feeling nauseous and wanting.

He searched in his pants pocket and came up with a half-full vial of methadone. He uncapped the thing. But instead of drinking it down, he poured a small blot of the pink liquid over the gray rug. *Why am I doing this?* The lock turned and Max came in.

Max definitely wasn't alone this time. There was a tall, unnaturally pale, thickly built fellow with him. The Russian was pointing at the rug where Chase had been dumping the methadone.

'You're making a mess.'

'Where are we?'

'Do you have someone you care for, Chase?'

As Max asked this, the man that Chase already thought of as 'the albino' walked over and pushed him toward a corner of the room away from the window and forced him down. Max came and squatted in front of Chase. The albino stood sentry, watching neither one of them but looking stern, like he'd considered engaging in some system of belief and finally said yes to it because he thought he must.

'I don't feel too good.'

'You keep saying that,' the Russian said, 'and you think anyone should care. We got business to discuss.' Saying this, he tossed some things on the floor. They were Chase's notebooks, six of them, the ones he'd given Mette for safekeeping. He hadn't noticed them in Max's hands until they were spread out between the two of them.

Chase gave a cry, barely audible even to himself, and made a feeble attempt to make for the Russian. He was easily pushed back. Then Max gave the albino a nod and the fellow slapped Chase in the face. It wasn't a very hard slap, just enough to put him in his place. It still hurt, his face feeling like fallen fruit from the intermittent beatings of the last few days.

The Russian looked up at the albino and then at Chase. 'What do you say we talk about what you can tell us.'

'I can't tell you a bloody thing. I thought we had a deal.'

Max's man had started giving Chase that sort of misaligned look camels get when they are chewing something. He looked worried. So did the Russian. There were sounds from behind the door in the other room. Shuffling of feet, maybe someone talking into a phone. Chase was too unsteady now to think about it clearly, but he could feel something was wrong. They were taking too long; they weren't trying to beat the information out of him. They seemed too preoccupied.

There was a knock on the door and the albino walked off and left them alone. To Chase it felt as if he were dipping back through layers of time. They'd always be here, he thought – the silent albino, the Russian and Chase himself,

178

studying his own throbbing face between intervals of dreadful sleep.

'We're wasting each other's time here,' Chase said, forcing himself to talk.

'Talk about waste.' Max pointed at the notebooks. 'What's the use of all this? Wasting good paper. As if anybody cared what you thought.'

Chase wanted to know if they'd hurt Mette, but instead he found himself murmuring something inane about how every man needed to discover his worth through something, even if he had to fill reams of worthless paper to get to it.

'I don't disagree, Chase. A man can be reborn out of anything, a poem, a painting, a book. This is why you and I are here, isn't it?'

'Are you referring to the *Hallaj-Nama*?'

'What else.'

'Tell me first what you've done to her. I left my notes at her place.'

'I suppose she's fine. She won't even miss them, I don't think. But, Chase, how can you stand having her work in that bar? Really!'

He was going to protest that he didn't have her working anywhere, that it wasn't his call to make. But he said something else – it just came out, and as he said it he knew it to be the truth, an ugly one: 'I care for the girl, yes. But if you think you're going to make me trade the book's whereabouts for her you're wrong. I haven't known her *that* long, and even if I had . . .'

'The Iranians wanted to bring you one of her fingers, but I convinced them not to.'

'You're a gentleman.'

'Who'd want damaged goods, right?'

The albino was back. He whispered something into Max's

ear so that the Russian rose immediately and both men stood over Chase appraising him with uneasy looks.

'Who's the mute?' Chase asked, watching the albino.

'Ask him yourself.'

The albino took a step towards him and Chase instinctively put a hand up to his face thinking he was going to get hit again.

'These,' the fellow said in a gruff voice, indicating the notebooks. 'They're yours. Why did you leave them with the woman? You have something to hide?'

An Iranian. Chase would have asked him if his name by any chance was Zaal, after the famed albino character in the Persian epic *The Book of Kings*. He refrained, comedy not being an option now.

'I have nothing to hide, or you'd know it by now. But I guess I have a regular fan club right here. All you guys reading my humble notes.'

'Your notes have no interest. We want to know where the *Hallaj-Nama* is.'

'Well, it's certainly not in my notes.'

'Where is it?'

Chase had one eye on his own notebooks in front of him, and another on the Iranian's boots which had a perfect toe-shot to his face. He started to wriggle and back away on the floor. At the same time he said forcefully, 'Like I said, I thought I had made a deal with Max here.'

The man looked at Max, who now looked like he was obliged to say something: 'What deal?' he said to Chase dismissively.

'The deal.'

'There is no deal,' the Iranian said angrily. He turned and stared at Max. 'You are a fool,' he barked. 'I told them in Tehran not to do business with you. Russian scum!' Then he picked up Chase's notebooks from the floor and stormed out of the room.

Max said something under his breath in Russian and started to follow the other man out.

Chase called to him, 'How long do you guys plan to keep me around here?'

'As you can see,' Max said sourly from the door, 'that all depends on how many chefs there are in the house.'

Chase lay flat on the floor. The door was being shut. 'Hey!' he called again with some urgency. 'What about the girl?'

'What about her?' The door closed and the lock turned once more.

Bad sleep. When he woke up, there was very loud salsa music coming from somewhere out on the street. Distant voices. Spanish probably. It was dark out. Cold in here. His stomach was churning and he needed a bathroom. He crawled up to the door and started banging on it. Soon he heard footsteps and rolled himself away from the door. A light snapped and there stood the Iranian. He grabbed hold of Chase, just about picked him up and threw him against a wall. In the other room somebody put the radio on and turned the volume high.

'I need out of here,' Chase cried. His eyes and head hurt in the light. He heard the salsa and radio and cursed Kari under his tongue.

The Iranian approached him again. Chase was almost flat against the wall, barely standing. He received a slap and rode with it to the floor. His nose was bleeding.

'I'm not telling you anything.'

'Where's the Russian?' the fellow asked him.

'Say what?'

'He's gone. What deal did you make with him?' The

Iranian kicked him in the ribs. Chase scrunched up and struggled mostly to protect his face. He was trying to digest that bit of news and not get hit at the same time. The Iranian kicked him some more. 'What did that Russian swine read in your notebooks? Why is he not here? What did he find out?' Chase was tuning out. The boots had ceased to have an effect on him. Somebody else came into the room and tried holding the other man off. They spoke hurriedly. He heard one say to the other, 'We need him alive.'

There was loud hammering from outside, a black woman's voice saying she was going to call the police if they didn't turn that radio down. The Iranian had stopped kicking him. Chase pressed his face into the rug and tasted wet dogs and rain. He would have liked to inch over to where he'd spilled the methadone earlier and start sucking on that carpet. He wanted to blubber and whine. He cursed Kari again for leaving him alone like this.

And then, as abruptly as it had all began, it ended. Quiet. The last thing he heard was the Iranian's voice saying, 'Who's the note from?' *What note?* Chase thinking they were still discussing his notebooks. And then, 'We'll be seeing you again.'

The lights were out. No more salsa music from outside. Late. Chase doing a grunt's crawl through one room then another until he got to the bathroom, raising himself halfway and then passing out. Fat lips. Sore ribs. Cold.

Later, Kari's fatherly voice in his ear. 'Okay, kid. Sorry to put you through this. We can get out of here now.'

'You abandoned me.'

'It had to be done. I counted on you being tough. You were, or you wouldn't be alive now.'

'Oh man,' Chase moaned, 'is that supposed to make me feel better?'

'Let's go. You did good. I'm proud.'

Chase said nothing more. He let Kari grab him under the arms and lead him out of there. Afterwards he wouldn't even remember they'd had this little exchange.

15

To wake up back in Roth's bed and see Kari watching over him – little could top that. Chase forced a smile out of himself. 'They didn't kill me.'

'They couldn't afford to. They'd have to go back to Tehran empty-handed or worse: not go at all.'

'You rotten man, you left me to handle it alone.'

'I had to be sure of how many they were, who they were,' Kari said half apologetically.

'At the risk of having me dead.'

'Kid, if I thought you'd crack, if I thought you couldn't put up with a bit of roughness, I'd say you deserved the worst.' Kari watched him closely. 'You didn't talk, did you?'

Chase groaned to himself. He touched his face and was surprised to feel it wasn't that much worse since the fight at Billy's. It was his ribs that hurt most – but at least they didn't seem to have been broken. He settled into that pain, aware of how it could turn to nourishment if you didn't fight it.

'How do you feel now?' Kari asked.

'Profound. How am I supposed to feel?'

The big man sighed. 'Take a look at this. Can you tell me what it is?'

Chase gave the most obvious answer. The thing was one of those six-socket plug extensions, the ones you bought from the hardware store when you only had one outlet and too many electrical gadgets for your room.

'I swept your place,' Kari started to say.

'Swept as in you looked for bugs here?'

The big man pointed to the white socket Chase was still holding. 'They call it the WP-6. Operates with a 110-volt outlet. I examined it. It's got the works. Adjustable audio-gain control, a built-in filter for speech frequencies, FM Varactor circuitry for a nice clean sound, DC-controlled oscillator, internal voltage regulation. Truly a thing of beauty.'

'Please! Quit with the science lesson.' He let the device Kari had been describing drop to the floor. 'You know, I don't even know where I was.'

'They had you not far from my digs. Mixed neighborhood. Anyone could disappear there.'

'You think they bugged this place?'

'They tried anyway. But it doesn't matter now. They're gone. I made sure of that.'

Chase was sitting up. What he wanted was wisdom, tailor-made to suit him and only him. He recalled all those books he'd seen on Roth's floor about how to go about being a detective. No one could teach you this stuff. Maybe experience counted, but mostly you just had to be born with something, a gift of some kind. He didn't think he had that gift. Not enough of it anyway. He said, 'What do you mean you made sure?'

'Spooked them,' Kari answered easily. 'I mean I made sure they knew they were being watched. Once I figured which unit they had you in, I had a note dropped under their door.'

'A note!'

'They mention it?'

Chase nodded.

'I told them if anything happens to you they might as well call the police themselves to come pick them up. Told them they could forget about ever making it back to Tehran.'

'You took a chance, Kari.'

'So I did.'

Chase realized he'd neglected to mention something important. 'One of them is a Russian.'

Kari took in that fact. He was silent for a while, thinking. 'It makes a lot of sense.'

'Care to elaborate?'

'Sure.' But then the big man didn't say anything for a while. He seemed to be still working it out himself. He got up to go fetch some water for both of them. Chase thought: It's not water I want; it's an answer.

Kari came back and stood in front of him. He handed Chase a glass and declared, 'When too many hunters are after the same prey, it's best sometimes to let the prey go. Leave the catching for another day.'

Chase was about to do a 'Huh?' and tell the big man to stop talking like a puzzle. But then almost right away he lost his focus, finding himself in an abrupt mental void with no margins. Maybe it was the drug they'd fed him, or the lack of his own medicine. He felt like he'd misplaced a valuable of some kind. Now he was only half listening to Kari saying something about whether Chase wanted the long or short version of it.

'No!'

'No what?'

Mette! She was what was bothering him. He jumped up and started darting back and forth across the apartment. Kari had not only pulled the cord on the phone and the answering machine, he'd actually dismantled the whole system looking for more taps. The entire place looked again like an earthquake had hit it. Chase turned to Kari.

'I need your help.'

'No kidding.'

'I'm talking about Mette. They had her notebooks. I mean, they had *my* notebooks, the ones I'd given her for safekeeping. You've got to help me.'

'Help you do what?'

How quickly moods could change. Now, for the first time since they'd known each other, Chase got a sense that Kari was finally getting tired, plain sick of his troubles. And who could blame him? He searched the other man's eyes for the trace of sympathy he'd seen there only moments earlier. They were blank now, except for a touch of disdain directed at Chase's pleading tone.

'There's a girl,' Chase explained. 'Her name is Mette. I think they're holding her. You know, like they do in the movies,' he added in a false tone to sell them both on the idea that he was still on top of his game.

'They didn't take any girl over to where you were,' Kari snapped humorlessly. 'I was watching everything.'

'They could have taken her elsewhere. My notebooks . . .'

'Your notebooks what? What do you want me to do, save your girl for you?'

Strange to hear it: *his girl.* Essentially she was someone he'd both managed and failed to sleep with a couple of times, and then entrusted some notebooks to.

'What day is it?' he asked, half mumbling.

Kari snapped again with impatience. 'Sunday.'

'I just want to know she's okay. And if she is, suggest to her she put as much distance as she can between herself and this town.'

'Noble guy. And what if she's not okay?' Kari asked, relenting a bit. 'What if . . . you know?'

Chase put out his hand. 'Please, friend, lend me your cell phone for a minute. Your beloved Allah has dialed Chase's number, so he can do the right thing for a change.'

'Tell Allah to keep his nose out of New York City,' Kari muttered as he handed Chase the phone.

Seven p.m. Back of Billy's bar. The look in Mette's eyes was familiar. He'd seen the same look in Kari's only an hour earlier, a look of exasperation with a child, a look she wanted him to read plain and clear: *What now, Chase? Why the cloak and dagger? Why do you come into my bar with hat and sunglasses on when it's already dark out? You're starting to be a caricature.*

He said, 'You're dressed to kill tonight,' pointing to the bursting cut-off jeans that barely covered her thighs.

'New uniform,' she answered. 'Economy's gone to hell, according to boss Billy, and the tourists are getting stingier and stingier with their dollars. Don't come to work, he says, if you plan to wear anything below here.' She made a cutting motion across where her jeans began and ended.

A crackling noise from under his jacket. He took out the Motorola two-way Kari had forced on him, feeling self-conscious. Here was another one of Kari's toys in his hands. Mette watching him like he had lost his mind – Chase, the guy with the shades and the hidden two-way radio standing in the back of Billy's Corner Bar.

A mouse darted from under a beer keg. He followed its scampering while trying to attend to Kari on the other end of the receiver. 'You're clean,' Kari's voice crackled. 'But get out of there soon.' Mette turned to go. Chase grabbed her arm and she shook it off. He murmured an okay into the two-way and turned the thing off completely, feeling foolish.

Mette said, 'What is it you want from me, Chase? You come, you go as you please, acting like a kid. I didn't come to New York to baby-sit anyone. I'm tired. There's an empty counter over there, except for two lonely guys from God

188

knows where. One wants to marry me because he's had too many shots of Red Label. The other guy keeps saying to me he won't take no for an answer. I ask him an answer to what, and he stares into his beer and laughs like a nine-year-old. This is my life. It's grand, no? And in another hour Billy himself is going to arrive and if he sees you here . . . well, you know the rest of it.'

'All right!' he shouted. He threw her the house keys she'd given him. 'I didn't come here to take you away anywhere, and I didn't come to say I won't take no for an answer. I came to say goodbye.'

They had been coming to this point. She broke, crying softly to herself. She wouldn't look up at him while it went on. He gave her time.

'Why are you doing this to me, Chase?'

'Forget it. You just said you didn't want to baby-sit any-one.'

'Don't be mean. Please!'

'Hey!' He reached to pull her close. From the other end of the bar they could hear both suitors grumbling about Mette's absence.

'Lovely admirers you got,' he joked.

She laughed between some stifled tears. 'Don't kid around. Not now.'

'Baby, do you know what happened to the notebooks I left with you?'

She looked up at him questioningly. 'I thought you came and took them. I thought you'd . . . you'd decided to just dis-appear. I thought the five-thousand-dollar check you wrote me, I thought it was your way of easing the guilt trip. I ripped the check up, threw it away.'

'Good.'

'Good?'

'Don't take it wrong, but where I'm going I'll need all the money I can get.'

'Do you want mine too? I have five thousand of my own. I'm being serious.'

He shook his head. 'I want *you*. It wasn't me who took the notebooks. Someone broke into your room. I thought they'd hurt you or kidnapped you or something. I was beside myself there for a while.'

She was unconvinced. 'Why would they hurt me?'

'Question is why they wouldn't.'

'You're losing me again.'

'Long story. I have to go away for a while.' He stopped and looked into her eyes, kissing them. 'Would you go away for a while too? *Please!*'

She was delicate with her revelation: 'My ticket's already been paid for. I'm moving to San Francisco.' She gave him an uncomfortable look. 'A guy traveling through a few months back gave me his card, asked if I wanted to run his restaurant over there. He was serious. Called me again a couple of days ago. I said yes this time.'

She must have noticed the rigid look in his face. She added, 'Hey, you're the one who put the bug in me to move.'

'Will you have to sleep with him?' he asked in a voice taut enough to cut with a knife.

'Not unless the restaurant starts to fail. You wouldn't want me to be out on the street, would you?' Forced laughter, a joke, trying to defuse some of the awkwardness, not succeeding much.

'You do what's right. I want you to take this number.' He gave her one of Kari's. 'If you like – I mean if you get to California and decide you'd like to stay in touch, give me a buzz. It's not my own number, but I'll get the message from someone, no matter where I am.'

'Sounds like goodbye.'

He kissed her lightly on the lips. It was that feeling of self-consciousness again – *sounds like goodbye*. Had he been a distant observer, he might have cringed at how sappy they were. 'Do me a favor,' he said, 'give your boss the finger your last day here and throw your uniform in his face.' He pointed to the cut-off jeans.

'Bye, Chase.'

'Maybe I could leave from the back?'

'Maybe you could. There are all kinds of evil people trying to hurt you, aren't there?' she commented sarcastically for the last time. But the sarcasm was flat and she had tears in her eyes again.

Another mouse, or maybe the same one, scurried ahead of him. What a dump! *Go to California, little girl, and never turn round to look behind you.*

'You have the phone number,' he reminded her. 'Use it!'

She had started to go, but now she turned and called his name. He waited. She placed the piece of paper with the number on it back in his hand and made him close his fist. 'I'm not going to call, Chase.'

'Why not?'

'Because I'm already gone.'

'I bet you made that decision in the last fifteen seconds.'

'Of course I did. That's how decisions are made.' This time she didn't look back.

He shouted after her anyway. 'I'll come looking for you. I'm not done with us. And that's *my* decision.'

He was out on the street where it was dark. He turned on the radio. 'I'm outside now,' he called to Kari.

'Where the fuck you been?'

'Falling in and out, out and in, what's called love. You know, the way it's done when it's done badly.'

'What did you say?'

'Nothing. I'm heading home, Kari. Watch my back.'

Eleven p.m. Kari had been talking for some time. The big fellow kept getting up to roam about the apartment, needlessly looking for more electric bugs he might have somehow missed. Chase finally had a sense of him as a man who channeled an insatiable need for action into a haphazard search for unobtrusive entities like God. His search through the thicket of Islam rested on a foundation as thin as a toothpick, and ever since losing the faith he had not found anything to replace it. Until Chase had come along. But Kari was not after settling scores anymore. Gaining back faith was not his thing either. He only wanted to be doing *something*, because Dakari's Used Furniture was a joke that had never made him laugh and now was only a burden. Chase wondered about the ordeal Kari must have gone through after returning from Afghanistan. Pestered by the federals for a time – his skin always a red flag to some guy with a badge somewhere who took issue with Kari's size, his self-sufficiency, his casual brushing-off of authority. Kari was Joe Roth without Roth's penchant for self-destruction. Plus Kari had shed enough skins to know it was never too late to shed another layer when he needed.

As if to put a punctuation mark to what Kari had gone on about this past hour Chase said, 'So, there's a manuscript and too many hunters after it.'

'The Russian, I think, has been working for one group of Iranians, Lotfi for another. Sometimes there's nothing more violent than a family feud. These guys don't mind killing each other over a book. And that's precisely what they've been doing, with you in the middle of it.'

'They've all had a whiff of the money.'

'Haven't you?' Kari countered. 'Haven't I? Don't ever blame a man for wanting to catch fish.'

'Is the river that transparent then, Kari?'

'It sure is.'

Chase had been gradually coming around to an idea that he was sure Kari wouldn't like. He wanted to quit this business while he was ahead, while he was still alive actually. This he told the other man now.

Kari looked at him. 'Kid, to stay with the fishing analogy, let me tell you this: you don't take a man to the river, and leave him thirsty.'

'Ah! Is this about you then, Kari? If you like, I'll tell you where the manuscript is. Go get it. It's yours. I want nothing to do with it. I'm tired.'

Kari looked hurt, but he kept his peace. He asked, 'And what do you propose to do with yourself?'

'I could disappear. I've got ten thousand dollars. It'll hold me till I find something.'

'You don't get it, do you? They'll eventually find you. You'll get yourself killed. And how long do you think ten thousand dollars lasts?'

He had a point. And even if no one ever caught up with him, what then? Was it going to be back to night-clerk duty once the money ran out? The thought made him ill. Kismet. Whether he liked it or not, they were going to have to go to Istanbul. Still – and perhaps only out of sheer indolence – he would try one more time to dissuade them both.

But Kari was already thinking ahead of him, 'I know, kid. It's very probable they've spotted me. But that doesn't bother them now. What they're interested in is drawing you east. They're confident enough to believe they can deal with me when and if it becomes necessary. Until then they might even be happy to have me on board. They know that alone you'd probably lose your nerve and go to the law. And you probably would. Wouldn't you?'

'I might, at this point.'

'You see! They need me. *You* need me. And I suppose I need you to need me too. So . . . is it going to be Istanbul or is it not going to be Istanbul?'

'It is, I guess, going to be Istanbul.'

During the night the two of them took turns keeping watch. Chase toyed with the idea of calling Mette. He didn't. What would that accomplish? Mixed signals. They were something people died over. Died stupidly. Chase had the first watch. At four a.m. he went to wake Kari to switch naps with him. Tomorrow – today actually – it was going to be another day, in another country.

16

Thursday

He had always approached Istanbul with wariness. The place dazzled. And because it did, men with something to hide became ever more cautious here. The last time he'd been to the city was on his way back to the States on that Canadian passport from Tehran. He had missed his connecting flight on purpose – for two reasons: one, because he had expected there would be a call ahead from the Canadians to some New York office about a curious walk-in in Tehran, and two, because Istanbul was one of the most in-between places he knew of, and what he'd needed for a few days back then was to be nowhere. Istanbul was certainly that, a place where the Iranians would send him now and then to front for them back when they'd still trusted people like Chase not to skip town. He had told himself each time that one day, as a free agent and with enough money, he would come here as just another tourist, like the thousands of tourists you ran into no matter where you went in the Old City or across the Galata towards Taksim Square.

But that time, there hadn't been any money to speak of, so for a few days he'd rented what must have been the shabbiest hole-in-the wall in all of Istanbul, near the Fatih Mosque where the other guests were mostly hungry-looking Iraqis and Kurds trying to get themselves smuggled into Europe, insular desperados who kept to themselves and preferred to spend their time in what they saw as one of the less-depraved neighborhoods of the city. Chase had tried to buy himself some time, making the usual rounds on foot – the Blue

Mosque, Aya Sofya, Topkapi but, in the end when he'd gotten on that plane and arrived in New York the official men he'd been trying to avoid were still there at the gate, waiting for him.

Chase and Kari were to arrive on different flights. Their target was in the Kumkapi neighborhood, which sat on the south flank of the Old City, overlooking the Sea of Marmara.

'What do I do there?' Chase had asked. 'Do I just go in the coffee house, hand the guy the key and Tabib's code word and expect him to give me the box? What if the owner died since Tabib left the manuscript there? What if he doesn't want to give it to me?'

'It's a chance we have to take,' Kari had told him. 'The guy won't know the worth of what's in the box. He'll take it for granted it's just forged documents. It's usually that, nothing more. Anyway, he won't *not* give it to you. These fellows run their business on total trust. If word gets around that So-and-So can't be trusted as a safekeeper, he's as good as finished. You of all people, Chase, should know something about that.'

The last sentence was Kari's way of giving him a hard time for having been on the trafficking end of the fight in Afghanistan. Chase let that go. What Kari said was basically true. No – completely true.

Kari continued: 'Besides, no one would think your friend Tabib would be so dense as to leave the book in a safebox where half the Istanbul underworld comes to drink their raki and Turkish coffee. This is what gives you and me our advantage.'

'Let's hear about our advantage then.'

It was about historical monuments, which Istanbul was full of. But the two of them could not be too close to one another at any time. This, according to Kari, made their advantage a little shaky; all the more so because 'East of New York City a black dude my size stands out like an Egyptian mummy ambling down Broadway.'

Chase was to concentrate on the old Christian quarter of the city, Fener, where there were still plenty of shuttered-down buildings, mostly churches, any of which they could use for what they needed to do.

'You'll have to find your way in, kid. You have to make it look like you *need* to get in that church. Let them stay behind you. I'll be behind *them*.'

'You, the Egyptian mummy?' Chase said bitterly.

'I *will* be there. I promise you this: neither you nor anyone else will know it's me until it's time to know it's me.'

'I want radios on us then.'

'I can't trust you with that. They see you using a two-way, they'll start looking for me in the vicinity.'

'What then?'

'Improvise. Let the watcher think you've found what you came for.'

'And get my throat slit?'

'Won't happen. Not with Kari behind you.'

'You forget we got more than one set of eager beavers following us.'

'Which is why we might have to do this more than once. In other words, you might have to find more than one closed-down church in the Old City. Once we know we're completely clean, that's when you hit the coffee shop.'

Chase wanted to tell him that somehow the plan didn't exactly put his mind at rest. But he'd drawn a blank, unable to think of anything better. If they lost each other, Chase was to show up at certain places at a certain hour – the Hüsaym Bey Mosque near Valens' Aqueduct precisely one hour afterwards; the main gate of Istanbul University two hours later; outside the Pierre Loti three hours after, or else just go back to his hotel room and wait. Chase didn't even dare ask the obvious: how was he to know if they'd lost each other if Kari was following him and he couldn't tell where the other man was?

No more questions, no more dilly-dallying. He wanted it over with. He wanted the manuscript. He wanted to never be in withdrawal again. 'Don't screw up, kid!' Kari had said. What was there to screw up, except another life gone bad? Gone the way of Istanbul's defunct churches. Gone the way of Constantinople and Byzantium. Gone the way of every little thief in the world who never realized they shouldn't steal unless they knew exactly what to do once they'd done the stealing. Gone the way of a dead Tajik named Tabib, locked up in the vault of some cemetery where the borough of Queens and the freeway came together.

The whole world had turned brackish and green and it looked as if Istanbul would drown under the angry clouds hanging over it. It rained and rained. A downpour that was said to have been going on for ten days straight and would probably continue for another ten. This last according to the wisdom of old men who sat disconsolately by doorways of decrepit buildings waiting for a ray of sunshine so they could resume their love affair with tea and backgammon in the city's exterior gardens. Mist, too thick, and not romantic by half, hung over the Golden Horn and the Bosporus. Across the water, Asia sat in a fog as if it didn't exist. Everything was wet; dirty brown puddles chased away the bravest of pigeons and prayer-bead sellers. The squares remained empty, and somber men gathered inside blue-tiled mosques to whisper – he imagined – about the end of days. But then he recalled that this was the city where men had spoken of the end of the world a thousand years before anyone else.

He couldn't leave his room. The place was another ramshackle affair in an obscene concrete structure from the seventies. But at least he was close to his destination. The Kemal Pasha coffee house was directly opposite the hotel. It stood mostly empty. The tourists seemed to have vanished into thin air or chosen to remove themselves to less soggy destinations. Hard rain beat on the lone window of the room, crowding out the sound of a Turkish soap opera on TV. Someone had told him that a block or two away were remnants of the ancient walls facing the Sea of Marmara. But you could not see that far. Rain had spoken for the city and Chase had nothing to blunt his need. He was in the grip of a bad bout of withdrawal. He let two days pass without much leaving the hotel. He felt incomplete. Addiction was a kind of memory. It didn't really go away but only lengthened with time. The body forgot nothing. So he twisted about, drenched, too awake, on a bed smelling of smoked fish. He was sorry that he had not wanted to chance bringing some medicine with him, and now he hadn't the nerve to go copping for anything. Kari of course would be watching. Chase had expected him to call the room after two days, demanding to know what Chase was doing cooped up. But Kari didn't call. The big man knew better.

Two p.m. Great sheets of rain flapped through the main avenue. The hotel took its name from the street it was on, Ibrahim Pasha something. Less than a minute out in the chill Chase was soaked completely. He walked along Türkeli Boulevard due east, ducking into alleyways and dead-ends to see what gave. Just rain in abundance. Empty restaurants advertising Russian belly dancers who would have done better to stay north of the Black Sea. Resigned men and women walking quickly past, ño longer bothering with umbrellas. The traffic was as light as it would ever get in Istanbul. You saw the faint yellow of cars chasing the fog and felt sorry for the lonely, barely visible uniformed figure who whistled at the top of his lungs at the oncoming traffic.

Shivering whores in the Laleli district still peddled themselves. Trash swam by the feet of naked mannequins lingering in the rain outside of wholesale shops for fur and leather. Chase ducked into a sex hotel called the Sphinx where an Arab vendor had himself a doner kebab stand. The first bite of the sandwich lent the sickness new wind. He got on a tram and headed further east. There were few people on it and he couldn't tell which, if any, would be following him. He sat in the back of the car and watched the mist collect itself as the tram knifed through it. How would anybody find anybody here? What if Kari had already lost him? He considered showing up at their first alternate spot but then quickly dismissed the thought. What they were doing now needed doing. He mustn't forget that. He was tired. His socks were wet. He took off one of them and filled it with a fistful of bulging Turkish coins. He stuffed his improvised weapon in his pocket, got off by one of the stations near the Walls of Theodosius, where ruined brickwork jutted out of greenery as if the earth had regurgitated the loss of itself. Did any people fight harder to preserve themselves than the Byzantines? Everywhere there was absence in this city. Ghosts and ruins.

He caught the tramline going back the way he'd just come and got off again at Laleli. The whore looked like she needed a plateful of sugar to stop her from shaking. Under her eyes were deep black marks. They were not from any beating.

'You speak English?'

'I take dollars,' she said. 'Only twenty. It is a bad day.'

'You don't even know what I want.'

'Yes?'

She was maybe twenty-five, going on twice that. Chase had noticed her standing in front of a wholesaler across from the Sphinx an hour earlier, shuddering before a sopping mannequin with a missing arm, talking to it.

'We go there,' she said, pointing to the hotel.

'No. I need something.'

'Me?'

He lifted her chin and ran a thumb across the defeated hollow of her eyes.

'I want *something*.'

She understood. He must have looked too desperate to be a cop. Her gaze was a washed-out blueness that had no illusions about Istanbul or Kiev or wherever it was she came from. He didn't want to know her name. But she did want to know where he was from. When he told her America, her interest peaked.

'Twenty just for me.'

'Okay.'

They sloshed through muddy passageways to Ordu Boulevard. When he slipped her the wet twenty-dollar bill she took it to her nose and sniffed at it. She pointed to a mosque across the street and then to herself.

'In there?' Chase asked surprised.

'Me no. You.'

She took out a cell phone and talked briefly into it. A minute later a feeble-looking young man ducked his head out of the building and nodded towards them.

'It's him. He help you.'

The mosque was almost deserted. It was a less grandiose affair than many of the other holy places in the city. Chipped blue tiles adorned parts of one of the niches where three older men were quietly praying. It wasn't a place for tourists.

Chase followed the man into one of the private recesses where he turned his back to him and worried with his prayer beads. His neck was bird-thin and the white shirt he wore looked several sizes too large for him.

'You police?' he said.

Chase took out several lira notes and threw them in front of him. The man regarded the money almost without interest, and then asked again if Chase was the police.

'No, I'm not the goddamn police.'

'That is better. You American?'

'I need something. What's available?'

The young man laughed. 'The obvious.'

'The obvious is not my thing.'

'Then talk with me is not your thing. Go away and your money too.'

It had to come to this. Him, standing in the niche of some drab mosque in Istanbul, trying to convince a junkie he himself wasn't one.

'I'll take what you have. Anything.'

'Here is anything.'

A roll of tinfoil fell on the floor of the mosque next to Chase's money. He sat beside his man and regarded him.

'Is this what I think it is?'

'It will help you. You need it.'

'How do you know what I need?' Chase asked.

He took his foil, the Turk his money. Then the Turk asked for more money and when Chase asked him how much more, the man pointed to one of the lira notes and put up three fingers. 'Too many zeros in Turkish money,' he said. 'It is like Turkish character maybe?'

'I don't know what you mean. Take it!' He handed the man three more notes. 'Can I try it here?'

'You can. You need it very bad. I can see.'

'You can see? How can you see?'

'How can I see? I can see like that song. American song. And then he actually burst into it, and sang with a perfect pitch: 'Carmelita, hold me tighter. I think I'm sinking down. And I'm all strung out on heroin. On the outskirts of town.'

Chase felt so odd just then that the only thing he could think of doing was to join the singing Turk. They both sang: 'The county won't give me no more methadone, and they've cut off your welfare check.'

'Ah! I see you are of us.'

'Perhaps. But this is still not my cup of tea.'

'Beggars not are choosers. Yes? When in Rome – no, when in Istanbul . . . You know it?'

With a worthless five-million-lira note rolled into a tube, Chase sniffed a very thin finger of the white powder he despised. The effect was immediate. His body had quit fluttering. His head had found itself. Another minute passed while Chase's new friend continued singing to himself – 'I hear mariachi static on the radio. And the tubes they glow in the dark. And I'm there with her in Encinada. And I'm here in Echo Park. Carmelita . . .'

And then the nausea arrived. The Turk noticed it.

'You are sick?'

'I told you this wasn't my thing. But it will pass.'

'You will be okay.'

'I know. It's the best we can ask for in life. To be okay.'

'Yes, man. Be okay.'

The Turk brought out his hand for a high five and Chase obliged.

'I am doctor of mosque here. In Laleli.' The Turk smiled sadly as he said this.

'Good man. Take care. Take care of your mosque.'

Chase could hear the Turk still murmuring the song with

his back to him. Then he called out: 'Where is Encinada, friend? Where is Echo Park?'

'Other time zones, same problems,' Chase shouted back.

The sharper edge of the sickness had already passed by the time he was walking into the rain again. He hurried back towards the hotel, gripping the foil tightly in his fist to keep it from getting wet. *Carmelita, hold me tighter* . . . Kari would not be pleased with his performance so far. No one would.

17

Friday

Eleven a.m. The rain hadn't let up. He washed down some hard black coffee in a café next door to the hotel. Wet again. Sloshing up and down one hill after another, Chase slowly made his way toward the northwest end of the Old City, consulting a water-resistant map to show whoever was curious that he had a specific destination in mind. A little past noon the mosques of Istanbul came alive. Standing at the peak of a hill near the old Christian quarter, he got a momentary glimpse of an unmoving ship on the other side of the Golden Horn before fog overtook it. There was now a full clank of muezzins. He followed a road that paralleled the length of an Ottoman mansion where milky vapors suspended themselves between the iron gates. The rain slowed to a trickle for a bit, footfalls drifted away ahead. It was perfect weather to kill or be killed. At the bottom of the hill he came across a faded orange square of a building that jutted out of a crooked dead-end street. There was no sign to tell you the place had been a bustling church once, except for a small cemetery in the back where tombstones lay. There was a forbidding black door which Chase tried opening to no avail. This was going to be as good a place as any and it mattered little to him now if it was a church or not. A group of teenagers hurried down the path and out of view. Once they were gone, he climbed over the waist-high gate by the cemetery and made for the back of the building.

An odd assortment of carved capitals and column fragments sat under a canopy next to a second gate, this one surmounted by a cross. There was a long, rectangular, blue stained-glass window just above one of the columns. Since it was already broken, Chase didn't hesitate and made a crawl-through by shattering the rest of it with one of the stone fragments. He had to grapple sideways and pull up, then edge himself over the broken glass into the church. Some light came from other broken windows. Remnants of a mosaic beard, with its Christ or saint missing, could be seen beside a wrecked panel. Everything else had been removed. A thorough pillage job dating back to who knew when.

From a mosque nearby more calls. The prayer echoed in the dampness of the defunct church like a corrupt song. It settled nowhere. Here he was, what next? He would have to go back out the same way, through that broken window. What if someone was waiting below? From inside he couldn't see what was directly beneath the window. Maybe he could should just sit here, for hours. No one else would be able to enter the small church without his hearing them. He wrapped the wet sock with its fistful of Turkish coins in his grip and waited.

The patter of quickening rain. The prayer calls retreating. And as they did, the sound of searching footsteps in the yard. They came right up to the window and halted. Another five minutes passed. Whoever was there was not going away. Chase was tempted to call Kari's name. But Kari would call *him* if it came to that. Then the footsteps seemed to retreat. They went as far back as the cemetery gate, stopped and turned around, determined this time.

Chase saw the hands searching for a good grip over the ledge he'd come up. They looked like powerful hands. All he had on him was the wet sock with the coins. He tried to hold his panic in check. He saw the hands pulling up on themselves but the fellow still had trouble pushing past the ledge's narrow space. Chase held back until he was completely horizontal. As the man turned his head slowly to face the interior, Chase seized his jaw and pressed it into the broken glass.

The man's curse came in Arabic. He tried to drop himself back out onto the cemetery grounds, but Chase had already grabbed his hair and was pulling hard. Once the torso was in, he worked the Arab with the sock and wouldn't let up on him.

No gun. Just an eight-inch knife he'd been carrying outside his belt. His name was Adnan. Chase wouldn't have known this from searching in the man's pockets. The fellow carried nothing. Chase knew the name because he knew the man. Because he had once worked with him.

'Who sent you?'

The fellow had always been strictly muscle. One of those Arab fighters who'd gone for opportunity instead of the fight. Loyalties shifted, so did causes. The man was Lebanese Hezbollah who'd been sent to Tehran for training back when Tehran was still putting its money where its propaganda was. Plenty of guys like him stuck around where they'd been sent, gradually falling in with the minor pushers in intelligence. They'd earn their pay doing dirty work, like beating up college kids who demonstrated against the government. Then at some point they might drift further east, marrying a couple or three or four Afghan refugee women near the border and littering unwanted children they seldom saw. They became somebody. They worked with anybody. They were for hire.

The Arab tried raising himself on his knees. Chase gave him a kick on the neck so he dropped down again.

'Who sent you? I said.'

'Fuck you, Chase. American garbage. Low life.'

'What are you, high life? Since when do you do anything besides give it to war widows in Allah's name?'

The man's face made a cracking noise as Chase savagely stomped him. It was overkill. The man screamed. Chase rolled him over the ledge so that he fell about six feet, crashing into one of the columns before landing on his back on the cemetery lawn. Chase jumped after him, knife in hand.

'I won't ask again – who sent you?'

'Drop the knife!' a familiar voice said. It came from behind.

Not exactly surprised but still feeling thwarted, Chase turned to see Max. The Russian keeping him in his gun's sight. Chase let go of the knife and just stood there for some seconds trying to process what was happening. Max here. Kari not here, or perhaps almost here. He was going to have to buy some time.

He said to the Russian, 'Do you see any manuscript in my hands?'

There was a flicker of doubt in Max's eyes and his grip on the gun seemed to slacken a bit. He took a step forward. 'Where is it?'

'Not on me.' Chase had collected himself after the initial jolt of seeing the Russian at the cemetery. He shrugged and said, 'Yes, it's most definitely not on me.'

The bullet whizzed past Chase's foot and bore its way right through the left eye of the prone and half-conscious Arab. There was a slight tweak of the body, then a barely audible groan. They waited for him to die. He did.

Chase and the Russian stood eyeing each other from a yard off. Chase held his breath. From behind the dead-end side of the church Kari had been making his approach. He wore a fishing cap pulled low over his forehead. What was visible of his skin looked strangely tanned, the color of brass, as if he'd rubbed turmeric on his face. He appeared just acceptably strange. Chase would have known him had he seen him on the street. But he'd never seen the big fellow coming, not until this minute.

'Nice shot!' he said to Max. 'But that Arab wasn't your problem. Now you've gone and killed one of your former employer's men. The Iranians will chase you to the ends of the earth for this.'

'As far as they'll know, I didn't kill the Arab. You did.'

'You had it all figured out, didn't you? Disappearing like that in New York.'

'No point hanging around there if the book's here,' the Russian said. 'But I have to give it to you, Chase, I didn't count on you getting away from the Iranians.'

'The Iranians got nervous and left. So . . . here we are, Mr Max – you, me, and Istanbul. What do you say?' Chase could feel that Kari had gotten much closer to them, but he didn't dare look past the Russian.

Max started to wave his gun and say something. By then Kari had come up just behind him. He wrapped his arms around the Russian's massive neck and with a quick jerking motion snapped it. It looked simulated. The entire thing had taken but a second, yet it felt as if it had taken place off-stage somewhere far away and not two feet from where Chase had been standing.

An awkward interval where both of them just sort of milled about the scene of violence. This was the fourth, no fifth dead man they'd had to endure so far. Finally Chase uttered something about them having to leave. There was only mortality here and exhaustion. Fog horns blowing beneath them on the surrounding waters. The rain starting to pour harder than it had all day long. Maybe it would cleanse their sins.

'No one's around. Don't worry,' Kari said matter-of-factly. He surveyed the corpses at their feet for a while longer, then took the Russian's gun out of his hand.

'You look like a painted giant, Kari. You call what you've done to yourself a disguise?'

'It's better people laugh at strangeness than get frightened by it. There's too much nastiness in this weather for folks to stand around and point, anyway.' After a pause he asked, 'This the Russian?'

'Max.'

'Who's the other guy?' He pointed to the Arab.

'Another child born to bad luck, I guess. He's been living on the fringes in Iran for I don't know how long. At least twelve years. I worked with him in the old days. Border trade and things.'

'Nice set of acquaintances you got.'

'Seems all the guys who got their causes mixed up ended up where I did. The Lebanese sent this fellow to Tehran to learn something, and look at what became of him.'

'Yeah. And then there's you. Your mother's ideal son. May I ask why you were jerking us around for the past three days sitting in your hotel room? On second thoughts, forget I asked. I saw you with that rotten flesh in Laleli. Boy, do you have a problem you need to fix! Men dropping like flies all around us for something neither of us have ever seen and you going on like this. I must be getting stupid. I swear to God I must be getting stupid.'

'Kari, you ever think about women?'

'Let's get out of here. We'll go around back, the way I came.'

'I'm serious,' Chase persisted. 'Do you?'

Kari spoke calmly even as they walked away from the dead men. 'I think about them all the time. I think about them when I wake up in the morning, when I go to bed at night. I thought about them the whole time I was in Afghanistan engaged in holy fucking war. That was the problem. I was thinking about women while looking for God. Looking for God, thinking about women. What you really mean to ask is if I ever think about anything but what needs my immediate attention. The answer is yes, I do think. I'm tired like you are, and one reason I came all the way here is because the next time I think about women I want it to be the *only* thing requiring my immediate attention. I don't want to wait for when things get better. Things never get better. Like there's never a perfect time to have a kid or buy a house. Not unless you reel that perfect time right up to your doorstep, which is what you and me, we're trying to do now. Sometimes you gamble and stop to cut your losses. We haven't lost anything. Except an old friend. And that's in the past. You with me?'

They'd come to the edge of a tall brick wall while Kari had been sermonizing. Kari jumped onto the top and extended his hand to help Chase up. Then he repeated the question.

'You with me? Or are you not with me?'

'Long as you're with me.'

On the other side of the wall lay the same mansion that had led down the hill to the deserted church.

Kari jumped down and looked up at Chase. 'Don't sweat it. This here's the house of the dead. Like the rest of this neighborhood. There's just an old dog and he's too tired.'

'One more question.'

'Stop it!'

'I just want to know if you ever feel – you know – fear.'

'I do. And that's all for now. No more questions. Don't stray. Concentrate on the immediate.'

'Kari, everything I think is the immediate. That's my curse in life, like any old habit.'

'That's a pretty tall curse if you ask me.'

'I'm not asking. I know all about it'

*

Almost midnight. The Kemal Pasha was a shadow of itself. Rain beat cruelly enough outside to mostly drown out the appropriately melancholic music of the zither and alto saxophone combo in the back of the café. No local toughs around, let alone more adventurous West European tourists. A group of older fishermen played backgammon two tables away. It was a large place with sturdy old wooden tables laid out and empty. A bored belly dancer would get up once in a while to clack her shells at the sea-green walls. Not a soul paid her any attention. But the sight of her took Chase back to the night he and Tabib had sat in the basement of that Persian bookstore in LA, watching restless men drink vodka and stick dollar bills in the skirts of another dancer because they thought it was gallant of them to do so, not because they were the least bit interested in what she'd had to show. It was another dead art, this bellying about, Chase thought, like the stories of *The Thousand and One Nights*, groping for phoney sensuality in all the tourists traps of the Mediterranean where grown men dreamed in dollars.

He ordered a plate of eggplant paste and beer without touching any of it, watching the owner come and go. The owner was a short middle-aged guy with a sturdy face and the odd combination of a red silk vest and an apron. He seemed gentle enough with his workers but treated his friends – the backgammon players – with a roughness that bordered on plain disdain. A couple of times he forced himself into their game, tossing a few rounds of the dice, bringing the game to a noisy head and then getting up to attend to the kitchen where the grill was mostly gathering dust.

A half-hour after his food had been brought, the owner finally caught sight of Chase's untouched plate and came over to him. He pointed without smiling and said something in Turkish. Chase, who only had a smattering of that lan-

212

guage, understood what the man was asking but didn't know how to answer him.

'English, please.'

This seemed to annoy the man even more. He clucked his tongue and turned to go. Chase reached for him. 'Please, me and you talk.' He gestured with one hand so the owner comprehended. Then he called out to the belly dancer. 'You speak English?'

'I can,' she called back, shaking a hip and laughing for no reason.

The sight of a twenty-dollar bill quickly brought her over to the table.

Chase said, 'I need a translator. I need to speak with your boss. In private. Tell him this, please.' He reached in his pocket and laid the key that Tabib had given him on that LA/NY flight on the restaurant table. The owner's eyes zeroed in on the key for a moment, then he talked to the girl.

'He says you follow him to back.'

'I think I got that, honey.'

'I want twenty more. You are taking me away from customers.'

Chase looked around at the empty joint. 'Twenty more afterwards.'

The owner made Chase and the girl wait in a tiny white room where there was no furniture; they stood around avoiding each other's eyes while the girl played nervously with her earrings. In a minute he reappeared carrying a long metal box. One look at that box and Chase knew that Tabib had been playing him. The box was certainly long enough but it was far too narrow to hold any sort of a book or manuscript inside. It could be used to store cash, passports, things of that sort; what it couldn't be used for was what Chase had come for.

The girl said, 'He says you are supposed to give him the word.'

'The word? Ah, yes. Beethoven. Tell him it's Beethoven.' It was the password Tabib had given him when he'd told Chase the address of this coffee house.

The owner mumbled something so that the girl remained quiet. Chase figured there was no need to translate that particular name.

He asked for a few minutes alone and waited for them to leave before locking the door from inside. It took a while before he could bring himself to open the thing. The box was almost weightless and he couldn't hear much of anything move when he tilted it. Lifting the latch, he turned it over without looking for what might fall out. He didn't expect a whole lot. What he saw lying on the floor when he did finally bother to look was a passport. A burgundy-colored passport that had the stamp and seal of *The Islamic Republic of Iran* on it.

The photograph on the second page of the document was of him. Chase circa 1990, taken in Tehran when he'd needed forged documents to go back and forth between Mashad and Istanbul. There hadn't been a whole lot of change to him since that photo. Some hair loss. Bad left eye straining to stay focused for the camera. The collar of the brown leather jacket visible, the same jacket he'd worn from the Canadian embassy to the airport five years after the date of the photograph. The name on the passport belonged to one Mehdi Molai. Some pages had been stamped with visas from abroad. The last page, a three-month visa to France. It was a perfect document. Above suspicion to even the most professional eyes. The due date for its renewal was not until another two and a half years from now. Somewhere in this world, probably in a village outside of Tehran, there was a Mehdi Molai who hadn't a clue what a passport looked like and what it was used for. And now Chase had his name and his travel documents and in just over two years he could theoretically go to any embassy or consulate of the Islamic Republic and have himself renewed. Why had Tabib done this?

He held the palm-sized booklet upside down and rifled through it. Nothing fell out. He leafed through the pages again from back to front until he finally caught onto what he expected to find. Stuck to the lower end of that familiar page with the tedious decree from the Iranian government that said, *The holder of this passport is not entitled to travel to Occupied Palestine*, was a piece of paper folded several times over. He took it out carefully and opened it. It was a letter from Tabib, written, as Chase had guessed it would be, in broken but just tolerable English:

> My good friend don't angry with me. I must careful. This cost me time. This writing this. But I make sure you understand. For sure you come to end with us. If I tell you before this I know you don't want to go. Tehran you know I can't go there, back. But you have now no worry. The Iranians finished with you. They will not know. Because this passport is good. It is photos from before. I had. You can travel Iranian man. Before you did it. I know this. You know this. I could leave it, the book in Tehran. Other places too much risk. You I trust. If you alone reading this I am maybe waiting for you. Or else I don't know. Let's maybe think good. Call me like you like, but go to Tehran for me brother. Please. In life there is time when a man . . .

He skipped the philosophizing part of Tabib's letter and glanced at the end where a Tehran address and specific directions were written. Once he'd memorized it, he took the paper, put it in his mouth, chewed and swallowed. *Call me like you like.* Call you where, Tabib – at the Mount Zion cemetery in Queens? He stuck the passport inside his shirt and waited for the girl and her boss to come back.

'Boss says if you are finished.'

'I am. I don't need the box anymore.'

'Twenty dollars please.' After he'd given it to her, she added: 'He says five hundred dollars for the box.'

Chase looked hard at the café owner. The man didn't flinch a bit.

From their kitchen he put a call to his hotel room where Kari was waiting.

'Come down. Bring five hundred dollars.'

'You have it?'

'I have something. I'll explain later.'

Fifteen minutes later Kari showed up at the café with their travel bags. All heads in the café turned towards him. Chase caught Kari's eyes and pointed to the proprietor. Kari went over to the man and respectfully laid five one-hundred-dollar notes on the table between them. The other smiled, offering his hand. Kari took it. They shook.

'Did you check out of the hotel for me?'

'I did,' Kari answered Chase.

'I left something in the drawer there. Piece of tinfoil.'

'I threw that away.'

Chase looked down. 'It's been a hard ride, that's all. I'm sure you understand.'

'I don't. Where's the manuscript?'

'The story only gets longer.'

'How long?'

'All the way to Tehran. I don't know why he didn't just take it out with him. Why leave it there?'

'The Iranians might have found out what he had on him on the way out. He couldn't take the chance. He left it in the

216

safest place he could. Tehran. But he couldn't tell you that's what he did. He knew you wouldn't bite.'

'So what do I do?'

'I can't follow you there, kid. Black man in Istanbul is one thing. He could be a tourist or diplomat. In Tehran . . .'

'What makes you think I'm going?'

'Because I'll bust your jaw if you don't. You didn't bring me this far to stop now.'

He started to answer, then looked around and saw that everybody was captivated by them – by Kari actually. Chase glanced at the café owner who had anticipated him. The owner motioned for them to follow behind him and then left them alone in the private room Chase had been in before.

'Look at this.' He showed Kari the passport. 'How am I going to Tehran on this?'

Kari examined the passport. 'It's legit. It's got your picture and everything.'

'That's the problem. It's got my picture.'

'Come on, kid! You think they got iris-scanning equipment in Tehran? You'll walk right past them and no one will know who you are.'

'No way am I going through that airport.'

'Your only other choice is the bus through the frontier. That's a two-day ride. And a whole hell of a lot of things can happen on the Istanbul–Tehran bus. No, you take the plane, if anything.'

'And you?'

'This is the end of the line for Kari. You know that and I know that. You go to Tehran, get the thing and get out. We go straight to the airport from here. I catch a plane back to the States. You – you take the first plane to Tehran. Meanwhile, we get you an open ticket right here for a return trip, just in case it's safe enough to fly out too. Tehran, Paris, New York.

217

The French visa in this thing is still good. You'll only use it for transit anyway.'

Chase was looking at his shoes again. 'Kari, you're sending me to my death.'

'Just say the word, kid. Say you want to come back with me and we'll go back together. Me to my furniture store, you to what? To Chinatown? And with what money? You think these guys will let up on you? Look! I'd go with you. But in Tehran I'd only be in the way. We couldn't move half a block without someone looking funny at us.'

'I don't know about this.'

'How about we go to the airport first and in the meantime you decide. New York or Tehran. I got my furniture store. But you – you only got men who are far from finished with you.'

'Are they out there?'

'No, I don't think so. Probably not in Istanbul. But they're somewhere. They're always *somewhere*. Anyway, it's your call, not mine.'

Pause.

'Let's go, then.'

'Where to?'

Chase said, 'You to New York. Me . . . to Tehran.'

'That's my boy!'

The restaurant's mood had picked up a bit. A busload of merchants, Bulgarians, had emerged from the rain with enormous loads of soaking-wet goods they'd probably be carrying back home tomorrow. The belly girl was hovering around them, waiting till they'd had a few shots. The backgammon players and the owner nodded at Kari and Chase. *Adios compañeros*.

'I'm hungry, Kari.'

'Eat in Tehran.'

'What did you do with the gun you took off the Russian?'

'I bequeathed it to the Sea of Marmara.'

'What do I do in Tehran?'

'You get the book and get the hell out. I already told you.'

'But they search your stuff at the airport over there when you want to get out. I mean, they really search you then. It's one thing going in, it's another getting out.'

'You'll figure something. You could go the land route north. That passport's good for anything. Catch a bus out of Tabriz through Armenia. Then switch to your American passport from there. Bribe visas at the borders if you have to. You can hit them in four straight nights. Yerevan, Tbilisi, Moscow. I could even come fetch you in Moscow if you want. Better yet, in Istanbul again. Now let's see if we can manage not to get ourselves shot before we get to the airport.'

They managed that much. During the next sixteen hours of waiting there were a lot more flights going to America than to Tehran, but Kari waited till Chase had gotten on his before changing the return on his own flight. Getting on the plane Chase immediately noticed that, save for a few Turkish businessmen, almost all the passengers were Iranians returning home. It helped that he hadn't shaved for several days and his own color was just tan enough to make him blend. It didn't help, however, that the last date of exit from Tehran on the passport was from close to two months ago and he happened to be returning with only a carry-on bag. *You got robbed in Istanbul.* Nor was it much comfort that his Persian-script handwriting was like that of a child's and he was going to have to fill in the inevitable customs form in that language. *Pretend you've injured your hand. Have someone else fill it for you.* Address? Any old address would do. If it ever got so that they wanted to hassle him on that point, he'd know he was already done for.

219

He asked one of the stewards to show him to his seat. The fellow guided him with neither a double take on Chase's accent nor the way he looked. This was going native, if anything was. He was slowly, inescapably being nudged further and further east – to Tehran of all places, the city he had worked so hard to get out of, the city he had vowed he wouldn't ever glance at on a map again.

'Excuse me,' he apologized to the Persian woman sitting to his left. Would she be so kind as to open his bag for him before he put it away. He explained carefully that his right hand had been sprained and he couldn't work it with the other to open the zipper and get his things in and out.

She smiled, did what he asked, and then turned to look out the window. Her hair was uncovered for now. In another hour she'd have to reluctantly put on her veil as the plane crossed over into Iranian airspace. Chase kept his 'sprained' writing hand tucked into his jacket the entire flight, à la Bonaparte.

18

Saturday

Ten-thirty p.m. Tehran. There were police states, and then there were the Iranians. Their country was too chaotic, too schizophrenic; there were too many loci of power working against each other for an efficient system of fear to flourish. This was nothing like Baathist Syria or Iraq where you couldn't open your mouth; it was no communist East Germany or Russia. Even as far back as ten years ago, Chase could remember Iranians openly heaping curses on their own government and on the mullahs, the religious clerics who mostly ran things. From what news he'd had of the place since he'd been away, things could have only gotten more muddled.

He caught something of that insolent air as soon as they stepped off the plane. Mehrabad was usually a sleepy old airport that would quickly get overwhelmed if two flights arrived within a half-hour of each other. Chase's flight from Istanbul was one of three that had landed in quick succession tonight, the other two were from Bombay and from Frankfurt. He walked through a pandemonium of shouts and near scuffles. Kids braying at their mothers. Women who had just come from abroad already looking fed up with the head-gear that made their scalps sweat. Men shoving one another to get through the queues and past the worn-out passport officers who'd barely glance at any of the faces. Who'd want to come to Tehran anyway? Folks wanted out of here, not into it.

Luck was with him so far. He looked up the line and saw

that the customs agents were too busy to pay much attention to who had too much luggage and who didn't have enough. Already a fight had broken out between several of the porters. Chase had to smile. Some things never changed. The porters all wanted the arrivals from Frankfurt, figuring those were the travelers with the real money. Forget Bombay and Istanbul.

He had some Turkish liras and more than enough American bills. The airport's pale yellow lighting made everything appear depleted and wrong. Across the hall, there was an enormous picture of Khomeini, the dead leader of the Islamic revolution. The turbaned grand cleric gazed down on the travelers less like a father or a tyrant than a man who still carried, in the after-life, a grudge and a chip on his shoulders.

A one-eyed old man holding a huge suitcase bumped against him begging his pardon, then bumped him again before moving on and not apologizing a second time. An old sense of infirmity had begun to settle on Chase. He thought he was probably wobbling his way toward the inevitable: the passport guy would suddenly decide to look up and a flicker of momentary genius would make him swear that Chase was a foreigner. An American! This airport and its bedlam took on a sinister aspect now. What if they were watching him? It was almost impossible that they were not – back in *this* country, which had given him so little before, nothing in fact. He could smack himself. *Do you think that the door of freedom is as wide as the door of entrance?* The line of people crawling slowly up ahead. No going back. These Persians had an expression for something like this: A man ought to stick to eating his own slice of bread and leave well enough alone. Only two weeks ago he'd been doing just that, eating his own bread, not butting into anyone else's business and staying put on the night shift at the hotel. Now here. Simply getting out of the airport in one piece meant nothing either. There was good reason someone would want to coax him into believing he wasn't being watched.

The passport agent didn't give him a second glance. At the baggage area they were only too glad not to have to search another passenger with four suitcases and half a dozen yapping children. Chase made his way outside of the terminal building and breathed in the Tehran air. First time in over seven years. Foul and cold, it stuck to the nose. He had no particular destination in mind. This time of night the city was a dead place. Tehran, unlike Istanbul, had no nightlife to speak of. Actually, it did. Too much of it. But it all took place behind closed doors so that the authorities could pretend they were upholding the laws of an Islamic state, and the citizens could pretend the pretence was working.

An address occurred to him. An old acquaintance whose house had always been an open one, a place that stood by itself with no nosey neighbors and where no one asked to see your passport before giving you a room. He'd be able to put his head down for a few hours. He spotted a cab and waited for it to start to take off with its two passengers. At the last moment he ran up and asked the driver to put him in front where the seat was empty. When the other two passengers protested, he offered to pay for their ride as well and then stuck two ten-dollar bills in the driver's face. More money than if the guy were to travel this route back and forth till morning.

The journey seemed to go on forever. They wove along one freeway after another, most of them recent additions that were unrecognizable to Chase. The man and woman in the back chattered softly between themselves. The driver meanwhile seemed quietly focused on the grayness of his city, a grayness that muscled its way into your consciousness, even when it was midnight and dark everywhere. Chase couldn't be bothered anymore to check if they were being followed. He shut his eyes and thought of the notebooks he'd lost. He could always write more. The exercise didn't cost much.

They dropped the two passengers at an address in the Yusefabad district, an area of several high rises towering over a small, unlit shanty town right beneath them. Twenty minutes later the driver let him off at the extreme north end of the city in Darband where Tehran suddenly ended, the temperature fell sharply and the mountains began.

A considerable two-story white stucco house was set back from the main road and partially hidden from view by a row of old cedars. He pressed the buzzer. Soon he heard the familiar crunch of gravel under a pair of feet as they approached the gate. A thin sleepy fellow he didn't recognize appeared, looked him up and down without saying anything, then decided Chase was not worth bothering with and went to close the door in his face.

'I'm here to see *Khanum*,' he told the man quickly, using the term 'lady' on purpose. Only someone in-the-know about the goings-on at the white house would know to say this.

The man rubbed his eyes and seemed to be giving Chase consideration. Down the road car lights were approaching. Chase made his decision. He squeezed past the fellow inside and shut the gate himself. He saw now that most of the lights in the house were out, which was something strange for this time of the night.

Chase felt the other man's hand on his shoulder. 'Where did you say you were from?' he asked Chase.

'I didn't say where I was from.'

'Which embassy then? You look too poor to be European.'

'I'm American.'

'What?' the man cried with both anticipation and alarm.

'I'm just kidding. Look!' He searched his pocket and came up with enough dollar bills so that the man relaxed. Chase asked, 'Will you take me to Khanum now?'

'Khanum's not in tonight.'

'Khanum's always in on Saturday nights,' Chase said firmly.

The man took a step back in surprise on hearing this further piece of inside knowledge. A few minutes later they were standing outside the front entrance to the house while the gatekeeper made his case to someone inside.

The house, like most well-to-do Iranian homes, was decorated with an abundance of cheesy statuary and outsize fake gold furniture. He followed a silent and cloaked old maid up one set of stairs past a long corridor of railroad rooms to the very end. She showed him inside and asked if he wanted some tea.

'Some tea and the Khanum, please.'

The room was a boudoir on a bad day. A red velvet spread covered the enormous giltwood bed that took up half the space. A pair of cracked oval mirrors stood over a slightly crooked dressing table. The cracks in them were in the exact same corners, as if a dissatisfied client had taken pains to mete out his anger in equal portions. The owner of the place was an old-time whore herself who'd moved her operation uptown and into semi-secrecy when the religious militias had closed the downtown red-light district after the revolution. She had done very well. At the time Chase had known her, she'd been one of a handful of operators that serviced the various embassies in town, supplying pictures of young women and boys who would be available at a moment's notice for foreign diplomats who despised the idea of being posted to a dreary place like Tehran rather than, say, Rome or Tokyo. She had to pay a 'special tax', of course, to both the Morality

Militia and the regular gendarmerie, to keep herself in business. She also let the men in uniform have freebies. They, in turn, supplied her with a fairly steady supply of girls who'd been raped and would otherwise have to be kept in 'special homes', which were in fact jails for tainted women.

But Madame Effi had also dealt at the margins of the opium trade. This was how Chase had first come into contact with her. The intelligence service, which sometimes worked with, and sometimes fought against, the border and narcotics police for control of the traffic, would use people like Effi's contacts in the various embassies to make connections and set up blackmail jobs to get the drug to Europe by any means possible, including the diplomatic pouch. Ironically, it was Effi's being 'involved' that made her place choice – she made a living out of staying inconspicuous.

Effi herself presently floated into the room without knocking. She was a woman of gigantic proportions and styled herself after a certain Persian singer who had died of a drugs overdose in exile several years earlier. Her make-up was laid on badly, and as thickly as Chase could ever recall. She wore a feathered red gown that matched the velvet spread. She gave him a false hug and pushed him onto the bed.

'Chase, you devil, I thought you were dead.'

'Effi my love, I've just come halfway around the world and you're the first person I wanted to see.' He was sickened by himself and the false tone of their conversation.

'Wait right here,' she told him.

She went out to call some orders and quickly returned.

'Chase, rumor had it some people were not too happy when you disappeared the way you did.'

'There's always somebody to take offense. What can I say, I was homesick. But everything's okay now. I've paid the right people – but let that just stay between us.'

'And may I ask why you're back?'

'I am homesick again, for Tehran this time.'

'Why don't I believe a word you say?'

'Ah Effi! I'm an honest man. It's just you're so used to your crooked cops and all those diplomatic receptions you go to, bantering with thieving consuls and their underlings.'

'My love, things have changed. Just look at Effi's place. Run-down. Everything is run-down. So it's Saturday night, but even for the first night of the week this place is dead. No one here at all. Not a single customer.'

'I noticed. What happened?'

'Too much competition. The only receptions I'm invited to nowadays are with Pakistanis and Syrians. Those miseries don't exactly have money, you know. But what they have plenty of is attitude.'

Effi took her time relating all the woes that had befallen her in the past few years. She wasn't fond of her country opening up to the outside world, not even a little bit. All that had done was to bring her more headaches. 'Nowadays, every cunt wants to be her own boss, Chase my dear.' The West Europeans had all but forgotten her, she claimed. And when a fresh batch of diplomats arrived they were quickly referred to other houses. Her only real customers now were domestic business travelers from smaller towns and second-rate clerics and seminarians who required her well-deserved reputation for being discreet.

She kept on talking. Chase thought of what a bizarre conversation this would appear to anyone who didn't know a country like this better. The world seemed to always be running on several orbits at once, and unless you delved deeply into the underbelly of some location, you would never, ever know what that place was all about. So few men really knew. Kari knew. Roth had known. Chase liked to think that he

227

himself did too. A place like Iran was one of smoke and mirrors where nothing was ever as it seemed. Robed priests got on their Friday pulpits and talked endlessly about chastity and Allah, while men and women made a point of having meaningless sex only because they'd been warned not to. Alcohol was banned as anti-Islamic and yet bootleg vodka made the rounds in almost every home. Meanwhile, to be a prostitute was a political act; a lot of women did it just out of spite for the mosque. It really was the world of *The Thousand and One Nights* here, and if he'd lingered for so long before, it was mostly to find out where this story would end, if it ever would.

The tension of the past few days slowly began to lift. He was thankful for that. Thankful to fat Effi who plied him with food and Armenian wine.

He caught her winking grotesquely under the red lamp that hung above them: 'Do you come with dollars, Chase, or with local money?'

'Only with dollars, my darling.'

'That's very good. Would you like me to make a quick call and have someone sent up to your room? The taxi service is excellent nowadays, you know.'

'I need a good sleep. Maybe next time.' Saying that, he let a hundred–dollar bill settle on the tray between them anyway. Effi didn't turn down his small gesture.

They heard the rumble of a slow car on the gravel path just then. She looked at Chase and beamed through all her rouge and powder.

'Maybe the night is not a total loss,' she observed. 'Stand to the side of the stairway and see what I was talking about. Customers from hell nowadays.'

He followed her out of the room. The second floor was built so that it looked downstairs through a full circle. The banisters were rickety now, but Chase had heard of a mythic time in the 1970s – before the Americans were kicked out and oil was still flowing at a premium – when larger homes in Tehran, like this one, would hold masked balls, where members of the royal family would be occasional guests, and champagne for those parties would be imported on overnight flights from Paris. The house, of course, had fallen on hard times after the revolution, but not hard enough that Effi could not resurrect it for her own purposes.

A pair of staircases going in opposite directions from below divided the second floor in two halves. Effi turned off the lights at Chase's end before descending the stairway. Downstairs she talked briefly into a house phone and after a while went to open the door herself. Chase – feeling becalmed, even resigned to betrayal – stood in the shadows upstairs and watched as Effi swung the door open to a large man with a distinctly pug nose, a man who wore a brown camel-hair robe and a black turban and who invited himself in without offering Effi much of a greeting or demanding one in return. Effi still did not shut the door, as if she were expecting someone to follow. Someone did. In a minute another man wearing pretty much the exact same set of clothes as the first man walked inside. Both were obviously clerics. The second man – who was smaller, younger and deferential to the first one – whispered something in Effi's ear. She nodded, one of her red feathers slightly rubbing on the man's black turban as she did so. Chase thought that the three of them standing there like that, each dressed as they were, resembled a cast of some insane opera. He watched them ascend the opposite stairway without exchanging another word until Effi opened the door to one of the rooms on that wing and let the two visitors through.

Chase waited in his own room for Effi to return. He tried

to imagine the two holy men waiting as he was on the other side of the house. What could you say about a world that happened only in interiors? He'd seen variations of what he'd just witnessed many times before in this country, and yet each time it still jolted him. It made him think there were worlds within worlds and perhaps it was better never to have walked through some of them – just as in *The Thousand and One Nights* the hero of some story or other was always warned not to open a certain door, but he always did open that door and always did end up getting himself destroyed.

Effi was in the room looking at him. Chase, feeling drained, asked, 'Why does one of these mullahs need another to bear witness when he comes into a whorehouse?'

The room was cold, but she still fanned herself. All of a sudden her expression had changed into one of exhaustion with the world.

'Chase, you still know so little. We Shiite Muslims figured it all out a long time ago. If you can't beat the oldest profession in the world, tax it. The big mullah you saw has a weakness for moon-faced girls. He comes here with the little mullah who will marry them, officially, for the duration of the night. The little mullah gets his commission for his work. Completely legal. Effi too gets her cut for the space and discretion she provides. And the big mullah gets to be temporarily married to the girl until morning, after which he goes wherever he goes, having done nothing against the will of God. All perfectly sanctified.'

'And the girl? Is she here now?'

'Every year it gets harder and harder to find moon-faced girls in Tehran. They're all into dieting and having nose jobs and freelancing on their own. Effi's tired of it all.' She heaved a sigh. 'You're a good boy, Chase. I always liked you. Are you sure you don't want a moon-faced girl tonight?'

He didn't know what to say. He thought that even if Effi got him the moonest-faced girl in all of Tehran, he still wouldn't be able to do much about it right now. 'I'd only fall asleep on the moon,' he said. 'Another time.'

She smiled. 'It's good to have you around again. In the morning we talk more.'

He sprawled on the bed closing his eyes. Once alone, within minutes that light feeling he'd gotten from the Armenian wine turned sour on him and he thought of the remainder of his purchase from the Laleli mosque, that Kari had so cruelly thrown away. He could use it now. Or he could call Effi back and she'd have something for him within minutes. *No. Lie quite still. Don't think.* Think he did. He'd fetch the book and get out – whatever it took. A couple of hundred miles north of here you had plenty more sorry countries to disappear into – Turkmenistan, Azerbaijan, Armenia – or a boat ride across the Caspian Sea would take you to mother Russia. Just get yourself across one of those borders and call papa Kari to come get you. It will be that simple.

He slept for some hours. When he woke up it was nearing seven in the morning. It had started snowing outside. It could snow up here in the hills and still be sunny only a mile down the road. A covered plate of rice and chicken had been set aside for him on a tray. He ate some of the food and left another hundred-dollar bill for Effi with a thank-you note telling her he'd be back in a couple of days for one of her moon-faced girls. He left the door closed and, instead, made a quiet jump for it from the bedroom window to the garden. He recalled that a cherry orchard led all the way down from the rear end of the grounds to a seldom-used gate on the south side. When he got there, he was greeted by a lone sheep tethered to a tree, probably waiting to be sacrificed for some religious festival. Effi had a longstanding custom of feeding the neighborhood poor on those occasions. For no reason – other than he felt like it – he untied the sheep and let it out the gate before him. *Door of freedom!* He closed the gate. The sheep walked one way, Chase the other, to catch a cab downtown to the blackmarket moneychangers.

19

Sunday

Ten-fifteen a.m. He sat in Café Naderi, watching the back of the head of the man who only fifteen minutes earlier had changed three one-hundred-dollar bills for him down the street from here into 240,000 tuman. This part of town, about a half-mile up from the grand bazaar, was a lot more crowded than the northern boundaries where Effi's house was and where he needed to return for the book. The café was a semi-historic place fallen, like everything else, on hard times – once famed for long-past literary evenings where writers would gather to order beer and Piroshkis from the Armenian proprietor, while discussing Kafka aloud and the works of Marx and Engels in hushed whispers.

Now, the place and its dilapidated garden were so empty that every time a customer walked in, the two ageing Armenian waiters would almost come to blows with one another trying to get the guy to come to their own sections. Like Tehran itself, smoke hung in the café air and wouldn't go away. This was a city that lumbered on, breeding asthmatic children who peddled Winston and Marlboro cigarettes at traffic lights with hungry stares. It may have been a place of intrigue, but certainly not romance.

He gave the money-changer another few minutes. Finally the man turned around to acknowledge Chase's presence. Chase must have been his best customer all morning and the young fellow had taken a risky break from the day's competition to come inside. He nodded with satisfaction to himself when he saw Chase walking towards his table, cup of coffee in hand. Strangers who came to change three hundred dollars in the Naderi district's sidewalks could often be after something more.

'What can I do for you, brother?' the money-changer whispered to Chase.

'A gun?'

'Not my game. Sorry!'

'I don't really need a gun.'

'What is it you need then?' The man looked more intently at Chase and commented, 'Your accent is a strange one. You from the south?'

'I come from Mashad.'

The money-changer laughed. 'There is no chance you come from Mashad. I come from Mashad.' He paused for a second and added, 'Stranger!'

'I also eat pork and don't pray five times a day. I like to sleep with men's wives. Safer that way. Does that bother you?'

'I'm a money-changer. Nothing human bothers me.'

'You want to make some more money?'

'I'm a money-changer. I always want to make more money.'

Chase shoved a ten-dollar bill his way. When the fellow didn't respond, Chase tripled the offer.

'What can I do for you, stranger?'

'What you can do is very simple. There's a man outside the café. Let's just say I don't like how he looks. Why don't you go outside and check to see if he's still out there or not. He's got a shaved head and wears a green coat. He's about your height.'

'I don't need to check anything. This is my street, and I can tell you that your man is out there waiting for you.'

'Then I want my man not to be waiting for me anymore. No questions asked.'

234

'No questions.'

The money-changer pocketed the bills, left his own bill for Chase to pay and got up to leave. 'Give me a few minutes,' he said.

In those few minutes Chase had some time to rethink the path he'd taken from Effi's place to here. Getting off the cab at College Square and having to pay for the ride in dollars again. Then walking the rest of the way to see if he'd spot any tails. He had noticed that fellow in green right away. The man was trying too hard to stay close to Chase at the busy downtown underpasses and traffic circles. He could have belonged to anyone, even to Effi. But none of that mattered to Chase at this point. What was clear was that he'd already been spotted; or maybe they'd been on him the entire time. It was over, or nearly so. Yet he didn't feel hopeless. Not at all. One could disappear quickly in Tehran. It was that kind of a place. And either he'd die trying, or he'd get the job done one way or another. Afterwards: get out! Get out of fucking Tehran. Out of the Middle East. Rip off their historic art wherever it lay and get lost. He'd carry the Pyramids away and hawk them at a Sunday flea market in Chelsea if he could. National treasures of proud civilizations be damned. What civilizations? What pride? He knew better. There was only the likes of Effi left in these places, Effi and the horny mullahs who came for their weekly share of moon-faced girls.

When he came out of the café he saw that his new friend had already managed to move half the money-changers to this end of the block. They were all gathered in a tight circle somewhere between the sidewalk and an open sewer arguing excitedly among themselves. Chase caught a brief sight of the tail in the midst of those bodies. Green coat had seen him too. But as soon as he tried to cut through the crowd, the pool of money-changers fiercely hemmed him in and their voices grew more loud. You couldn't have asked for a better lot of fellows to do a job like that.

Chase didn't waste any more time. Across the street he saw a cab that was waiting for a single rider. He offered the cabbie 2000 tuman to take him uptown without picking up any more passengers. As the car was moving off, he turned to watch the crowd of men by Café Naderi shifting to and fro. The cab carried the smell of the previous female passenger's perfume. Chase allowed himself to relax a bit and sank into that cheap scent.

'Where uptown exactly?' the driver asked him.

'Drop me off at that sports club, Persepolis, I think it's called.'

'Where have you been, friend? They changed the name of that sports club to Martyr something or other a long time ago. Too many names of martyrs in this country, if you ask me.' The man seemed to be making a genuine complaint when he said this. Then he started to drive.

Chase remarked, 'Our whole country is named after martyrs, isn't it?'

'True. So very true. It's like they'd run out of names. This city is named after a bunch of dead eighteen-years-old boys who went and got themselves blown up so they could get to heaven on time. Say, you're not from Tehran, friend, are you?'

'No, I'm from Mashad.'

'You don't sound like you're from Mashad.'

'I know. Everybody tells me that. Guess I've been away from home too long.'

Noon. The cemetery was a quarter-mile south of the sports club where he'd been dropped off. There was a stone plaque above a boarded-up gate that noted the years 1914 to 1918. Probably a memorial to British dead of the Great War on the Syria and Mesopotamia fronts. He'd read about all that – Lawrence of Arabia, the siege of Kut, General Allenby's capture of Damascus, the end of the Ottoman Turks and . . . the creation of this piss-hole, the Middle East. Behind the cemetery was the little-used summer residence of the old British embassy. Chase had always known about this summer residence but not the cemetery. The road that it was on connected one of the main north–south arteries of the city to poorer neighborhoods further to the east. Almost seventy years earlier when the British traveler Robert Byron had been staying here, he'd written about the residency and the village of Golhak across from it. Back then it had been a full day's coach ride from Tehran proper. Today Golhak was right smack in the center of town, and the small cemetery – pushing against the din of traffic on Dowlat Avenue – was like a mistake someone had forgotten to take off the map.

He walked among the rows of graves as the muezzin began his noonday din at the Golhak mosque less than a hundred yards down the road. Across from the mosque was the local police station. The cemetery itself was separated from the British residency by a high wall, forgotten and unattended. Probably not visited since the English gave India up and went home. Chase searched the names – five rows back and six to the left, according to Tabib's note (*look for this name: Simpson. Robert Simpson*), passing cracked headstones that bore identities of men who had been buried on a plot of land that now some local real-estate developer would pay a fortune for. Names of the dead: Paul Heaton. Peter Laverack. Stanley Mariot. Robert Simpson. 1894–1915.

The headstone, as Tabib had indicated, was already loose. It was unbelievably heavy, though. From the side street

Chase could see men on their way to the mosque. The muezzin had begun repeating his final batches of *Allah-akbar*. Traffic was stalled on Dowlat Avenue and the sound of car horns under the downcast skies bled through the call to prayer.

He set Robert Simpson next to Stanley Mariot and took the book out from inside the unlocked metal box that had been buried underneath the headstone. He had imagined the thing to be much thicker than it was. The binding felt wooden. It had a strange blue-luster painted color to it, giving it the appearance of old ceramic. He saw that the folios inside were separated and almost evenly divided between the miniatures and the text of the Muslim Sufi saint, Hallaj's apology for the devil. The sayings were numbered, some longer than others. He examined the paintings first. Not being an expert, he couldn't be sure about their age and authenticity, and whether they'd been drawn by a master craftsman or not. But it was true what Tabib had said of them. They were full of devils. Whole armies of them in every state of revelry you could imagine. There were demons surrounded by all the heavenly young virgins – *houris* they called them – that the Prophet had promised the faithful. But these houris were in hell, not in heaven, and they were not complaining a bit about that either. On the contrary . . .

He felt woozy with the richness of the images. The writing itself was in Arabic, a language that wasn't all that familiar to him. But next to each numbered paragraph was a handy English translation ripped out of a book that someone – probably back when the manuscript had been in Kabul – had slipped in there for reference. He glanced at the esoteric title of the piece that read: *The Cycle of Endless-Time and Lasting Equivocation*. Below that was a piece of verse that sounded equally arcane:

For he understands —
in the understanding of the understanding —
what is justly legitimate
in regards to intentions.

He could just about imagine Tabib getting his hands on this oddity, trying for a minute or two to grasp what it said, giving up and deciding on the money instead.

The money, at least a part of it, was in the paragraphs, 37 of them, which could easily be read in the translation pages in under ten minutes. They looked like an inspired and, at the same time, incredibly far-fetched explanation of good-in-evil that Lund had told him about.

Chase stood there among the graves leafing through the paragraphs. It all seemed like a fantastic jumble of reasoning that, nevertheless, could pretty much be broken down to one simple idea.

Yes, it was true what both the Koran and the Bible said about The Evil One: yes, Satan had refused God's command to bow down before Adam. But, Hallaj argued, by this very refusal Satan had only confirmed his absolute love of God who was the only being before whom he would ever prostrate himself. Satan, in other words, was not a rebel; on the contrary, he was the supreme worshipper of God. Meaning: Satan had gotten a very bad rap throughout history and his getting condemned to hell was not fair at all. If anything, it was downright evil.

Chase read:

— Allah said to him: 'Prostrate yourself!'
— Eblis said, 'Not before another than You.'
— The Creator said to him: 'Even if my curse falls on you?'
— Eblis said, 'All choices and my choice itself are yours, because You have already chosen for me, oh Lord. If I am prevented

239

from prostrating before Adam, You are the cause of the pre-vention.'

Sound of a chapel bell from the British residency. Sunday. Another faith and its chimes. Meanwhile, the too-familiar hum of men with naked feet praying to Allah at the Golhak mosque down the street from the cemetery.

He held onto the manuscript but put Simpson's headstone back in its place and smoothed the earth around it. He had an uneasy feeling now about that orange cab which had been idling in front of the gate for the past few minutes. Orange cabs didn't linger like that. The men inside it wouldn't be able to see him where he stood, but he could easily see the car. The manuscript just about fitted under his jacket. He came out from the other side of the fence onto the dead-end side-street and walked to Dowlat Avenue, hurrying toward the police station where a young recruit stood guard with a rifle strapped to his shoulder. The street was full of cars. But the cab shifted quickly in reverse, zigzagging past the oncoming traffic towards the police station and Chase. There was no time to waste. He ran across the street and made for the mosque, where all the doors were open.

The prayer was still in full swing. He could see the turban of the cleric way up front leading the congregation. Chase took off his shoes and carried them over the prayer space to the other side of the yellow-brick domed building, looking for a rear way out of the place. In one of the niches a great mound of Korans had been stacked every which way. They looked like they could topple at any moment. Muslim prayer was a pretty democratic exercise. People came and went, started late as others were already finishing. This made his loitering about while others prayed a non-issue. He waited for the moment when the cleric led everyone into one of the down positions of the prayer. At that precise moment he took the manuscript and stuffed it as far back as he could under the canopy of the holy Korans. Then he looked for a way out.

The back of the mosque led to a small paved enclosure with a fountain in the middle. A green wooden door was on the other side, probably left open for the people who lived below Dowlat Avenue. In a corner of the yard he saw another sheep, tethered, ready for sacrifice – *you again, in Isaac's place*. At first he took an automatic step toward the animal, but then hurried away from it and the mosque.

The road came to a quiet residential street that ended at a tiny square where a pastry shop, a butcher, and an odds-and-ends store were bunched together. They had him. He saw the orange cab coming up towards him from the opposite direction as he passed by the butcher. He slowed his pace and rounded the corner, making no attempt to run for it. It would have been pointless. There was nowhere to go. The orange cab screeched to a halt at his feet. Two burly fellows got out. One of them quickly pushed Chase into the back seat and the other got behind the wheel.

'Where is it?' the driver asked matter-of-factly.

Chase shrugged. He turned to the man sitting beside him. 'Where is what?' he asked.

'Where is it?' the man echoed the driver's question while patting Chase down.

'I don't have it, do I?'

'Don't make a move, you pimping American bastard.'

Okay. Chase thought it best to oblige them.

It was a fairly short ride. The house they took him to was in the vicinity of a bridge that had to vie for the title of one of the most peculiar names ever – Pol e Seyyed Khandan, or 'The Laughing Descendant of the Prophet Bridge'. The driver got out and pushed the gate open. It was a small one-story house in another peaceful neighborhood. They left the car in the driveway. The garage was on the inside. Its door was open and crammed with what looked to Chase like car parts and small motor engines. A fellow, who at first glance looked to be from Africa, appeared at the top of the steps. He had a goatee and wore the kind of white jellaba one would almost never see in Tehran.

'Chase!' the man calmly called to him in English. 'Do you know you've caused a world of trouble. What is the matter with you? Since when did you become such an expert at eliminating people?'

Chase had to keep his astonishment in check. He was standing face to face with Saladin, a long-time American convert to Islam who was wanted on a murder charge back in the States.

'I didn't know you were involved in all this, Saladin,' Chase answered briefly, not bothering to correct the detail that, in reality, it wasn't he who had done any of the actual eliminating.

'I don't see the book on you.'

'Didn't have time. Your boys were being too obvious outside that old British cemetery in Golhak.'

'That's where it is?'

Chase looked around at the men who'd brought him here. 'These fellows speak English?'

'They're deaf to the language.'

'It's there. Take it, it's yours. I'm tired of running.'

'Running and getting away. You're good at that, aren't you?'

'Not good enough apparently.' Chase indicated the men waiting by the car. 'Are they yours?'

The other American didn't answer but motioned for

Chase to follow him inside, leading him through a sliding glass door which he then closed.

'Don't try anything. I have a gun. And for all my fondness for you, being, well, a compatriot and all, I will put a bullet through you with or without the book.'

'Then you'll have to go digging in the entire British cemetery with your two boys.'

'My boys!' Saladin laughed bitterly. 'They're on loan from one of their ministries. Don't ask which, I don't know myself. They're what you might call a forced loan. I don't know what is what in this country anymore. And I don't bother asking a lot of questions either. Ever since Lotfi disappeared, they're all scrambling. Meantime they're letting me, the foreigner, run this thing so if there's a bigger mess I'll be the one to get burned. My boys – give me a break, Chase!'

'So why are you doing this?' Chase asked, genuinely curious.

'Oh man, look at my life.' He pointed to the living room where a hodgepodge of mismatched furniture garishly sat. 'I asked the Iranians for a proper house, not an apartment, and look what they gave me. The furniture is from confiscated property. Am I a beggar, I ask you? A charity case?'

'Maybe that's what they think of you by now. You should have known, man, most defectors come to regret their move. That's just how it is.'

Saladin looked at him. 'Sit. You want some tea?'

'I want to hear what you plan to do with me.'

'You know, it's good to speak English. I'm tired of these people. Twenty-two years ago when I first came here they said they would name a street after me. They said they wanted to give me a wife. A house by the sea. What I got instead was a brain-deadening job at one of their newspapers, managing the translation section of their propaganda department. When I told them I deserved something better, they got defensive. I've been cooped up last few years with little to do. They feed me, they clothe me, they give me enough money, they pretend to defer to me, but I'm still bored as hell. They won't let me leave here.'

'You *can't* leave here,' Chase reminded him.

The other man looked away saying nothing.

'Do you regret what you did, Saladin?'

'I might have regretted not doing it.'

It had been inevitable during the earlier years that at some point Chase would run into Saladin in Tehran. Back then they had been among the odd handful of Yanks in a country that was barred to just about all Americans. Chase couldn't even recall what Saladin's name had been before he'd changed it. Over two decades ago, fresh with a convert's zeal, Saladin had carried out the political assassination of an Iranian exile in Orange County, California, on behalf of the then one-year-old Islamic Republic; then he'd gotten himself to Tehran before the police could catch up with him. You had to figure that not long afterwards Saladin's existential spiral had gone into high gear. For what a convert often needed was attention, attention for the leap he'd made – leap of faith, literally. But in Tehran Saladin had quickly become just another foot soldier who did his part for the cause and was forgotten. They appreciated him here, but he was no more special than, say, your average Arab operator who did a job in Amman or Beirut and then came to Tehran to retire and be left alone. A man like Saladin, however, didn't want to be left alone. If he did, he would never have converted. He wanted to wear his change of faith like a seal and he wanted his assassination, his rite of passage, to be remembered as an act worthy of not just one but ten streets named after him.

Chase said, 'Really, what do you plan to do afterwards, kill me?'

'Kill you?' Saladin shot back in his quick and highly-strung voice. 'Let me tell you something, Chase. Everybody here is after something. All I want is out of this country, and for that I need money, lots of money. Why do I want out? Look at the color of my skin. I got tired of being pointed out on the street. Little kids want to come pull my nose. Pull blackie's nose. 'Cause they've never seen one. A nigger's a nigger wherever he goes. Too black for here. Too light for Africa. And the US-of-A was never exactly my country to begin with. I just want out. Buy my own little island somewhere where no one can bother me. God! half the time I walk around this town wearing a woman's *chador* so people can't see my face. I've gotten pretty good at wearing them chadors too.'

'What happened to the faith then, brother Saladin?'

'Don't get fucking cynical. Faith died. A long time ago.'

'Is that why it was okay for your men to steal all the money I had on me just now?'

'Hey, I told you they *ain't* my men. Anyhow, brother Chase, you're the one who made the whole thing more difficult for everyone. You should have just handed over that fellow Tabib. Like these Persians say: you eat too much melon, you better not complain when you get the runs and shit runs down your leg.'

He thought how Saladin could just as easily be talking about himself and the choices he'd made so far in his life, starting with that assassination back in Orange County twenty-two years ago. Chase looked outside, but couldn't see either of the two guys who had brought him here. The outline of Saladin's gun was visible under his jellaba. Maybe he could try rushing his fellow American. He'd either be overpowered or shot or he'd manage to grab the gun and try doing something. The odds were awful either way. He had nothing

– his money and both his passports were gone. Saladin's men had taken everything.

He said to Saladin, 'You know, I have a friend back home. In New York. You remind me a lot of him; you talk a lot like him.'

'How is that?' Saladin asked almost contentedly. You'd have thought the fellow was truly glad to have a bit of America with him right now. Two Americans sitting across from each other in some home on the other side of the world, surrounded by gaudy furniture that was someone's idea of generosity to a man who had fought for the faith and supposedly still believed. Saladin believed in nothing. For him even the long-ago assassination was just part of a reverie that, in the end, lacked profit. And why convert without some concrete profit – profit either for Kari who had once tried so hard to become Islam's warrior, or this man with the sad gray eyes and the gun under his jellaba?

'This friend of mine in New York,' Chase went on, 'he too bought into what you bought into, Sally. But then, like you, he lost it. I mean he just plain lost it. Faith, I mean. You guys should have a talk together. Brothers in disappointment.'

Saladin was looking at his watch. His attention had suddenly jumped and he seemed to be elsewhere. Watching him Chase knew he had come to the end of something here. He had a notion of Saladin as the loneliest man he'd ever known – lonelier than Roth, lonelier than Kari. A man who didn't even have anger or ache from his loss of faith to keep him going.

Chase waited. So far, the adrenaline rush of the day's events had made him forget how bad a state his body was in. Now the wind of the wing of withdrawal was back. He felt defeated.

Saladin had got up and walked to the glass door and turned

to Chase, 'I read all six of your notebooks, you know. Couldn't put them down. Took me the better part of a day.'

Chase almost jumped. 'What did you say?'

'Yeah, Chase. You sit there on your high and mighty pedestal judging me. You think I don't see it? To you I'm just a traitor to our country. What are *you* then? You think I made a bad move one time and killed somebody and now I'm sorry for it, and you think what would Saladin give to be able to go back home and order himself some ribs and home fries. You're so full of shit. You know nothing. Because I tell you, there's this thin blue line,' Saladin brought his right thumb and forefinger together to make his point, 'between a man who becomes the servant of the state and the other who says *fuck you* to the state. And the end result, unfortunately, just happens to be the same: nobody wins, neither the one man nor the other. Look at me, I'm stuck here in nowhere land, and your friend Joe Roth, like you say in your notebooks, he's dead too.'

This time Chase did jump. 'Sit down!' Saladin shouted, and Chase sat back down. 'That's right, baby. Just the other day the Iranians handed over your notebooks to yours truly to translate, to see if there was anything worth looking into, maybe the location of the manuscript, for example. But there was nothing. Nothing and everything. There was the story of your pathetic life. But I have to say, you got a knack for it, Chase. I really did read the whole thing from start to finish in one shot.'

'What about Joe Roth?' Chase said, barely keeping his voice from rising.

'Notebook number four I think it was, you write about how the guy was like a father to you – the father you never had. Let me tell you, your father got set up and I know who did it. They did it right here in Tehran.'

'What's the point of telling me this?'

'Because,' Saladin let one arm drop violently, 'I may not survive this and I want *somebody* to know my mistake was no worse than anyone else's. Your friend Roth took the high road – he did it here in Tehran in 1978 – and look at what happened to him.'

'Dammit Saladin! If you know something about what happened to Joe here, spit it out.'

'Shut up! You're in no position to make demands.' Saladin looked at his watch again. 'Anytime now.'

'Anytime what?'

There was a buzz and they saw the two men outside reappear from the back of the garage and go over to the gate. After negotiating a while they opened up and a patrol car drove through. But then there seemed to be a stand-off between Saladin's guys and the newcomers. Four men had gotten out of the patrol car. Three of them were packing weapons. There was no gun-pointing, but it was obvious they were all government agents and there was some sort of tense stand-off between the two parties. The fourth man out of the car was the albino, the fellow who had kicked Chase back in New York and promised they'd be seeing each other again.

'Make your mind up real quick, Chase. You got one shot and it's right now. You realize as soon as you tell them where the book is they'll kill you.'

'What's my other option?'

'I'm the only hope you got left.'

'That's a terrifying thought.'

'Shut your mouth. My offer's this: ride with these people for now, and once I save your skin, which I will, in return you'll let me know where the book is.'

'It's in the cemetery.'

'I need a more precise address.'

248

'What do I get out of doing this?'

'You live. And maybe you'll also get a cut of something.'

They heard steps approaching. All six men, led by the albino, were about to enter the house.

Chase stood up nervously. 'Christ! You got a deal, man.'

'Good.' Saladin reached and yanked at the bottom of Chase's pants so that he fell hard on his back. It knocked the wind out of him and he groaned loudly. 'Sorry, Chase, but we gotta make it look right.' Saying this, Saladin went to give him a kick in the stomach. Chase rolled away and barely missed Saladin's foot. As he did he got a glimpse of the glass door being slid open. The albino was the first one in. He rushed at them, shoved Saladin aside and stood looking over Chase.

'I told you I'd see you again.'

'You're clairvoyant.'

'Shut up.'

'Everybody tells me to shut up.'

The albino waved two of his men over. 'Take him.' He turned to Saladin. 'We will deal with you later.'

They stood Chase up and tied a sack over his head. Someone shoved him forward and he tripped on purpose and fell all over himself again. He didn't want to get up anymore. He didn't want to move at all. This time one man held him under the arms from each side and they dragged him along. Chase let his weight sag and closed his eyes inside the sack. The thing smelled of rice and urine. He heard tap–tap–tap as his feet hit the stairways and he was hauled to the car. How had he come to be here? Ten years ago he had asked himself the same question in the same city. *Are you thinking of me, Mette?* He recalled the *Hallaj-Nama* under all those Korans in the mosque. It might stay lost there for ever and no one else would know just how exquisite the argument on behalf of the devil could be, and how inviting hell could appear. Maybe it had been worth it, after all; he didn't blame Kari for having talked him into coming here.

20

It was as bad as Chinese torture, having that fat clock to stare at all through the night. Every time he turned in his cot he'd see it. He tried to avoid it for as long as he could. But once it turned dark, he couldn't help glancing at the thing every few minutes. Altogether the setup they had him in was not too bad. The room had its standard Persian carpet. There was a bookshelf full of religious texts and a large pitcher of water. But no bathroom. Once, when he had expressed loudly to no one in particular that he needed to relieve himself, the door had opened immediately and a very deferential young man dressed entirely in black had led him across a courtyard to where he needed to go. The courtyard was barely lit under a faint glow of moonlight. The air was crisp, and for once he didn't feel the ubiquitous smog that made simple breathing a challenge. Chase stood a while out there in the open next to a placid little prayer fountain and watched the sky. The young man who was with him had made no attempt to force him to move. Instead, he'd waited with his head almost bowed, respecting Chase's appreciation. It was an idyllic image, something from a past Chase knew of only from Orientalist paintings. You didn't see these kinds of homes anymore. Not in Tehran anyway. Fountains and courtyards and slender columns and arches that were there purely for delight. After he had gone back to his room, it was even harder to sit still and not gape at the clock. The young man had brought him food at some point. It was extraordinary food, fit for a king. A mound of crusted rice with skewered lamb and varieties of pastries with tea. He had asked the young man to eat with him, but the fellow had only smiled and left the room, walking backwards as if Chase were some distinguished captive who had to be treated with special care.

The clock showed eleven. Chase was still staring at the food he hadn't touched for three hours. It just sat there on a tray by the door giving off aromas that made his heart bleed. Eating would make him heavy, heaviness would make him want to get comfortable, and comfort was a luxury he didn't want right now. He thought of little else but his notebooks and what Saladin had said to him about Roth – Roth here in Tehran all those years ago, Roth having been set up. *Or is it me who's being set up now?* Then it was midnight. He fidgeted and stayed uneasy. By three he was ready to nail his face to the walls. By five, though, he had quieted down. He managed to put opium thoughts out of his mind. *Desire is making me feel like a work of art, Mette. I will find you; giving in no longer has its charms, you know.*

Nearing six, just as a cock had started to crow, he finally fell asleep. When he heard the door to his room being opened, he thought he must have been out for a long time. He glanced at the clock and saw that he'd slept for just about four hours. Someone had already collected his untouched tray and now another young man, equally deferential, stood at the door. Chase expected him to say something. He didn't.

'*Bale?*' Chase asked in Persian. 'What is it?'

'Agha will see you now,' the young man said.

He didn't know who Agha was. It was just a general masculine term. Agha could be anyone. A wave of hunger passed through him to be replaced by a far more immediate wave of withdrawal, his legs feeling as if they were not his at all. He was accompanied by the new man to the outhouse again at

252

the other end of the courtyard. There he put some water to his face and when he came out he saw the cock he thought he'd heard earlier darting about the fountain.

He breathed in the still fresh air. 'Nice place here,' he said to the young man.

'Yes it is. It is a sanctuary. We are lucky to be here.'

'We?'

The young man didn't answer but stood to the side and extended his hands to lead him to another section of the courtyard.

They had to wait another twenty minutes outside a hall where everything seemed to be made of cut glass. Chase looked and saw dozens of himself receding from view. There was an odd combination of ghostly stillness and a sense of martial rhythm to everything here that made him want to get goofy, to jump and make faces. Meantime, he couldn't stop yawning. The young man noticed this and turned discreetly the other way.

The tall, mirrored doors they'd been waiting behind were now opened from inside. There was more activity here than Chase had seen since he'd been brought in. All the young men there, five of them, wore black and had neatly trimmed beards. There was a quiet efficiency to their purpose, as if they were used to going through the motions of being in this room every day, fixing the location of furniture, dusting, appearing busier than there was any need for. They led Chase to an armchair and made him sit while they went about their business. Another ten minutes passed and then, save for one of them, the young men quietly disappeared.

Chase noticed the watcher who had remained with him stiffen up when soft footsteps were heard from behind some curtains. He saw the cleric's black drape precede him into the room. Then the mullah's face appeared. He wouldn't look at

Chase for a minute while he whispered something into the young man's ear. When he did finally acknowledge Chase, the look he offered was one of conciliation, as if they were old antagonists who had somehow come to terms with the nature of their differences.

Chase felt numb, a numbness where he'd never have to question again why he was here or why his body was betraying him.

The Muslim cleric, a man probably in his early sixties, said to him, 'If it is difficult for you, we can carry on this conversation in English. I have my translator here.'

'I can speak,' Chase said. Then he added *Haj Agha*, as a polite form of address meaning 'Sir,' more or less.

The mullah smiled. 'I have felt all along that you are a man who can understand us. Perhaps work with us.'

'Haj Agha, I'm curious: am I being recruited by the Iranian Ministry of Information and Security?'

The cleric, whose sunken eyes made him look long-suffering and tired, actually laughed. 'Please let us not hurry, Mr Chase. There's so much yet to discuss.'

'A manuscript, I believe.' Chase said, assuming a flowery, pseudo-classical style of Persian now – it would be more in line with what the cleric was used to. 'Forgive me, sir, but I look around this magnificent place and what I cannot figure out is why the book would be worth so much to you.'

The cleric gave him a long look, measuring him the way these mullahs were wont to do. Finally he said, 'Why don't you tell me, Mr Chase, why you think the book might be so important?'

The fellow was fishing, though not so much about where the book was but about how much Chase knew about the book itself. It came to him abruptly: face to face with the mullah, having the man stare fixedly at him like that, Chase wondered again why they weren't just beating the where-abouts of the book out of him. If they hadn't done so, it was because of something else. And that something else had nothing to do with all these hare-brained notions about Satan and whatnot. The only thing left now was to pretend to come clean. It might buy him time, or it might make the cleric think Chase was trying to buy time because he knew more than he let on. It was as if the two of them were playing a game of poker, except instead of holding cards the mullah held a Muslim prayer bead in his hand which he rotated round and round. With a nod then, Chase skirted the meat of the question the cleric had asked and instead started by telling him the story of Lotfi and Tabib and Lund – all of them dead. He left Kari out completely. He mentioned Max and the dead Arab in Istanbul and finally Saladin. 'Have you done away with that man, Haj Agha?' Chase asked warily, meaning Saladin. The cleric understood.

'Saladin did us a favor once. So we forgive him for his recent poor judgment. But he will have to end his days in Tehran, whether he likes it or not. It is, in the end, for his own good really. He has acted greedily, as did Mr Lotfi and some of the others who have worked for us in the past. We will deal with all of these people at some point. At the same time I remind you that we are never ungrateful to our *friends*, even if they do go off the righteous path – once, but not twice. That could include you, Mr Chase.'

Listening to the man, Chase wondered exactly to what clique in the Iranian intelligence apparatus the cleric belonged. It was one thing to hear that a country was run by its clergy, it was another to actually walk into a secluded office of, say, the Ministry of Security and be met by a mullah with a turban and a prayer bead, waiting to have you interrogated. Such images disoriented you, made you wonder if life on earth was not permanently on the verge of turning into a comic strip.

Chase said, 'It sounds to me, Haj Agha, that you may have domestic problems to contend with. Problems with your own people.'

'No harm in telling you what is common knowledge. We certainly are troubled by lack of discipline, fragmentation, by people who are no longer interested in following rules, codes of conduct. So many people these days, here and elsewhere, have forgotten their original sense of purpose. Now they are only after money.'

'But you are not?'

The cleric smiled. 'Take a look around, Mr Chase. Does it really look like it is money we need here?'

'Then – forgive a humble man's curiosity, Haj Agha – but truly, why are you after this manuscript if not for its value?'

'Why? Because the devil's work is not something we take lightly.' When Chase showed no reaction to what he'd said, the cleric asked him, 'Do my words frighten you, Mr Chase?'

No, it wasn't the cleric's words, but the nature of his deception. A man in his position did not need to explain anything to Chase; the fact that he did only bore out the obvious: it most certainly was *not* the devil's work that bothered these Iranians, but something else. What?

'What are you thinking, Mr Chase?' the cleric asked patiently.

'I am only thinking, sir, that a book is just a book,' Chase said, letting the mullah ride the crest of his own bluff. 'I am thinking that it is perhaps beneath men of your station to make a mountain, as they say, out of a molehill. Everyone knows that that fellow Hallaj's writings about Satan were published long ago; now they're all over the world. What is one more version added to that?'

256

'I do see your point, and it's a valid one. But let's put it this way, Mr Chase: a man might worship, say, a doorknob in private and you could let him be. But once he produces a book – and not just any book but one with supposedly astonishing one-of-a-kind illustrations – about why that doorknob should be worshipped, that is when you and I start getting worried. Do you really think men like myself here have nothing better to do with our time than worry over what one misguided fellow wrote about Satan? That would only make us ridiculous. We are not stupid men, Mr Chase. But we do realize that the threads of a society can come undone from something as seemingly innocent as a book, especially when that book glorifies Satan. Do you dispute this?'

It wasn't his place to dispute anything. If they wanted him to believe that they only wanted the book in order to destroy it, then let them. He had no say in that. All Chase knew was that the cleric and he had arrived at a point where he would have to say something concrete, something that would signal he was done fighting a losing battle.

'The book is at the British cemetery in Golhak,' he lied. 'I'm sure you already know that.'

The cleric nodded. Chase thought: why have I lied? He could think of any number of motives, the absolute least of which was that maybe, just maybe he wanted to save an important work of art from possible destruction. But how likely was he to be able to escape and take the book with him? And even if he did, how likely was he to get out of this country in one piece? There wasn't going to be any repeat of his Canadian embassy performance this time around.

The cleric had been speaking to the young man and soon the others were back in the room. The mullah nodded to someone else in the back also. Chase looked around and saw that it was the albino, waiting, unsmiling. The mullah turned

257

to Chase again: 'You and I are not finished. We will see each other after you have shown us the book.' He got up to go.

'Haj Agha!'

The cleric turned and waited for Chase to say what was on his mind. Nothing was on Chase's mind, nothing immediate anyway. He was surrounded by six men. That was about it. And if there was anything on his mind, it had to do with homesickness; he was homesick for Chinatown and 43rd Street, for Mette pouring him a drink and fixing him with her scolding gaze . . . homesick for Kari and Uncle Seyyed and White Horse whisky. For an instant he thought he'd tell the mullah he'd stuffed the manuscript under all those Korans inside the mosque down the road from the cemetery. But was that considered sacrilege? Would the cleric have him flogged or something worse, because he'd left the devil's work alongside God's?

Chase made a bow and said that he too hoped to see the great man again. The mullah nodded and walked off the same way he'd come. 'We're not small men,' he called to Chase. 'We believe in something. We want to preserve that something, Mr Chase.'

Chase thought there were tons of things he could say in answer to that. If belief, for one, made men big, then the world must be populated with several billion giants. But the mullah sounded so sincere about the devil that it made his case almost plausible. Almost.

The first young man who had stayed outside of his room last night came and lightly grabbed his wrist. The albino called from the door: 'Now we go to the cemetery,' he commanded.

'Yes, now we go there.'

21

They had driven in a plain white car with regular license plates. The three men who rode with him were silent now, and severe. The albino sat in the front next to the driver, and Chase heard one of the young men call him Agha Ziya. So that was his name. Chase watched Ziya sitting there impassive, not once turning around to address him. No point in talking anyway; they were intimates already.

He had expected that more of them would come along for the ride, but these security types were not like the militias; they preferred to blend in and do things quietly, without too much fanfare. Chase went on sweating, sneezing, yawning, wishing for anything. He gazed out of the car and saw drabness on a sprawl. Tehran was just a hugely exaggerated version of what it had been seven years ago. It started with the air, of which there was none. Then the traffic, which was impossible. And a sea of humanity that appeared cheerless and completely unused to itself – unlike other megalopolises, say a Bombay or a Mexico City, where people took for granted that no matter how impossible life became it was still somehow liveable. Tehran was a city of suicides.

Now they were standing around the grave Chase had indicated to them – Robert Simpson, 1894–1915. The driver had remained in the car, parked just outside the cemetery. Standing over Robert Simpson's headstone, Chase was flanked by Ziya and the fellow who had brought him food the night before. If he was ever going to make a run for it, it would have to be now. But run where? He was sure he'd barely be able to jog past the graveyard's last row of tombs before he ran out of steam.

He'd made a show of looking for the name on the headstone among the other names in the small cemetery. Finally he stood pointing. 'It's this.'

'Are you sure?' Ziya asked.

'I don't forget the names of the dead.'

Ziya moved to the side while the other man put his foot by one end of the headstone and went to pry it loose. He had expected the stone not to budge much, but the thing came right off, as Chase had known it would, sending the fellow tumbling backwards. The headstone fell on his ankle and he gave a short howl.

Chase shrugged. 'We've got to remove that dirt too.'

They did. All three of them together. It was loose, unpacked earth that Chase had only churned and smoothed back the day before. The other two men didn't seem to think much of this. They were too caught up in what they were doing. In a minute Ziya was holding the box the manuscript had been in until yesterday.

'There's nothing in this.'

Chase shrugged again. 'It's supposed to be in there.'

'It's not. Are you blind?' Ziya shouted. 'Why did this headstone come off so fast?'

'It's an old grave.'

'Don't be smart. We know you were here yesterday. Did you already move the book?'

'Move it where? That fellow Saladin would have had it on him if I had. Wouldn't he?'

It was midday prayer hour again. The mosque had started to sing. He thought he might just as well tell these guys where the book was, get them out of his hair, be done with it. Now Ziya threw the empty metal box at Chase and both men came at him. Chase stood there. There was no point in resisting. They were angry and he was an American and they felt swindled right now. Maybe afterwards he'd tell them the truth, or he wouldn't.

He felt a hard blow to the side of his head before he saw it coming. The blow seemed to clear his head for a second and he welcomed it in a contrary sort of way. He stumbled back but didn't fall. They came at him again, pushing and kicking. He fell backwards now over one of the graves. The headstone had the name of someone called Salisbury, the first name having been rubbed off. It seemed unfair having only half a name like that. He didn't know what to think. Maybe they'd just shoot him here and get it over with. No way was he going to give the book to these guys now. He felt dogged about it all of a sudden. He told them to go to hell in English first and then in their own language. That did it. Ziya stood away, but signaled the other man who now fell on Chase, holding him down and throwing a handful of dirt in his face. Chase was blinded. He felt a thumb pressing hard into his Adam's apple. This blocked his windpipe off and he heard himself gasping. *Adam, why couldn't the devil have just bowed before you and saved us all this shit?* Then the pressure on his throat eased off. He heard a thud first then a low suffocating sound, then everything was still.

He lay there, struggling to see, little clods of earth in his eyes and mouth and inside his shirt. He recalled how he hadn't changed clothes for days. The mosque was singing again. What if somebody decided to steal a Koran from the mosque and took the *Hallaj-Nama* by mistake? *Don't be silly! No one steals Korans from a mosque. Or do they?*

'Get up, Chase. We don't have all day.'

The voice definitely wasn't Ziya's, and it spoke English. 'Sally?'

'I said I'd save you and so I have.' Saladin reached for Chase's hand and stood him up. 'Can you see?'

'In a minute.' Chase wiped the soil off his face and spat. His head was bent so that he noticed the dead man lying on the ground before he actually saw Saladin. The fellow lay by Robert Simpson's grave, his throat slit open and one arm dangling into the small ditch where the headstone had been before. There was a bloody knife next to his head. 'Is he dead?'

'Call him a martyr. They like that better over here.'

'How did you know we'd be here?'

Saladin motioned behind Chase. He turned to see Ziya standing there, dead-faced as usual. 'You?' He would have liked nothing better than to put a bullet in the Iranian's head right then. Instead of feeling lucky to be alive, he felt indignation at all the faces disloyalty could wear.

'Take it easy, Chase. We don't have time now for proper introductions.' Saladin was crouching, surveying the area and taking away his victim's gun from him.

'Don't bother,' Chase said. 'The book's not here.'

Ziya stepped up and grabbed Chase. 'Where is it, then?'

Chase tried shaking himself loose, but the Iranian drew his gun and shoved it in Chase's face.'

'Shooting me won't change a thing. You still won't get the book.'

'Forget about the book.' Saladin got up and walked towards Ziya and Chase. His head was down. He had started to say something else. 'We have to get . . .' he ate the rest of his words, then reached quickly right under Ziya and swung his fist from a down position into the other man's abdomen. He held, twisted and pushed harder and twisted again. Stunned, Chase stood and watched Ziya go down open-mouthed, sucking air. It was like someone had pried his jaws open and cut his tongue off. As big a man as he was he hadn't madc a sound. Chase could only see the curved handle of a knife lodged deep just below his heart. The Iranian lay silently on his knees as if he were meditating. He made another slight gasp, and as his head lolled forward and he was about to drop on his face, Saladin pushed him back, pulled the knife out of him and stabbed him again. 'Out of here.'

'Huh?'

'We have to get out of here. They've got a surveillance perimeter four blocks away. And there's a fellow just outside who's going to get a bit uneasy when his associates don't show up soon. So . . . Chase, you got a couple of choices. You either come with me or you walk out of this cemetery and see what happens to naughty Americans in Tehran.'

Chase was totally speechless. He only managed to bring out, 'But I thought . . .'

'Forget what you thought.' Saladin gave Ziya a kick. 'It was this bum's bad luck to think he could work with me. I never liked him anyway.' He looked at Chase. 'Wake up! You coming?'

'Which way do we go?'

Saladin reached into his coat pocket and brought out a long black chador that would cover him from head to foot. Drawing the cloth over himself, he said, 'We're going through the back of the British residency. I don't have a better idea. Do you?'

Chase glanced one last time at Ziya and the other dead man. More body count – he was spending too much time in cemeteries of late.

The two men hurried off.

Monday, six-thirty p.m.

Chase was watching Saladin's outline hover just outside. Trees rustled in the wind and cats wailed loudly. His notebooks sat beside him on a crate in a large room with nothing else in it. Saladin had told him that the place was one of those homes confiscated from the rich after the revolution. It was in the Elahiye neighborhood – a convenient jaunt from the cemetery. Apparently so many different government organs had fought over the property for so long that it had somehow gotten lost in the shuffle and no one had ever claimed it. Not even thieves or Afghan squatters. The place was dusty and cold but not impossible. Mice scuttled about inside. You could hear them. Chase had tried lying down on an ancient waterbed in one of the bedrooms, but found it leaky and smelling faintly of something dead.

Outside, the cats howled desperately all of a sudden and a minute later Saladin came back in and stood there looking at him.

Chase said, 'What is it? Am I supposed to thank you now for saving my life down there in that graveyard?'

'I don't need your thanks.' Saladin pointed outside. 'It's dark now. We'll give it another hour at most, make sure the last prayer's over with. Then we hit the mosque. You better not be lying to me, Chase. If that book's not there . . .' His voice trailed. 'That mosque is just too damn close to where we were today. It's practically across the street.'

'It's there all right.'

'Where in there?'

'I guess you'll have to take me along to show you.'

They listened for a while longer to some more infernal sounds of cats preparing to fight outside. The animals sounded like ferociously angry infants. They put the chill into Chase. For several hours the two men had sat in this cold house, exhausted with themselves and with what lay ahead. The thought that they might be ambushed right here had kept them from talking much. Chase, who badly needed sleep, forced himself to go the distance with Saladin because he wasn't sure of what the other man would do. With the onset of dark, he relaxed a bit. Soon it would be time.

He asked, 'Why do these people want the book so bad?'

'The devil bothers them.'

'That's what the mullah I met with today tried to have me believe.'

Saladin came and sat close to Chase. 'You believe him?'

'Not a bit. What's the story, Sally? I must know the truth if you want to see that book. I'm serious.'

Saladin lit a cigarette and blew it impatiently at Chase. 'Man, what do you want me to say? There's supposed to be a bunch of names hidden in there somewhere. That's what I hear.'

'Names?'

'Use your brain, professor. Don't sit there and ask me what kind of names. What kind do you think?'

The realization came to him even before Saladin had finished his sentence. It left him staggered, appalled. Finally he thought he understood what all the killing had been for. Saladin caught the fear in him.

'So, Chase, I guess now the question is did you or did you not see a list of names in that book? That's what's important.'

'I didn't, but then I didn't look too closely. How many names are we talking about here?'

'Don't know. No doubt enough to make a lot of folks in Washington very nervous if they find out this list exists.' Saladin sighed loudly. 'You messed everybody up, Chase. That's what you did. It all was a tangle of guys not knowing what they were really after and then you came along and made it that much worse. But Lotfi and me, we were working together good. We just wanted the book for its own sake. I swear I didn't even know about the list till later. Then Lotfi gets killed and I get the security people in Tehran knocking on my door and I know this is no longer a simple case of Saladin trying to make a buck for himself. I find out the Iranians got this Russian character working for them and he goes and disappears too. After that, I was damned if I did and damned if I didn't. I had a feeling the book had to still be in Tehran, so I waited for you and you came. Then I got a lucky break and that big white fella we put to rest today showed up with your notebooks.'

Chase tried to cut in: 'About that . . .'

'Wait. I'm not finished. The fella says let's work together. Just me and him. He says the Russian has gone awol on them and I know what the guy is thinking. He's thinking the book is worth something and he's tired of being underpaid by his government. He's got your notebooks. He wants me to read them closely to see if you've written something to point us in the right direction. So I read. Nothing there. But I know you're coming and I tell the man to relax, Chase will be here. The rest you already know, 'cause you were there.'

Chase got up and went and stood by the window. He saw a white cat scramble past the front door. Just ahead were little mounds of leaves that had collected by the foot of trees for some distance. You could hear the sound of cars further off. He might be able to close his eyes and imagine he was elsewhere – standing on 11th Avenue in Manhattan listening to the hum of the West Side Highway, and soon he'd stroll back to Times Square and head to Billy's Corner Bar and order a scotch from Mette and she'd pass it to him without a charge because he was favored. He could imagine all that if he thought it could change the landscape. It couldn't. He was here. Right here.

What foolishness, all of it. And it was exactly the kind of

thing he'd been interrogated about so many times before by men like Jay Shanker. *Do you know of any Muslim sleeper cells in the United States, Chase?* What a question to ask someone! And even if he had known, it would have been as good as a death sentence to say yes to that. Do I know of any sleeper cells? Sure, they're right down the street playing ping-pong. You could laugh those cross-examinations off and keep faith in the basic sanity of a system that said you were innocent until proven guilty. *Sorry guys, I don't know of any cells, unless you're talking about red and white blood cells and such.* And so they let you walk off to your little hotel room where you could lock out the world until . . . until you found out there was a one-of-a-kind manuscript and there really were names – a feast of names – and both were yours for the taking if only you could manage to survive.

Saladin called to him. 'Chase, man, you're sweating like crazy. What's wrong with you?'

'I'm trying to kick the old habit, but – you know how it is – the habit's kicking me instead.'

'Why didn't you speak up? Here!' Saladin reached in his pocket and threw Chase a piece of foil. When he opened it, there was a nice finger-cut of opium in there.

'You carry this stuff on you?' he asked.

'It's as good as money in this town. You want a guy to sing for you, just throw him one of these. I'm hoping your song's the right melody for me before the night's over.'

'All the same, I wish you hadn't given it to me.'

'Hey,' Saladin put out his hand, 'you don't have to take it. Just trying to help out, you know. We're partners now.'

'Sure. Just like you were partners with the guy you killed in the cemetery today.'

'Low blow, man. Low blow.'

'True, anyway.' Chase put the foil in his pocket. It was like insurance for him. His hope was that he could keep going without it. It hadn't been easy, but he was enduring. Last night had been the worst, tonight was a little better.

There was so much on their plate; he didn't know which to address first. He called to Saladin from where he was. 'Why did they put the names in the manuscript in the first place? What had the Uzbeks to do with it?'

Saladin spat. 'Who knows! Probably some preacher up in the hills somewhere couldn't get to, or no longer trusted, regular mail or an overseas phone call or the internet. But what did the fellow have to do? He had to get the names to a contact across the sea before the Americans bombed him into oblivion in Afghanistan. Which the Americans most probably have done by now. The guy knew his time was limited. The Uzbeks and their little book were the answer. And you got to admit, it was a beautiful solution. It's not as if someone's gonna lose a book like that or tear it to pieces. Or maybe the fella who put the names in there just liked the irony of it all – slipping his list in Satan's book. It was an elegant enough solution anyway, until your friend Tabib went and broke the link by stealing the manuscript.

'Did Tabib know about the names?'

'No one did, except, I'm guessing, maybe a single contact in the States who'd have known what to look for in the book. That is all. Tabib and his team, they were only carriers. They had no idea what they were carrying. The Uzbeks got cold feet in Turkey once Tabib went missing with the book. Your buddy Tabib had put a dictionary in its place and those idiots never could tell the difference. They showed up back in Tehran and now the Iranians, the kindly hosts that they are, are giving them cold water to drink at some undisclosed location.'

'What about the Iranians themselves?'

'They're opportunists. They found out too late about the list or they'd have stopped Tabib and the Uzbek team right here in Tehran before they left. But ever since they found out, the Iranians have been all over it.'

Chase had to ask the obvious question: 'Why is it so important to them? It's not even their list.'

'Were you born yesterday? It's for leverage, what else? It's like an insurance policy. There's probably over a hundred guys, alone or in small cells, waiting for their orders in the States, wondering why nobody contacts them. What Tehran wants to do is take over the operation, fill the vacuum. Wouldn't you do the same if you were in their place?'

Chase shrugged. He knew where Saladin was going with this – not a good place at all. 'I don't know,' he muttered. 'I don't know anything.'

'Man, you need a crash course in geo-politics, don't you? I'll give you one right now. Look at what's been going on lately in this neighborhood. The Iranians, they take one look to their right side and see the Americans sitting pretty all of a sudden in Afghanistan. They look to their left and see Baghdad, a target if there ever was one. Sooner or later it's going to be the Iranians' turn, because that, my friend, has always been the biggest prize of all in the Middle East. The Americans lost this country twenty-three years ago; they figure it's time to take it back. As for the Iranians, they figure what they really need is that insurance policy, ace in the hole. That's what them names are. The Iranians wouldn't do anything unless they had to. And those names waiting quietly in the US of A right now, they're what I'd call precision-guided missiles, except they're made of flesh and blood. My guess is that these guys figure if Washington decided to hit them one day – which they might – then they could hit right back and quick, from inside and with deadly precision. Now, that

269

would put the fear of God in a few people on Pennsylvania Avenue, wouldn't it, Mr Chase?'

Chase didn't answer. He wanted fresh air, a shower. Mostly, he wanted not to have to think about all that Saladin had just said. He wanted a time-out. At least he finally had some new clothes. Saladin, who'd obviously planned everything, had seen to that. There had been fresh clothes and some food waiting when they'd gotten here. Except that mice were all over the food and Chase, who'd been starving, hadn't touched a thing. Now he went to open the door to go outside and Saladin told him to stay put.

'I need to breathe, is all. Where would I go anyway? I've got no money, no passport. I couldn't get five miles out of the city.'

Two candles had been burning where Saladin was. One of them went out as Chase opened the door and a cold wind came in. He heard the click of Saladin's gun, closed the door and backed off. They waited there in the darkness.

'Shoot me,' Chase said, 'and you'll be condemned to Tehran forever. You'll never find that book.'

'Don't make me shoot you then.'

Chase came and sat back down across from the other man. 'You realize we're done for. We'll never get out of here.'

'Wrong. I know how these guys think. They'll be heading east to the Afghan border after you. They'll figure that's the area you know best.'

Chase grunted. 'Wishful thinking.'

'I've lived here a lot longer than you. Half my life. Do you know what that means? Half my life!'

'My sympathies.'

'What I'm saying is, they'll be too busy for a few days looking for one of their own to blame. It's always been like that here. They're more scared of each other than anybody else. That's their weakness. And that works for us.'

'So how do you propose we get out?'

'One thing at a time. I want to be holding that book in my hands first.'

They sat still, facing each other. Chase could see the silhouette of Saladin's head dance to the light of the candle on the wall behind him. The absurdity of their situation didn't escape Chase. They were two Americans hiding out in an abandoned ancien-régime home in a strange country waiting for their luck to finally come through. They were bound together now, both desperately needed each other. No doubt Saladin had forged travel documents and an escape route all planned out. But he'd never be able to get very far wearing that chador, acting as a woman alone. Then again, if he took the chador off, revealing his skin color, they'd catch him before he'd taken two steps. He was going to have to have Chase with him to do the talking while he hid behind that veil.

This logic made Chase feel a little better about his own prospects. The time had come to bargain. He said, 'I want that list.'

Saladin's ears pricked up. 'What?'

'It's the only deal I'm willing to make with you.'

'You want to be a good American and deliver the list to the law?'

'I haven't figured out how, but yes, I want to do that.'

'You damn fool! No way. The list is not your worry or mine. How will you explain where you got the list?'

'The law doesn't have to know it's coming from me. I'll just mail it in or something,' Chase said unconvincingly.

All of a sudden the air hung heavy between them again and it dawned on Chase he'd given his hand away by asking for the list. It made sense: Saladin didn't just intend to sell the book, he'd sell the list too, probably back to the Iranians. And to do that he couldn't afford to have Chase alive after Iran. A rush of panic made Chase hold his breath. He looked at his watch. Seven o' clock. He realized then that he was going to have to break down for the time being; it couldn't be helped, if he had to stay alert he'd need to rid himself of the aches and pains. So while Saladin watched, Chase took the cut of opium out of his pocket, twisted a small ball off its head and dropped it in his mouth. He was not used to eating the stuff. It tasted like the poison it was. But he swallowed and immediately had the dry heaves. Saladin laughed, cradling his gun in his lap. That was good. Let the man laugh at him.

'You poor bastard, Chase. What did you think, that the US Department of Justice would salute you for giving them the list? Did you think you'd get your name in the papers and become America's favorite local boy who made good? America doesn't give two shits about you and me.'

'Don't compare yourself with me. I'm not the one who's wanted on a murder rap. You don't even believe in your Allah anymore, Sally. So twenty years ago you went and killed some innocent guy for nothing. The minute they find out you're out of Iran, Interpol will be on your tail.'

'Who's gonna tell them?' Saladin asked in a menacing tone.

Chase shrugged. 'You'll run out of luck one of these days.'

This seemed to anger Saladin more. He got up and stood over Chase. 'First, I don't operate on luck. Second, difference between a guy like me and you, Chase, is I put my money where my mouth is, and all you do is babble, babble, babble. You want to be a real hero, do you? Just like your old friend Joe Roth.'

Now Chase stood up too and pushed Saladin back despite the gun. 'What about Joe Roth? What did you mean earlier when you said he was set up in Tehran?'

Instead of answering, Saladin jumped at him and smacked the butt of his gun in Chase's shoulder. Chase fell back a bit, but held his ground. His upper arm stung. He was not going to back out of this one. He spoke up, 'What happened to Joe Roth in Tehran in '78, '79?'

'What happened is he got fucked,' Saladin almost shouted. 'He got fucked by his own people – *your* people, and supposedly my people.'

Fucked! What a way to put it. Roth himself had called it getting buggered. *Iran my first piece of bad luck, Afghanistan the second . . .* And all these years later fate had brought Chase here where it had all started for both of them, Roth and himself. Kismet!

He asked, 'Why did you bother to bring my notebooks along?'

Saladin let the gun point down. Hitting Chase seemed to have calmed him down again. 'No use leaving them for the Iranians,' he said. 'Anyway, bringing them was my goodwill gesture towards you.'

'You're too kind.'

Saladin started to walk to the door. 'Come on, Chase. It's time.'

Chase didn't move. 'I'm not going anywhere until you tell me what you know about Joe Roth.'

Saladin went over and blew the candle out. Now the two men were standing in total dark. 'You're messing with me. I should have never said anything to you.'

'You got nothing to lose by telling me. We got time.' Chase was feeling the early effects of what he'd swallowed. It was as if somebody were holding him upside down. If he had had anything to eat it would be all over the floor by now. It was always like this when you got so low as to have to eat the stuff. First you'd be retching and feeling queasy. But, afterwards,

273

you'd feel like dancing. It was a matter of waiting the misery out. He could tell Saladin was on the verge of violence again. He also knew he was in no shape to deal with that sort of thing right now. He walked up to Saladin, put a hand gently on the other man's shoulder saying, 'I gotta know. There's nothing more to it than that. I'll show you the book after that. It's all yours. I'm finished.'

Saladin lifted Chase's hand off his shoulder and dropped it. He took another step closer so that the two of them were nose to nose. 'You're crazy if you think you'll come back to this godforsaken place and do what I think you mean to. But, just in case, the man you'll be looking for, his name is Ali Kasrai. He's some sort of a deputy mayor now in Tehran. He shouldn't be hard to find.'

'You talk like you don't plan to kill me after all.'

'I ain't decided not to yet. Depends on you, Chase.'

'What about Roth and this fellow Ali Kasrai?'

'Not much to tell. I did a bit of research after I read your stuff. Kasrai was one of them student leaders when the revolution was happening. Marxist, Leninist, Trotskyist, Maoist – some shit like that. I'm not really sure. He was on the left anyway. A communist of some kind. Back then Joe Roth was one of the Agency's boys here. Hell was breaking loose in this country. Washington was about to lose its numero uno ally in the neighborhood, its puppet, keeper of peace in the Persian fucking Gulf. Roth dealt with everybody back then. Talked with them all – the priests, the communists, everybody, because that's what a good agent is supposed to do. Right? That's what they teach them: don't limit your options. So your pal is here sending word back to Langley telling them it's a mess over here. Telling them they should reconsider a bit, they should open up channels of communication with *all* the players. But in Langley they don't want to hear this, especially when it comes to dealing with commies. In those days dealing with commies was a big no-no; you didn't do it, period. It was against the rules. But the rules were garbage and Roth went against them because he thought it was the right thing to do. The man was a sucker, but his heart saw clear. He knew things were gonna get awful bad. And they did. The Americans got kicked out and the Iranians stormed our embassy here and took it over. I mean, completely took it over! You were still just a kid then, but do you know how much "highly confidential" crap came out of that alone?'

'Is that how you know about all this?'

'That and other sources. I tell you, man, there are people in Tehran who make a business of selling the past. Everybody's past has a hole in it. Me and you included. This guy Kasrai, Mr Deputy Mayor, back then he was just waiting on the fence to see who'd come on top.' Saladin spat. 'The guy wasn't a communist, he played communist until it paid off. And as soon as it didn't, he switched sides. He took to the priests and grew his beard. Back then it was musical chairs, brother. The priests wanted their main competition, the communists, out of the game. And in Washington they figured if they had to swallow the bitter pill and lose Iran, they'd rather lose it to the Muslim priests than commies in Russian pay. When Roth started to make noises about all this, somebody back home had this bright idea of shutting him up. So they found Kasrai. A willing, two-bit, no-good little devil. Kasrai sent your friend Roth a letter on behalf of some Marxist student organization. Somehow a copy of the letter found its way to headquarters back in Virginia. That wasn't enough to convict Roth of treason. It was his job, after all, to make contact. But it was enough to accuse him of bad faith. Afterwards, what happened? You already know what happened. They recalled Roth and put some of the blame for the Iran debacle that was making the rounds on the one guy who'd seen the storm coming and tried to warn Washington about it.'

An awkward silence. Saladin waited for him to digest all that. For a moment the hurry seemed to have gone out of the world.

'Thanks,' Chase said softly. There was nothing else to add to that. In the darkness of this place he recalled some years back when he and Roth had both been living at the hotel in Times Square and had gone out for a walk in Central Park on a bright summer day. Roth gave a ten-dollar bill to an old bum who'd approached them and when Chase asked why he'd given that much, Roth had said that it was because his life and the old man's life had come together in that very instant in time and that he had no choice but to give what he gave. It was kismet, he'd added and laughed. Chase saw that now: criss-crossed lives was what they were – Saladin and himself, Joe Roth and that fellow Ali Kasrai. Would this Ali Kasrai even remember the small service he'd rendered those many years ago, wrecking a man's life? Deputy mayors were busy men, after all; they didn't have to remember much if it wasn't convenient for them to do so.

Saladin tugged at Chase's sleeve. 'Come on, man, let's go. I know, it's something, what I just told you. But at least now you know – only you, me and maybe half a dozen other men here and there. Don't blame it on Ali Kasrai. Blame it on the guys back home who probably paid him to do it.'

'If I have to blame, I'll blame whoever's available and has enough blood on their hands to get blamed,' Chase said walking to the door.

'That's real good. Now I wonder if you still want to be a hero like Joe Roth and tell about that list to anyone.'

'I told you I'm finished,' Chase mumbled. But he didn't know himself what he was finished with, nor was he sure if being finished only meant he intended to start something new.

22

It was nearing eight at night. Not only was the mosque not slowing down for the evening, but it happened to be packed full of mourners just then. And they were still arriving in waves. The black they wore, both the men and women, was in stark contrast to the blazing lights of the mosque. There was a carnival quality about the whole scene. Just outside the mosque some local men were stirring food in great iron pots to hand out to the poor afterwards. Someone of eminence had to have died for them to make such a fuss. The loudspeakers were live with lamentation. Across the street at the gates of the gendarmerie, the young soldiers on duty looked like luminous toys wearing uniforms far too big for them. Further down, the cemetery for the British war dead stayed obscure.

Chase and Saladin had been standing there for at least five minutes. Saladin had the chador wrapped tightly about himself. They could have been man and wife. But Chase still felt totally exposed like this. He was certain Saladin must be feeling it too. Soon they'd either have to go in or go away. 'Are you sure you want to do this tonight?'

'I'm done waiting,' Saladin growled. 'Let's go in.'

'Look at these people. We'll stand out.'

'Let's go in and see just how much we stand out.'

Saladin nudged him with the concealed gun. Ideas, all of them bad, were bobbing around in Chase's head. What if Saladin was going to kill him after all? He let the other man push him slowly into the courtyard. They bumped and rubbed against other people.

Chase turned and spoke with some desperation. 'We can't go inside the mosque like this.' He meant the chador Saladin was wearing. 'There's a separate area for the women.'

Saladin now did what Chase was afraid he might do. He swung them around the back of one of the outside pillars where there was no light and quickly took off the chador and rolled it inside his pants.

Chase closed his eyes and swore. 'You're crazy, man. You'll get us both killed.'

'It's too late for anything else. I want the book and I want to be out of Tehran *tonight*.'

The fellow meant what he said. There was fire in his eyes; he must really be tasting the book now. Chase stepped ahead of him and they walked past more black-clad mourners into the interior of the dome. Here, it was even more brightly lit than outside. You'd think a marriage was about to take place, not a funeral. It was typical of these Shiite Muslims – the way they turned bereavement into ecstasy, and ecstasy into false tears.

They took their shoes in their hands and stepped across the carpeted prayer space. There was a waft of rosewater and sweets. Thankfully, no one seemed to pay any particular attention to Saladin and his skin color. A mosque was a mosque; there was no hierarchy to it, everyone was welcome. They had to maneuver through fat little boys running around while their mothers remained hidden somewhere out back weeping, weeping especially loudly so they'd be heard. A cleric was up front running his hand over his hennaed beard, talking to some people. Here and there a few men were praying by themselves in the niches while the neighborhood hungry loafed about and waited for free food to be handed out. It was an odd jumble of the best and the worst of the country Chase had known so intimately, and for a passing moment he felt like joining them in all their follies. He turned to Saladin and pointed to the recess where the Korans were kept. They'd already separated the area with a thick black drape for the women.

'What's back there?' Saladin asked.

'They keep their Korans in there. They've divided it up for the women tonight. That's what they do on nights like this.'

'I *know* that's what they do, and I'm not interested in their Korans.'

'Your book is underneath them.'

Saladin nodded appreciatively. 'You better be right, Chase. Let's go.'

They walked casually past the divider. They were alone now and standing shoulder to shoulder. Chase saw just how uncomfortable Saladin looked. He was staring at the looming stacks of holy books and seemed suddenly unsure. He took his gun out and pointed it at Chase. 'Hurry up!'

Chase gave him a questioning look. 'What is our deal then? You aiming to kill me or what?'

'Never mind that.'

Chase considered his own situation. Strangely enough, he didn't really feel like he was under the gun. He didn't have anywhere near the sense of rush Saladin had. It was as if everything that had been happening to him since coming to Tehran had been happening to somebody else, that he was only a witness, and that this moment, here with Saladin, was a finale that took place in a world far removed from them all.

Chase smiled. Saladin's edginess was making him want to test the man's intentions. If he didn't do it now there might not be another occasion when he could. He asked, 'How can you be sure the book is here? Maybe I lied. Look at all those Korans.'

'Don't push me, Chase. I know it's here,' Saladin said breathlessly. 'Here somewhere. I feel it.'

Chase started to laugh. 'You know, in a few minutes these people are going to be doing whatever it is they do. Pray to their God, *your* God. The women are going to come in the back here and see two guys, foreigners, and they're going to see one of them holding a gun. In case you hadn't noticed, there's a police station about twenty yards away from the mosque.'

'I'm warning you.' Saladin stepped up and shoved the barrel of the piece to Chase's nose.

'All I want is what's my due,' Chase said without much conviction in his own request or that Saladin would honor it in the end.

'You'll get what's yours,' Saladin said quickly. 'Where is it?' He pushed Chase away and started throwing piles of the holy books to the floor.

'Not a nice thing to do,' Chase observed.

'Shut up! Get over here.' He grabbed Chase's hair and threw him at the Korans. Chase was faced with a mass of the things. At the back of his skull he could feel the pressure from Saladin's gun.

'You got one minute,' Saladin barked.

Chase spoke as he threw the Korans to the floor: 'I already read some passages from the manuscript. I especially love this part – I got the thing memorized: Moses says to the devil, "You abandoned the Lord's commandment and he deformed you." And the devil replies, "That is but the ambiguity of appearances, Oh Moses!" Ain't that something? What kind of an inspired nut would write stuff like that?'

Saladin hammered him on his back with the butt of the gun. The pain was like getting stabbed. Now he yanked Chase back and went at the Korans by himself again. He was scattering them every which way, crazily. He was opening some but seeing only the words of God, not the devil. He'd spit in disgust and carry on. He was in a complete frenzy, as was Chase's ill-timed laughter, which grew louder with the sound of the muezzin over the loudspeaker. They could also hear the rest of the mourners shuffling their way towards the inner courtyard.

'You're a fool, Sally. Do you know what they do to people who desecrate the holy book?'

Saladin turned and kicked Chase down, rolling him over the Korans and stomping on his neck. Chase laughed all the more maniacally. They'd both arrived at the threshold of madness. Something would have to give soon.

There was a loud *Allah akbar* over the loudspeaker. The mourners responded in kind. The buzz of their proximity on the other side of the black curtain made Saladin stop for a second and then he doubled his effort, flinging himself at the Korans like a raving lunatic. At the same time Chase saw the curtain starting to part, revealing the long black cloaks of the women who were about to enter the divide.

He got up quickly and stood facing them by the curtain, his head half turned so they wouldn't notice the blood dripping from his nose and mouth. He explained to the women that some children had been throwing the holy books on the floor. The books needed to be set right before the ladies could enter.

By the time the women had retreated and he turned around, he saw that Saladin had just about toppled all the books to the floor. Under a stack of four enormous Korans close to Chase's feet, the manuscript lay. He thought it was bluer than anything he'd ever seen, the *Hallaj-Nama*.

Saladin looked exhausted. Chase – not quite understanding what he did – picked up the manuscript, opened it arbitrarily and began reading from one of the pages:

I am Satan. If the Lord punishes me with His fire for all of eternity I would not prostrate myself before anyone, and I would not abase myself before any person or body because I do not recognize any opposite to Him! My declaration is that of one sincere in love.

Saladin's head shot up. He got a glimpse of the manuscript in Chase's hands and clomped over the slighted shells of the holy books to get to what he was after.

'Give it to me!'

Chase did what the other man said. Saladin pushed his gun into his belt. Chase watched him open the blue book to one of the miniature pages. Saladin's arms were shaking. It was his moment and Chase let him treasure it. Then he picked up from the floor the heftiest hardbound Koran he could find. The thing was massive, its cover having been slipped into a second binding made of elaborately carved wood. He waited.

'Sally!'

No answer. He wasn't sure yet what he meant to do. He called again. Now, as Saladin began to look up, Chase swung one edge of the book as hard as he could smack into the side of Saladin's head. It was a lucky shot. The sharp, cutting rim of the heavily bound old Koran caught Saladin hard on the temple and sent him flying into the pool of the other Korans on the floor. There was another loud *Allah akbar*, as if to fill in the time lying dead between them. They were both still for a few seconds. Then Saladin slowly got up and looked at Chase with dazed eyes. The manuscript dropped from his hands. He tried to reach for his gun, but couldn't find where it was. Chase, too, was in a cloud of his own. He was standing there watching, not taking a single step towards Saladin. Several more quick successions of *Allah akbar* from the loud–

speaker, to which the mourners on the other side of the curtain responded. Saladin fell.

He was lying on the stacks he'd thrown to the floor, drenched in blood. It was as if he'd been knifed or been crushed by a bat, and not hit by a mere book. His eyes were wide open. Dead.

It took him some minutes, but Chase finally came to himself. Trembling, he set aside the manuscript and started going through Saladin's pockets. Money – a nice fold of about two million tuman, or eighteen hundred dollars. There was also the gun and a cell phone. No documents, however. No passports.

He stood there, his head racing. There was something else. What? The manuscript lay at his feet. He glanced at it and then fell to his knees again. He skimmed every page, looking behind him every once in a while to see if there was any commotion behind the curtain. But the mourners were taking their time. He finally saw the original famous page Lund had shown him in New York and which he'd first set eyes on in the Persian bookstore. *I'm looking at the real thing*. Still, once he'd gone through all the miniatures and the text pages, he sat there staring at the cover of the book feeling cheated. He ran his thumb over the inside of the jacket. Nothing seemed out of place. He stroked the cover as if he were appraising the thing. It had to be done: he pressed a little harder into it and then began pulling from the book's edge, careful to pull only on the cover and not the pages themselves. It was hard going, but with a little more jerking and twisting one side of the manuscript split off and dangled in a neat line and he noticed for the first time that the streak had been sewn back, recently, and brushed over. He hadn't vandalized too much, only reopened the manuscript's wound. He turned back the cover. The list was there, a thin yellow sheet pressed between the two surfaces. The names were penned in blue ink in precise tiny letters, divided in groups of threes to fives. Altogether he counted fifteen groupings. Somewhere between fifty and seventy names. Each cluster had a single post office box address appended to it. All of them American addresses.

Out from the back way, like the first time he'd come through here. The women were waiting behind a second set of dividers and he moved quickly to avoid them completely. In the rear courtyard where it was empty and dark he saw a small moving shadow in a corner. A sheep. They would probably sacrifice it tonight or tomorrow morning and feed it to the neighborhood. Chase went up to the animal, untied it and gave it a slight bump in the rump to send it scurrying out of the mosque's back door.

Soon he was hustling down the back streets of Golhak. In one hand he had Saladin's phone. He dialed Kari, praying that it allowed access to overseas calls. It did. It must be around noontime in New York. Kari picked up the phone on the very first ring. He'd been waiting for Chase's call.

'Kid, I was starting to lose hope.'

'Don't.'

'You've taken care of business?'

'I think so.'

'Where are you?'

'Some street, far away,' Chase said distractedly. 'There isn't much light here and I've got to walk fast – but listen, big man. Listen to what the devil had to say. It's written here; it's all written here, plain as day: "I am Satan. God isolated me, made me ecstatic, confused me and finally expelled me, and all because of my love for Him."'

Silence.

'You all right, kid?'

'Huh?'

'You all right?'

'Never felt better. How's our business doing?'

'Come again?'

'You know, *the business*. Kismet.'

Kari's voice relaxed. 'Oh, okay, I guess. I've been staying at your place looking after things. But how did you know I was looking after the business?'

'Because that's what you do, Kari. You look after me.'

He heard the boom of Kari's laughter from halfway across the world.

'You had two calls,' Kari said. 'Some fellow named Najjar called. Said something about the Russians hounding him again. He didn't sound too pleased with the guidance you gave him. Another fellow called – Khan his name was. Left a message thanking Joe – I mean you. He said you'd been right and he and his wife were back together again.'

Chase saw the lights of two of the regular motorcycle patrols making for the police station up the road. He turned right into one of the narrow alleys of Golhak village and made himself small. 'One out of two,' he whispered.

'What?'

'The clients. A fifty percent success rate so far. That's not too bad a start.'

'It's all right. Why don't you come home, kid. I think you've done fine – whatever you've done.'

Chase was standing on the Shariati Road by now, a main street. He looked for a cab, not sure where he'd go. He fumbled in his pockets, the damaged manuscript tucked between his left ribs and arm. He'd managed to wipe the blood off his face so he wouldn't stand out. And he had enough money finally. But he still felt a mess. He needed to wash up and think of what he wanted to do. Tehran was a city of roughly fourteen million people. Anyone could get themselves lost in it and stay lost for a while. But Chase didn't want to simply be lost. He wanted out. A name kept dancing in his head. That name was Ali Kasrai's and it wouldn't let go of him. He would have told Kari about this name, but he couldn't take the chance on an international call.

'Are you there?' Kari was asking him.

'Guess what I did? I saved two sheep here. I'm the anti–Abraham.'

'Come home, kid.'

Chase put his hand up for a cab coming at him from two lights off. There were so many things he wanted to say. *I have the list. I finally have the list. This is my redemption song.* Except Kari wouldn't know what he was talking about. *Has Mette called?*

He spoke into the phone quickly now, 'I don't know, big guy. You really need to take a look at this book. Satan . . . I mean, it seems to me the fellow was really in love, only with the wrong guy. The wrong God.'

There was a gap in the connection, and then he heard Kari say, 'It happens, you know. It happens all the time. With all kinds of people deciding on the wrong God. They can't help it. No one can. Why don't you come home now, son. Or if you want, I can come meet you somewhere like we said before. Okay?'

The cab came to a stop next to Chase. There was no one else in it. He'd have to make the driver a nice cash offer for the ride.

'I'm coming home, big guy.'

Then there was a gale of static before the silence on the line. Chase looked for his watch and couldn't find it. It must have dropped during all that tussle. The driver saw what he was looking for and told him it was almost nine o'clock.

'What day?' Chase asked.

'Tuesday, mister. Where would you like to go?'

Epilogue

The news, once it hit the Tehran papers on Saturday, created a bit of a stir at first. Ali Kasrai, forty-five years old, divorced with no children, a midlevel politician and a deputy mayor had been found knocked over the head and murdered in his penthouse at one of the city's new luxury high-rises. Robbery was quickly dismissed as a motive, since nothing of value except perhaps some cash from the victim's pockets had been taken. The two guards on duty who had let the suspect upstairs swore that they'd first called the victim and made sure there was an appointment. There was. Or at least the guards claimed there was. But this brought up more questions than it answered. Was the act then politically motivated? Was it an inside job? Did it have to do with the domestic political disputes that were gripping the city these days? If so, then who really was Ali Kasrai and why would anyone go so far as to kill him? It seemed only a matter of time before some light would be shed on the case. But, if anything, in the weeks that ensued the newspapers seemed to become more and more silent on what had happened. Maybe powerful hands did not want the subject opened. No one could tell. And after a time, not only was it as if Ali Kasrai's death had never happened, but it was as if the man himself had never been.

That very Saturday when news of the Kasrai murder was starting to spread, the ferry from the port of Anzali was about a third of the way up its destination to Baku, Azerbaijan. The ferry had set out before dawn, fixing to be out of Astara, the last port of call in Iranian waters of the Caspian Sea, by late afternoon. From there to oil-rich Baku would take the rest of the night and the passengers would disembark in the early morning. They'd already passed the waterline into Azeri territory. Cold wind blew on deck and the ferry was not even half full. The captain of the boat, an old Daghestani Russian with a formidable mustache was not grumbling too much though, even if it was the bad season for this trip and there was almost no money to be made on the Saturday haul. The combination of summertime and Thursdays were the best. You got all these thirsty Iranians who'd head up to Baku for the weekend to drink themselves silly on booze they couldn't easily get back home. Then you carried their worn-out carcasses back to Anzali on Friday afternoon and let them recuperate, only to have them repeat the whole thing all over again the following week. Meantime, you paid the Iranian customs guys to turn a blind eye to the fact that you had alcohol on board and that you started selling the liquor to these Persians as soon as you set out. It could be a good living in the right season. But now was not the right season and on setting out, the captain had initially wondered if the trip was even going to be worth it.

But it was going to be worth it. At least this week it was. And it had to do with that wild-looking fellow who had caught up with him at the back of the Anzali teahouse and asked him for a ride. 'Ride for free you mean?' the captain had asked. Of course not, the stranger had answered. Then he'd started to elaborate and the captain had cut him off to tell him his Persian did not extend beyond a few sentences. 'How about English?' the stranger had asked. The captain nodded yes, 'A little.' By then he was starting to feel that this might be a trap set by the Iranian customs agents to make him fork out more money than usual. Yet something about the desperation in the stranger's eyes told him to wait and see. This might turn into a worthwhile haul after all. And it had. The stranger had said he wanted to buy himself a spot on the ship and the captain had told him to go right ahead and do it. The stranger did not respond, but just stood there and stared at him. 'I understand,' the captain looked toward the sea. 'No passport?' The stranger shook his head. Then he did something. He took the captain's hand and started putting money into it. He would take the money in nice thick folds from different pockets and slap them onto the captain's hand. Iranian money wasn't worth all that much, but after a while even the captain had to smile. It was more money than one hand could handle, so he put both out and the stranger, who looked like he must have spent the last few days stuck in the marshes around Anzali, kept feeding them. When they were done transferring the money, the captain had said what he thought was only a smart thing to say: 'More.' No more, the stranger had said. He could have taken that money and walked away with it. Leave the stranger who was obviously in a bad fix to fend for himself. But the captain was not a man who was willing to ruin his reputation over something like this. The boat was not going to be filled anyway, not even close. And who knew if this stranger didn't end up giving him as a reference to ten more like himself. To be safe, he would have to keep the fellow in the engine room till they passed Iranian Astara. He said to the stranger, 'You thief?' The stranger shook his head, even smiling a bit. The captain pointed to the bag the man had on him. 'Please!' The bag was unzipped. Hardly anything there. No contraband. A slightly torn book, some other notebooks and dirty clothes. The captain was satisfied. 'Okay. I take. Baku. Good?' Yes, the stranger said with obvious relief. Baku was very good. 'Come.' The captain motioned for him to follow. 'We go.'

Soon after they had passed the Iranian border the captain came down and told Chase he could come up now if he wanted. Chase was grateful. He'd been sitting in that space breathing in oil and fumes and wanting to throw up the end bit of opium he'd swallowed. *This is the last of the habit, Mette. I've learned how. I swear.* Over on the deck he crouched by himself looking like a ghost. He heard a couple of Iranians, who believed he must be a Turk or Russian, laughing at him. They thought he was either seasick or had had too much to drink and now he was going to make a mess. One of them said to the other, 'Don't get too close to him.' Chase smiled. He watched the in-and-out coastline, held tight to his bag and its precious cargo, and despite the numbing fatigue felt altogether not too bad about himself. He might have run out of luck these past few days, or worse: he might have faltered. But he hadn't. With the manuscript in his possession, he'd forced himself to hang around Tehran long enough to find the telephone number he needed. He had made that call to Deputy Mayor Ali Kasrai, letting the eager fellow convince himself it was America come calling for his services again after twenty-three years.

Afterwards . . . having to stay calm on the bus ride north and staying put until he found a willing captain who would smuggle him out of the country. Yes, he had the stamina, even if it came in fits and starts. Any passage could be taken, any habit broken. He knew *that*, if he knew anything.

Meanwhile, on the ship, he looked into the distance for the shoreline again. He didn't see it, but the shift in focus finally made him sick and he did what the Iranians talking behind his back had been afraid he'd do all along. He let go, but gladly – knowing that afterwards, in only a few minutes, when he was no longer sick, he might even feel like dancing. One of the Iranians now asked the other what time it was. Chase shouted out loud, 'Who cares what time it is. We're on the fucking sea.' He said this in English and they didn't understand him. But they did laugh at him again and he let them. They were all voyagers together, after all.

The captain had told him that in the morning when they got to Baku, Chase would have to slip off at some point and swim ashore by himself. But he knew that the water around that port was sick with floating oil, and Chase had something on him that begged to stay dry at any cost. It was always a question of cost in the end – wasn't it? And of whether you were willing to pay. Chase was willing. And he knew that when morning came he would convince the captain to find him a dryer way to get ashore. He would do this; he was not feeling unlucky. Whatever happened, happened: kismet.

The following extract is from Salar Abdoh's first novel,
The Poet Game – *a book which plunges the reader into the*
murky world of Arab terrorism. Originally published in 2000,
it anticipated, in an uncanny way, the al-Qaeda attacks on the
World Trade Center a year later.

The Libyans who surrounded him were humorless fellows. It was nothing to get restless about, Libyans were notorious for this. In early 1992, when the Office had penetrated the inappropriately named 'Lightning Battalion' in a northern Tehran suburb, he'd come in contact with a lot of these socalled Exchange Students from various Arab countries. The Lebanese were hotheads, the Syrians were cautious, old-hand PLO guys were capable of degenerating in a flash, the Egyptians could be serious and smart, yet also egotistical and clownish. But the Lemons, as the Libyans were called, were a breed apart. No talk, little action. And definitely not the kind of freedom fighter you'd want to cover your back in times of trouble.

One of the Libyans said something in Arabic and nodded in the direction of the cemetery they were passing. Sami had seen it from high up when the plane had been circling over Kennedy Airport. From this vantage point the sprawling graveyard had a certain authority to it, but from the plane it had appeared as something indecent and incomplete. He thought, How is one supposed to explain this idea to a Libyan brother? Then he wondered if he shouldn't say something for the sake of politeness. Neither of the men in the back responded, however, to his comment about being hungry. Finally the one in the passenger seat, a fleshy character who seemed to be the boss, turned to face Sami.

'It's Ramadan. You don't eat.'

The finality of the statement should have piqued him, but he didn't feel up to it. You usually had two sorts of Arab operatives to deal with: one set acted as if having an agent from Iran was like having the Prophet's own right-hand man at the helm, while the other lot were pugnacious and sneering, treating the Persians as if the ancient battle of Qadissiyah between the two races had never ended.

For the time being Sami was content to exert little effort. A more energetic emissary might already have been collecting brownie points trying to please these boys. He tapped the fat Arab who had addressed him.

'What?'

'You speak my language?'

'What, Persian? That's not funny.'

'Then I'll say it in English: fuck you; I'm going to eat anyway.'

The fat man gave a shrug and the ones in the back shifted uncomfortably. The car sped along a wide street. Sami read 'Jamaica Avenue' on a street sign. For no reason that he could think of, seeing this sign made him think of Winston Churchill. There had been a street in Tehran called Churchill, the name of which they'd changed after the revolution. He wondered why somebody would want to call a street in Brooklyn, Jamaica. He could ask the stone-faced Lemons – *Limu* in Persian – but he doubted if it would initiate conversation. He settled back into the seat, wondering if somebody was going to offer him a cigarette so he could refuse – but no, it was Ramadan, month of fasting, and they probably expected him to pray alongside them. This wasn't a comforting thought.

They passed a traffic light as a Hasidic man was getting

into his car. This caused stirrings of tension in the car, like the push of a wrong button. The driver, a dark-skinned young fellow with Berber features, muttered something under his breath.

'I always knew I should have learned Arabic when I had the chance,' Sami said.

Without turning around, the fat fellow up front repeated the tail end of Sami's sentence, 'When you had the chance.'

'Yeah, in Lebanon. 'Ninety to '92. I've paid my dues, helped the brothers.'

There was more silence while they turned into a side street. Then the big fellow started to ask him about dues. 'What is "dues"? You speak well English? How come?' But he didn't stop for an answer. The four of them slid out of the car at the same time. Sami followed.

It was a three-story redbrick building with a black iron gate that opened to the side of the first floor. The street was nicely tree-lined, and brown-skinned kids played in it. For a second he was scandalized at the apparent amateurism of these people; was this an Arab neighborhood? But then he heard the staccato exchange of Spanish. And soon he was even more relieved as a Chinese woman went pushing a stroller on the other side of the street. This made him recall how little he really knew. Until last week he'd been back to working on one of the Colonel's pet projects in Tehran, mostly translating reveal-all memoirs by former agents of this and that Western intelligence service. For internal consumption of the Office, of course. As if any agency worth a dime would let its real secrets be given away that easily. Nevertheless, it was a job and it beat chasing Interior Ministry guys all over the city.

A big-breasted, light-skinned man with a goatee and a Bokhara cap opened the door, looking rather too self-consciously pious. An American, Sami guessed, searching for Islam's regimented enlightenment.

He found himself in a small room with a barred window boarded up from the outside. A floor mat and an old yellow blanket had been thrown in a corner for him to sleep on. A Koran lay atop a short stool. A closet with no door stood empty save for a few plastic clothes hangers bunched to the side. This was evidently intermission time. How long it lasted was up to the Libyans. He was a houseguest without a key, being welcomed to Brooklyn, New York.

He'd been incarcerated before, but only during routine Office exercises. What was not so easy to figure was whether this, too, was an exercise or not. So on the second day, out of sheer boredom, he began to delve into the Koran they'd provided him with, readying himself for the long haul. They probably had him under some sort of observation, though he couldn't tell how. He gave a name to the man who had received him inside the house – Hazrat, or Prophet – just to fix his face in his own mind. Hazrat set out a food tray for him without saying a word – at an hour which Sami guessed to be dusk – two days in a row. On the third day Sami tried to break the ice.

'Your hospitality is beginning to weigh on me, brother,' he whispered in a sarcastic voice.

The hesitation took the form of Hazrat's setting the tray by the door, and then arranging and rearranging its position as if it were less food than an offering. Sami reached for a piece of sweet date – they were splurging.

'Are you scandalized at me, brother?' he asked as the other was leaving the room.

They didn't give him much of a chance after that. When the door burst open it dawned on him that old Hazrat had forgotten to lock it. Not that he would have tried to get out. Stretching over on the mat, he said in Persian, 'Fellows, if

298

you treat your friends like this, I'd hate to visit you at home in Tripoli.'

A runt of a Libyan with bushy eyebrows began to yell in Arabic and frisk through his clothes. Two other men stood around, pretending to debate something among themselves. This was the shake-up that Sami had been expecting for some time. He let himself be manhandled until a carefully shaven man wearing a pale blue suit appeared outside of the door.

'Tell the fuck to either shoot me or give me a cigarette,' Sami said, again in Persian.

The man in the doorway stepped closer and answered, also in Persian, 'But, Mr Amir, you don't smoke cigarettes.'

Sami muttered something to the effect that now they were getting somewhere. The runt shook him again and the man who had answered him in Persian said, 'He says you've come here to spy.'

'Well, we all have to get to America somehow.'

'Just live through it. These Libyans don't trust their own mothers, you know.'

The interrogation lasted an hour, during which time the other Iranian supplied Sami Amir with cigarettes which he lit up but didn't smoke. The fat Libyan who had sat in the front seat of the car came in shortly and put the questions to him in English. A second Libyan made as if he was taking notes.

'Your rank?'

'None. Sami Amir, Section Nineteen of Intelligence and Security. Travel orders, none. By the way, I'm hungry.' Here was one instance of a cigarette offer. Why was it smokers always assumed anyone could smoke his way out of hunger? 'Our aim is zero besides financial backing for fellow Moslem brothers here in the United States. You can ask and I'll communicate it with Tehran. When and if the time comes for anything, Section Nineteen wishes to remain ignorant of the specifics.'

'How did you come into the system?'

Sami looked across at the Iranian, who was watching him closely.

'It's all right,' the fat man said, looking past Sami at the boarded window. 'Colleagues should trust each other at times like these.'

'That's a negative. My window, so to speak, at Nineteen remains anonymous. If you're not already aware of that, then you are either terribly naive or you're a fraud. Either way means I'm done on American soil.'

The fat man laughed. 'What are these heavy words, Mr Amir: "terribly naive" – you speak English like a Yankee. And you look like one. How come?'

This was a signal that they were now into the 'serious' phase of their vetting and Sami had to give them the run-down of what they already had on him and keep to himself what they didn't. 'First off, gentlemen, my mother was an American, although I never met her.' Sensing no blatant aversion to this, Sami continued. A few times the fat man stopped to ask questions about things they had already gone over, especially about where he'd picked up his English. So Sami told him about the small Christian missionary–run boarding school in northern Tehran that the father he hard-ly ever knew had paid for over the years. He leaned into this part of his story, knowing the Arab penchant for collecting heartbreak. He talked of how after the annual stipend at the missionary school had stopped coming, the blind Irish Father O'Malley had decided to keep him on anyway, because . . . well, there was no because; sometimes people just did good deeds because they felt it was the right thing to do.

300

'Why did you mention Lebanon in the car? You were never in Lebanon from '90 to '92.'

'I was testing the extent of your knowledge.' Sami paused. He didn't want it to come out as a small victory on his part, but he said it anyway: 'And you can't say I haven't succeeded.' He offered an inappropriate smile.

The fat man pressed for the sake of argument, 'Is it necessary for you to test anything?'

'You're damn right it is.' He had meant to work himself into some sort of righteous anger, but now he felt it rising up for real. 'Section Nineteen sent me here, not my grandmother. Things are hard enough, and I had to get here on a bona fide visa. My own picture, my own name, passport, the whole works. They said I'd get my instructions across the water. So far all I've got is a slap in the face, hunger, and a gang of suspicious Libyans who seem to prefer to see me vanish. You tell me why?'

The quick outburst made them retreat from his room with a little more grace than they had entered with. The door stayed unlocked. After an hour's worth of soul searching he finally decided to venture out of his hole. The fat man and the Persian weren't there. But three other Libyans were busy practicing karate in the middle of the carpeted living room floor. One by one they stopped what they were doing to stare at Sami. The barrier of language divided these men of apparent common cause, Sami on one side and the Libyans on the other. He noticed the light-skinned Hazrat sitting cross-legged in the corner of the room, reading the Koran loudly to himself with exaggerated intonations. He read too flawlessly to be an American. Maybe he was a Syrian after all, maybe neither.

Sami called out to no one in particular, 'I'm going out for a walk; if I don't come back, it's not your fault,' imitating the last words of a high-ranking KGB defector to the Americans before the man had redefected to his own people. Sami had had to translate the public version of that story for the Office so the brass could read about it and gloat over hard-tocomprehend CIA bungling. Yet he doubted whether any of the men in this room could quite appreciate the joke even if their English was up to par. So he headed outside and was relieved to find that the night sky here looked no different than it did in most other places he'd visited before.

Hardly a block down the street he came upon a Chinese fast-food joint that cooked *halal* meat. This provoked a double take – a Chinese restaurant that served kosher food for Moslems! Less than a second later a Caribbean whore said something to him in Spanish. He didn't know what she said and couldn't even be certain if she was a whore. Ambiguity everywhere.

How did those Libyans handle such everyday encounters in America?

He ended up eating at an Oriental joint down the street. He ordered a dish called 'Hot Tofu Over Rice.' He left the tofu but ate the rice, though reluctantly. It wasn't very good rice. Not by a long shot.